"I have the claim to you, Miss Kellaway."

"I think not, sir!" she responded furiously. "Upon my word, you have a strange concept of possession! What gives you that right?"

"Those who put themselves up for sale, Miss Kellaway—" Seagrave began, only to break off as she interrupted him with no thought for courtesy.

"I am not to be bought, sir, nor have I ever been! You may take your insulting suggestions elsewhere!"

* * *

The Virtuous Cyprian
Harlequin Historical #566—June 2001

Harlequin Historicals is delighted to introduce author Nicola Cornick

Brand-new to Harlequin Historical, British author Nicola Cornick had her North American publishing debut in March 2001 with her Regency *True Colours*.

Be sure to look for the sequel to *True Colours*, *The Larkswood Legacy*, from Harlequin Reader's Choice in July 2001

and the sequel to *The Virtuous Cyprian, Lady Polly*, from Harlequin Historical in August 2001

DON'T MISS THESE OTHER TITLES AVAILABLE NOW:

THE VIRTUOUS CYPRIAN

Nicola Cornick

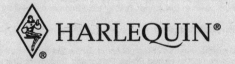

HARLEQUIN®

TORONTO • NEW YORK • LONDON
AMSTERDAM • PARIS • SYDNEY • HAMBURG
STOCKHOLM • ATHENS • TOKYO • MILAN • MADRID
PRAGUE • WARSAW • BUDAPEST • AUCKLAND

ISBN 0-373-29166-3

THE VIRTUOUS CYPRIAN

First North American Publication 2001

Copyright © 1998 by Nicola Cornick

Visit us at www.eHarlequin.com

Printed in U.S.A.

THE VIRTUOUS CYPRIAN

Chapter One

Nicholas John Rosslyn Seagrave, eighth Earl of Seagrave and Dillingham, was contemplating matrimony. It was not the abstract state that preoccupied him as he strolled along Bond Street in the afternoon sunshine, but his own approaching nuptials, confirmed that very morning by a notice in the *Gazette*. Miss Louise Elliott, his future Countess, was everything that his pride and lineage demanded: well-bred, accomplished and pretty, albeit in an insipidly pale way. He should have been delighted; instead, he was beset by the habitual boredom which had dogged his heels since his return from the Peninsular Wars several years earlier. All the delights of Town, sampled in full measure, had failed to alleviate this ennui. Now it seemed that his impending marriage could not lift his spirits either.

Some seventy miles away on Seagrave's Suffolk estate, it was also a somnolent summer afternoon, and the Earl's agent, Mr Josselyn, was dozing surreptitiously at his desk in the Dillingham Manor Court.

There had been very little business to keep him awake. A dispute over the enclosure of common land had been resolved with the offender reluctantly agreeing to remove his fence; a violent argument between two of the villagers over the antecedents of a certain horse one had sold the other had led to fines on both sides. The last matter of the afternoon was the transfer of a copyhold tenancy on an estate house to the nephew of the late occupant. Mr Josselyn shuffled his papers, anxious to be away. He cleared his throat.

'Mr Walter Mutch has petitioned that the copyhold tenancy for the house named Cookes in the village of Dillingham be transferred to him, by right of inheritance on behalf of his mother, sister of the previous lessee, Mr George Kellaway...'

The sonorous words echoed in the high rafters. Walter Mutch, a dark young man whom Josselyn privately considered rather wild, got to his feet with a show of respect. Josselyn examined him cynically. Mutch had never been close to his maternal uncle, but had seen his chance quickly enough to claim the house on Kellaway's death. Cookes was a fine property, set back from the village green and with several acres of orchard and gardens attached. Kellaway had been a gentleman of means, but his interests as a scholar and explorer had led him to choose to rent a house rather than maintain his own home during his long absences abroad. He had been a friend and contemporary of the previous Earl of Seagrave, and it had been natural for him to take a house on the estate. The copyhold agreement under which Kellaway had held Cookes was unusual, allowing for the tenancy to be inherited and not to revert to the Manor. Not that

Lord Seagrave would care about the disposal of a minor property like Cookes, his agent thought a little sadly. The Earl seldom visited his Suffolk estate, evidently preferring the more sophisticated pleasures of the capital.

Josselyn was suddenly distracted by a movement at the back of the room. The courtroom door swung open, the draught of fresh air setting the dust motes dancing and bringing with it the scents of summer. He frowned. Who could be disturbing the court session at this late stage?

'The petition of Walter Mutch having been given due consideration, this court agrees that the house called Cookes be transferred to his name from this, the fifth day of June in the year of our Lord one thousand eight hundred and sixteen, and in the fifty-sixth year of the reign of our most gracious sovereign King—'

'One moment, sir!'

The clerk's quill spluttered on the parchment at the unexpected interruption and he reached hastily for the sand box to help staunch the flow of ink. Josselyn was dazzled by the sunlight and shaded his eyes impatiently.

'Who wishes to speak? Step forward!'

The door closed behind the newcomer, cutting off the light. A whisper ran round the sparsely populated courtroom.

'Your pardon, sir.' A woman was coming forward to Josselyn's desk, gliding across the wooden floor like a ghost, garbed in unrelieved black and heavily veiled. She moved with youth and grace. He watched her approach incredulously. At the back of the room an older woman, also dressed in black, slid self-consciously into a seat by the door. The newcomer had reached the clerk's table now and was putting back her veil. Josselyn, and every male member of the courtroom below the age of eighty, caught his breath at the dazzling fairness that was revealed. Hair the colour of spun silver curled about a face that could only be described as enchantingly pretty. Eyes of a charming, limpid cornflower blue met his confidingly. Her nose was small and straight, her complexion peaches and spilt cream, and that soft pink, smiling mouth…Josselyn felt himself go hot under the collar.

'Madam?' All the assurance had gone out of Josselyn's manner. The whole room appeared to be holding its breath.

'I ask pardon, sir, for this intrusion.' Her voice was low, musical and slightly husky. A lady, Josselyn thought, even more perplexed. He adjusted his spectacles and fixed her with what he hoped was a professional regard.

'In what manner may we serve you, madam?'

Her voice, though quiet, carried to all corners of the room. 'In this manner, sir. My name is Susanna Kellaway of Portman Square, London, and I claim the house of Cookes by right of inheritance as the elder daughter of the late George Kellaway.'

Mr Josselyn might be a dry-as-dust old lawyer, buried in the country, but even he had heard of Susanna Kellaway. Who had *not* heard of the scandalous Susanna Kellaway, one of the most famous courtesans in London? The outrageous Susanna, who had been mistress to a whole parade of rich and famous men and whose career had reached new heights recently in a highly publicised and disreputable affair with the Duke of Penscombe? Josselyn found that he was almost gasping for breath. Could this bird of paradise really be the daughter of the scholarly recluse who had lived quietly in Dillingham for over thirty years?

Walter Mutch was on his feet, his chair clattering back. He had always had a hot temper and was several degrees below his late uncle's station in country society. He saw no need to hold his tongue. 'It's a lie!' he shouted hoarsely. 'My uncle never had a child! I protest—' He started forward, only to be restrained by his younger brother.

'There must be some mistake…' Josselyn began hopelessly, and looked up to meet the comprehension and wicked mischief in the lady's eyes, which told him more eloquently than any words that his identification of her had been correct.

'I assure you that there is no mistake, sir,' Susanna Kellaway said, with cool confidence. 'I have here my parents' marriage lines and the record of my birth. As I said, sir, I am the rightful claimant to Cookes!' She placed the papers in front of Josselyn, but they could have been written in Chinese for all the sense he could make of them in his current state of agitation.

The whole courtroom burst into uproar. Mutch was shouting, his brother pulling on his arm to try to quieten him. The clerk was banging his gavel and demanding order, but no one was taking any notice. All occupants of the room had turned to their neighbours and were avidly debating whether George Kellaway had ever had a daughter, and which members of the village could remember. And such a daughter! Josselyn looked hopelessly at the lady in question and saw that she was enjoying his discomfiture. She evidently appreciated both the effect she invariably had on men and also the drama she had caused. She leant across his table and he caught a tantalising hint of expensive perfume.

'My lawyer will be in touch to negotiate the terms of the lease,' she said with a charming smile. 'I bid you good day, sir.' And so saying, she turned on her heel and walked out, leaving Josselyn in the midst of the disarray, contemplating the ruin of his afternoon. He reached instinctively for paper and ink with a hand that shook. Normally he would not trouble Lord Seagrave with estate matters, but in this instance… He shook his head incredulously. He dared not risk leaving his lordship in ignorance of this astounding piece of news. Besides, the situation was too complex for him. He had no notion of how Seagrave would feel at a notorious Cyprian establishing herself on his country estate. Remembering the Cyprian and her melting smile, Josselyn came out in a hot sweat again. No, indeed—Lord Seagrave would have to be told.

'Whatever can have brought you here, Susanna?'

A less thick-skinned woman than Susanna Kellaway might have noticed the lack of enthusiasm in her sister's voice, but she had become inured to snubs over the years. Besides, she knew that Lucille's cool welcome stemmed less from disapproval of her twin than recognition of the fact that Susanna only sought her out when she wanted something. She gave her sister the benefit of her feline smile and waved one white hand in a consciously elegant gesture.

'Why, I came to commiserate with you on the death of our dear father! I assume that you had heard?'

A frown darkened Lucille Kellaway's fine blue eyes. She was sitting in the prescribed manner for her pupils at Miss Pym's School for Young Ladies, Oakham: upright with her hands neatly folded in her lap and her feet neatly aligned and peeping from beneath the hem of her old blue merino gown.

'I collect that you refer to the death of George Kellaway? Yes, I heard the news from Mrs Markham.' She sighed. 'I fear that I always think of the Markhams as our true parents, for all that our father paid for our upkeep and education!'

Susanna made a pretty moue. In the school's shabby parlour she looked both golden and exotic, too rich for her surroundings. 'For my part, I have no filial regard for either Gilbert Markham or George Kellaway!' she declared strongly. 'The former left us penniless and the latter never did anything for us, either living or dead! First he gave us away as babies, then he refused to have anything to do with us whilst we were growing up. When Mr Markham died and we needed him, where was he?' She answered her own question bitterly. 'Travelling in China! And we were left to make shift for ourselves! In my opinion, it's a most unnatural father who can treat his children such, dismissing them without a thought!'

Lucille Kellaway's own opinion was that there was no point in feeling resentful about their treatment at the hands of a man neither of them had ever known and could not regard as a father. George Kellaway, widowed when his wife had died in childbirth, had obviously considered himself incapable of raising two daughters on his own. It was also incompatible with his lifestyle as an academic and explorer. He was therefore fortunate that he had a childless cousin, Gilbert Markham, who was only too pleased to take on the responsibility for the children's upbringing. And they had been happy and well-cared for, Lucille reflected fairly. George Kellaway had provided the money to see his daughters educated at Miss Pym's school, and they had spent the holidays at the Markhams' vicarage near Ipswich.

Their father had never shown any desire to set eyes on his offspring again, but then he had been forever travelling in Europe and, when war broke out, further afield. It would perhaps have been useful to have had him to turn to on Mr Markham's death, for their adoptive father had left his small competence solely to his wife and the young daughter the couple had unexpectedly produced in later life. There had not been sufficient fortune to keep four people, and Markham had clearly expected Kellaway to support his own daughters. Lucille shrugged. What point was there now in regretting the fact that George Kellaway had been abroad on his cousin's death, and totally unable to help his children even if he had had the inclination? He had not even appeared to have a man of business to whom they could apply. Penniless, they had been obliged to make their own way in the world—and they had chosen very different courses.

'Did he leave you anything in his will?' Susanna asked suddenly, the carelessness of her tone belied by the sharp cupidity in her eyes.

Lucille raised her finely arched brows. 'His will? I

thought he died intestate—in Tibet, was it not? But since he had no property—'

Susanna relaxed again, the same little, catlike smile on her lips. 'Now that is where you are wrong, dear sis! I have been living in our father's house this week past! And a sad bore it has been too,' she added, with a petulant frown.

The entry of the school's housemaid with a pot of tea prevented Lucille from asking her sister to explain this extraordinary sentence. The maid cast Susanna one wary but fascinated look before pinning her gaze firmly on the floor as Miss Pym had undoubtedly instructed her to do. She put the tray before Lucille and backed out, but as she was leaving the room she could not resist another look at the wondrous creature draped over the parlour sofa. Miss Kellaway was so beautiful, she thought wistfully, with her silver gilt curls and warm blue eyes—and that dress of red silk…and the beautiful diamond necklace around her slim throat, a present, no doubt, from the besotted Duke of Penscombe. Fallen woman or not, Susanna Kellaway was much envied at that moment.

'Thank you, Molly,' Lucille said, a hint of amusement in her voice, and the maid was recalled to the present and could only wonder how so luscious a beauty as Miss Kellaway could have a twin sister as plain as Miss Lucille.

The door closed behind her, and Lucille considered her sister thoughtfully, seeing her through Molly's eyes. Susanna had disposed herself artfully on the sofa to display her figure to advantage. Lucille imagined this to be a reflex action of her sister's since there were no gentlemen present to impress, although she expected the drawing and music masters to appear on some spurious excuse at any moment. The dress of clinging red silk which Molly had so admired plunged indecently at the front and was almost as low at the back; completely inappropriate for the daytime, Lucille thought, particularly within the portals of a school full of impressionable young girls. That Susanna had even been allowed over the threshold of such an establishment had amazed Lucille, for Miss Pym had never made any secret of the fact that she deplored the fact that one of her former pupils had become 'a woman of low repute'. Miss Pym clearly felt that Susanna's fall from grace reflected directly on the moral failure of the school.

'You were saying, sister?' she prompted gently.

'Oh, yes, my sojourn in Suffolk!' Susanna stifled a delicate yawn. 'A monstrous tedious place, the country!' She stopped.

Lucille, used to her sister's butterfly mind since childhood, did not display any impatience. 'Did I understand you to be saying that you had been visiting our father's house? I was not aware that he owned—'

'But of course you were! We were born at Cookes! I understand that Mr Kellaway always lived there between his travels!'

Lucille frowned in an attempt to unravel this. 'Of course I knew of Cookes, but I thought it to be leased. Yet you say you have inherited it?'

Susanna smiled patronisingly. 'I have inherited the lease, of course! Old Barnes told me all about it—you remember Mr Markham's lawyer? I kept him on to deal with my business—why, whatever is the matter?'

Lucille had clapped her hand to her mouth in horror. 'Susanna, you do not employ Mr Barnes as your lawyer? Good God, the man's business was composed solely of country doctors and parsons! Surely you shocked him to the core!'

Her sister threw back her head with a gurgle of laughter. 'Which shows how little you know of business, Luce! Barnes was only too happy to take on the work I gave him! What was I saying—oh yes, it was Barnes who read of our father's death and drew to my attention the fact that I had a claim on the copyhold of Cookes. He is nothing if not thorough! And I thought—why not? There might be some financial advantage in it! After all, mine is not a very secure profession!'

Lucille put down the china teapot and passed her sister a cup. 'I see. So you have the right to claim the house and its effects as George Kellaway's eldest child?'

'So Barnes tells me. But there is no inheritance, for he spent all his money on his travels, and the house is full of nothing but books and bizarre artefacts from China!' Susanna looked disgusted. 'It's all of a piece, I suppose! At any rate, you need not envy me my good fortune!' She gave her sister her flashing smile.

Lucille raised her teacup and drank thoughtfully. 'But what are the terms of the lease? I collect our father held the house from the Earl of Seagrave?'

'Lud, who knows?' Susanna shrugged pettishly. 'I leave all that to Barnes, of course! Anyway, it is the dullest place on earth and if it were not for the fact that I may have something to gain, I would not stay there another moment, I assure you!'

She looked a little furtive. 'Actually, Luce, it was that which brought me here. You see, I need to go away for a little and I want you to go to Cookes and pretend to be me.'

Lucille, who had just taken a mouthful of tea, almost choked. She swallowed hard, the tears coming to her eyes. Susanna was watching her with a calculating look which made those limpid blue eyes look suddenly hard. There was a silence, broken only by the distant voices of some of the girls as they played rounders outside. Lucille put her teacup down very carefully.

'I think you must be either mad or in jest to make such a suggestion, Susanna.' Her voice was level and quite definite. 'To what purpose? Such childish tricks were all very well when we were in the schoolroom, but now? I would not even consider it!'

Susanna was now looking as offended as her indolence would allow. 'Upon my word, you have grown most disagreeable since we last met! This is no childish ploy; I was never more in earnest! Do you think I would travel all the way from Suffolk to Oakham for a mere jest...' she gave an exaggerated shudder '...and stay in the most *appalling* inns along the way just for the pleasure of it? Well, I declare! You are the one whose wits are going begging!'

There was some truth in this, Lucille reflected. Susanna could be relied upon never to do anything against her own comfort. She knew she should not give the suggestion a moment's thought, not even discuss it...and yet...

'Why on earth do you need me to consent to so foolish a masquerade?' Her curiosity had got the better of her, for Susanna was looking both dogged and determined, expressions normally alien to her.

'I need you to do it because I *have* to go away,' Susanna said with emphasis. 'Sir Edwin Bolt has invited me to go to Paris with him, and I cannot risk delay. I do not want to let him escape me!' She pulled a dainty face. 'The timing is most unfortunate!'

Something which might have been pity stirred in Lucille. 'Is Sir Edwin so important, then, Susanna? Do you love him?'

Susanna laughed, a bitter sound which matched the scornful sparkle in her eyes. 'Love! Lud, no! But he might be persuaded to marry me! And you know, Luce, we are neither of us young any more. Twenty-seven! I cannot bear to think of it!' Her unsentimental blue gaze considered her sister. 'I suppose you might continue teaching here until you died, but it's different for me. I need to secure my future!'

Lucille swallowed her sister's carelessly hurtful reference to her own prospects. 'I see. But I thought that you had claimed Cookes for that purpose…'

'Exactly!' Susanna rewarded her with a flashing smile, as though she had said something particularly clever. 'I cannot be in two places at once! My best chance lies with Sir Edwin—after all, he might make me a lady!' She did not appear to see the humour in her own remark. 'But at the same time I do not wish to relinquish my claim on Cookes in case there is some money in it for me! It really is so unfair! Why did our father have to die so inconveniently?'

Lucille's lips twitched at this supreme piece of self-centredness. 'I daresay he did not think of it,' she said, with a sarcasm that completely passed her sister by. 'Forgive me if I am being a slowtop, but I do not really understand why you feel you cannot leave Cookes now. Surely there could be no danger in you travelling abroad for a little now that you have secured the lease?'

Susanna pulled a face. 'But I know they want me out of that house! They wish I had never claimed it!' She saw her sister's look of scepticism and hurried on a little defensively, 'Oh you can look like that, Luce, but you didn't see those lawyers! They have been pestering me all week, trying to disprove my claim! I know they don't want me there! Why, they will break the lease if I give them half a chance, and then I may never be able to claim the inheritance I deserve! So I daren't go away without knowing that there's someone to look after my interests, and it's easiest for you just to pretend to be me for a little while! That way it looks as though I'm really interested in living in the house. After all,' she added, tactlessly, 'no one even knows you exist, so they would not suspect!'

Lucille felt as though she was struggling in a quicksand. 'But cannot your lawyer represent your interests? After all, he was the one who told you of your claim to Cookes in the first place. Would he not be the most appropriate person—'

Susanna was shaking her head stubbornly. 'But my lawyer is in Holborn! I need someone in Suffolk! I need *you*, Lucille!'

'But, Susanna,' Lucille said helplessly, 'the deception... It is fraud, after all! And if they were to realise—'

Susanna curled her lip. 'Lud, you always were so

pious, Luce! No one would guess! The only person you could possibly meet is old Josselyn, the agent, and even he has probably tired of trying to disprove my claim and will leave you alone! I thought you might like a chance to look at Cookes,' she added slyly. 'It is full of dusty old tomes that would no doubt be fascinating to you. For myself, I cannot bear bookish things, but I know that you are the most complete bluestocking.'

There was another silence whilst Lucille struggled against an inner compulsion. 'It wouldn't work,' she said, more forcefully this time. 'Why, we do not even look alike!'

Superficially, this was true. Lucille felt her twin's gaze skim her with faintly malicious consideration. She knew what she must look like to Susanna's sophisticated eyes: a country dowd in an old dress, angular where Susanna was generously curved, her silver fair hair several shades paler and drawn back in a disfiguring bun. They had the same sapphire blue eyes, but whilst Susanna made flirtatious use of hers, Lucille's were customarily hidden behind her reading glasses. Lucille's complexion was porcelain pale, without any of the cosmetic aids which Susanna so artfully employed—powder and rouge for the cheeks, carmine for the lips, kohl for the eyes... The effect was spectacular and could only serve to underline the differences between them.

It was three years since Lucille had seen her sister, and she felt that Susanna had not changed in either appearance or attitude. It was typical of Susanna to arrive without warning, demanding that her sister embark on some harebrained escapade just to oblige her.

Lucille, forever cast in the role of the sensible twin, had tried to restrain her sister's wilder schemes in their youth, but to little avail. Susanna was headstrong and obstinate, and had not improved with age. Lucille could still remember the horror she had felt when Susanna had announced defiantly that, their adoptive father's death having left them destitute, she would try her luck among the *demi-monde* in London. She had been quite determined and neither her sister's reasoned arguments nor the shocked disgust of their remaining family had swayed her. That had been nine years ago, and who was to say that she had been wrong? Lucille thought, with faint irony. Susanna had never been troubled by the moral dimension of her choice and materialistically she had done very well for herself.

Susanna got to her feet with the fluid grace that was one of her trademarks, and crossed to her sister's side, pulling her to her feet. They regarded their reflections in the parlour mirror, one a pale shadow of the rich colour of the other.

'You could be made to look like me,' Susanna said, slowly. ''Tis only a matter of clothes and cosmetics, and no one at Dillingham has seen me properly— why, I've told you, no one but Seagrave's agents have called in a week! So you see...' she gave Lucille a calculating sideways look '...you need consult nothing but your own inclination! It would not be for long, and I daresay you could do with a holiday from this prison!'

Lucille jumped, shaken, for her sister had hit upon the one truth which Lucille did not wish to acknowledge. Over the past few months, Lucille had been aware of an increasing need to escape the claustro-phobic confines and predictable routines of the school. She needed time to read, study, walk and be on her own, but she had had nowhere to go. In some ways the genteel world of the school, the endless classes of little girls, the restricted horizons of all the teachers, was indeed the prison Susanna described.

Susanna was virtually all the family Lucille pos-sessed and Susanna had made it clear long ago that her antecedents were not an asset in her chosen course in life, and she would be obliged to her twin if she did not broadcast their relationship. This suited Lucille, who could see that it would not be to her advantage to claim sistership with one of the most infamous Cyprians in London. The parents of her pu-pils would be outraged—or believe that she was cast in the same mould. It was a strange twist of fate that had cast two sisters adrift in the world for one to turn into a bluestocking and the other a courtesan.

Lucille sighed. She had no illusions that Susanna wanted to use her, but more than half of her was crying out to her to seize the chance Susanna was offering. The prospect of spending some time in the house where their father had lived and worked held a curious appeal for her. But an impersonation was both foolhardy and immoral, the voice of her con-science told her severely. But it would not be for long, temptation countered defensively, and she would not really be doing anything wrong…

'How long do you think you would be away for?' she asked cautiously, and was rewarded by a vivid smile from Susanna, who sensed that her battle was already won.

'No more than a week or two,' she said carelessly, resuming her languid pose on the sofa. 'And you would need to do no more than occupy the house. I do not imagine that anyone will call—doubtless it will all be a dead bore, but then you must be accustomed to such tedium far more than I!' Her disparaging look encompassed the faded respectability of the school parlour. 'Lud, how I detest this shabby-genteel place!' With a chameleon change of mood, she smiled on her sister once more. 'Oh, say you will do it, Lucille! You would so enjoy a change of scene!'

Lucille bit her lip at her sister's shamelessness. Unfortunately Susanna was right. Whilst the idea of the impersonation appalled her, the lure of Cookes definitely held a strange charm.

'All right, Susanna,' she said wryly. 'No doubt I shall live to regret it, but I will help you.'

Susanna glanced at the ugly clock on the parlour mantelpiece. Now that she had got what she wanted she did not wish to linger. 'Lord, I must be going or that old gorgon will be turning me out of doors!' She turned eagerly to her sister and clasped her hands. 'Oh, thank you, Luce! I'll send for you soon!'

She let her sister go and scooped up her fur stole and jewelled reticule. 'You must not worry that you will have to deal with anyone I know,' she added carelessly, with one hand on the doorknob. 'No one of my acquaintance would be seen dead in the country!'

'And the Earl of Seagrave?' Lucille asked suddenly. 'He is the owner of Cookes, is he not? There is no likelihood of him coming down to Suffolk?'

Susanna stared. 'Seagrave? Upon my word, what

an extraordinary idea! *He* has no interest in the case, I assure you! Why, Seagrave employs an army of agents and lawyers in order to avoid having to involve himself in his estates!'

Lucille turned away so that her sister could not see her face, and made a business of collecting up the cups and saucers. 'Do you know him, Susanna? What manner of man is he?'

Had Susanna had more interest in the motivation and feelings of others, this enquiry might have struck her as odd coming from her bookish sister. However, she seldom thought beyond her own wishes and needs. She wrinkled up her nose, frowning with the unaccustomed mental effort of trying to sum up some-one's character.

'He is a charming man,' she said, at length, 'hand-some, rich, generous… Lud, I don't know! He does not belong to my set—he is too high in the instep for me! But you need have no fears, Lucille—as I said, Seagrave don't care a fig about Cookes!'

Lucille stood by the window, watching as her sister ascended elegantly into the waiting carriage. Her thoughts were elsewhere. In her mind's eye she could see another June morning, a year previously, when the bright, fresh day had lured her early from her bed. Lucille's bedroom was at the back of the school, over-looking a quiet lane and the courtyard of the local coaching inn, The Bell. Lucille had thrown her case-ment window wide, relishing the light breeze on her face, the quiet before the routine of the school day began. She had been leaning on the sill when there was a commotion in the inn yard and a spanking new curricle had driven in, its driver calling for fresh horses.

Lucille had stared transfixed as he had jumped lightly down and engaged the landlord in conversation whilst the grooms ran to change his team. He was tall, with the broad-shouldered and muscular physique of a sportsman; a figure which showed to advantage in the tight buckskins visible beneath his driving coat as he swung round to view the progress of the grooms. The early morning sun burnished his thick dark hair to a rich chestnut and illuminated the hard planes of his face. Lucille had caught her breath and suddenly, as though disturbed by her scrutiny, the man had looked up directly at her. It had been an extraordinary moment. Lucille had stood frozen, the breeze flattening the transparent linen of her nightdress against her body and stirring the tendrils of silver blond hair that were for once loose about her face. It was as though they were only feet apart as the man very deliberately held her gaze for what seemed like forever. Then he grinned, his teeth showing very white in his tanned face, and raised a casual hand in greeting before turning away, and Lucille slammed the casement shut, her face aflame with embarrassment. And it was only later, whilst out in the town, that she had heard that their illustrious visitor had been none other than the Earl of Seagrave...

Lucille found that she was staring blankly out into the empty street. A wave of heat washed over her at the memory of the encounter. Never had the even tempo of her life at the school been so disrupted! Accustomed to seeking a rational explanation to everything that happened to her, Lucille was completely at a loss to explain the startling compulsion that had drawn her eyes to Seagrave in the first place and then held her captive staring in such a shameless manner! And then for him to notice her standing there immodestly in her shift! Well, Lucille thought, tearing her mind away, there was no danger of the experience recurring. Susanna had reassured her of that. Which, a small corner of her mind persisted in telling her quite firmly, was a great pity but perhaps for the best.

The atmosphere in the crowded gaming room was tense. There was no doubt that the Earl of Seagrave had had the run of the cards; several less fortunate players had been forced to retire, their pockets to let, grumbling wryly about his diabolical luck. His dark gaze was intent, a slight frown between his brows as he concentrated on the cards. It was a face of character, perhaps a little too harsh to be classically handsome, the dark, gold-flecked eyes deep and unreadable.

Another hand ended in his favour—and from the doorway, with disastrous clarity, came the stage whisper of some luckless sprig of nobility:

'Lucky at cards, unlucky in love, they say... It's all over the Town that Miss Elliott is about to throw him over...this business of the Cyprian...too blatant, only a week after their betrothal...on my honour, it's true...'

Too late, someone shushed him and he fell suddenly silent. Seagrave turned his head, and the crowd fell back to expose the speaker as one Mr Caversham, very young and cruelly out of his depth.

'Pray continue, Caversham.' All Seagrave's acquaintances recognised the note of steel beneath that silky drawl. His dark eyes were coldly dispassionate as they pinned his victim to the spot. 'Your audience is rapt. Miss Elliott is about to terminate our engagement, you say. Further, I infer that the reason is some…alliance of mine with a certain barque of frailty? Did your informant also vouchsafe the name of this ladybird? I feel sure they must have done, Caversham.'

There was a profound silence as Mr Caversham's mouth opened and closed without a sound. All colour had fled from his face, leaving him looking pitifully young and vulnerable. The Honourable Peter Seagrave, exchanging a watchful look with Lord Robert Verney across the card table, shook his head slightly in answer to Verney's quizzically raised eyebrows. They had seen Seagrave in this mood before and understood something of the devils that drove him. Peter put a tentative hand on his brother's arm and felt the tension in him as taut as a coiled spring.

'Nick, let be! The fellow's a foolish puppy who knows no better—'

Seagrave did not appear to hear him. He shook the restraining hand off his arm and got slowly to his feet. There was a collective intake of breath. Caversham was tall, but Seagrave towered over the younger man. Strong fingers reached for the neckcloth at Caversham's throat, drawing him inexorably closer in the Earl's merciless grasp.

'Do please reconsider your silence, Caversham,' Seagrave said, still in the same, smoothly dangerous tones. 'You possess a certain piece of information which I am anxious for you to disclose.' He gave his victim a slight shake.

Caversham was a fool but he was no coward. His mouth dry, his neckcloth intolerably tight, he managed to gasp, 'It is Susanna Kellaway, my lord! I heard…I heard that she had taken a house on your Suffolk estate… The story is all over Town.'

Seagrave gave him an unpleasant smile. 'True in all particulars! I congratulate you, Caversham!' The young man was released so suddenly that he almost fell over. Loosening his collar with fingers that shook, Caversham watched as Seagrave unhurriedly turned back to the card table, collected the pile of guineas, rouleaus and IOUs and sketched a mocking bow to his companions.

'My apologies, gentlemen. I find some of the company here little to my taste. Peter, do you come with me, or would you prefer to stay?'

There was a bright light of amusement in Peter Seagrave's brown eyes. 'Oh, I'm with you, Nick, all the way!'

The whispers gathered pace as they went down the stairs. 'Can it be true? He did not deny it… So *la belle Susanna* has thrown the Duke over for a mere Earl?'

Seagrave gave no sign that he heard a word as they left the club. His face might have been carved from stone. The brothers went out into the cold morning air, where a hint of dawn already touched the eastern sky. Once out in the street, Seagrave set off for St James's at a brisk pace which demonstrated that he was stone-cold sober. His brother almost had to run to keep up. Peter, who had been invalided out of the army after Waterloo the previous year, had still not quite recovered from the bullets he had received in the chest and thigh and after a few minutes of this route march he was forced to protest.

'For God's sake, Nick, slow down! Do you want to finish what the French started?'

That won him a glance with a flicker of amusement and although Seagrave did not reply, he slowed his pace to a more moderate rate that enabled his brother to keep up without too much difficulty. Not for the first time, Peter wished that his brother was not so difficult to read, his moods so impenetrable. It had not always been so. Now, for instance, he sensed that Seagrave was blindingly angry, but knew he would say nothing without prompting. Peter sighed and decided to risk it.

'Nick, what's all this about? When that idiot Caversham started talking I thought it was all a hum, but you knew all about it already, didn't you? You *wanted* him to tell everyone about Miss Kellaway!'

There was a silence, then Seagrave sighed. 'Your percipience does you credit, little brother.' There was a mocking edge to his words. He drove his hands deep into his coat pockets. 'Yes, I knew. Josselyn wrote me some garbled letter earlier this week to tell me that Miss Kellaway—' he sounded as though there was a bad taste in his mouth '—had claimed a house in Dillingham. I wanted to see how much of the story had become common knowledge.'

Peter was frowning. 'But if you already knew about the Cyprian, why did you not take action?'

He waited, and heard his brother sigh again. 'I did

not think that it mattered,' Seagrave said, with the weary boredom that was habitual.

'Did not think—?' Peter broke off. He was one of the very few who knew the depth of his brother's disaffection since his return from the wars, his apparent lack of purpose in civilian life. They had shared similar experiences whilst on campaign and Peter could see why Seagrave had been so deeply affected and had found it difficult to settle in a society that seemed to offer only instant, superficial gratification. Peter had the happy temperament to be able to recover from his harrowing experiences, albeit slowly, but Seagrave had always been much deeper, had dwelt more on all that he had experienced. It was as though some part of him had become shut away, unreachable and uninterested.

Nothing could hold his attention for long. He had the entrée into any *ton* function that he chose to honour with his presence. He had women fawning on him and a fortune to spend at the card tables. He could not even be accused of being a bad landlord and neglecting his estates, for he made scrupulously careful arrangements to ensure that all his tenants' needs were met. He just chose never to attend to such matters himself. No wonder then that a letter from Josselyn had met with such indifference.

Seagrave sighed again. 'I see now that I was naive in thinking that it did not affect me.' His tone was coolly reflective. 'It needed only for some busybody to hear the tale—as they have done—for it to be all over Town. And now Miss Elliott is to give me my *congé*! I wish I cared more!'

Peter frowned. He knew that Seagrave had never

pretended to have any more regard for Louise Elliott than the mutual respect one would expect to have for one's future wife, and he also knew that this had nothing to do with the exquisite actress which his brother currently had in keeping in a discreet villa in Chelsea. But even if his feelings were not engaged, the match with Louise was worth preserving if possible.

'Go and see the Elliotts tomorrow,' he urged. 'I am sure all can be put to rights. Louise is a sensible girl and will understand the truth of the matter.'

Seagrave's mouth twisted with wry amusement. 'Just so, Peter. I am persuaded you are correct. My future wife is indeed the sort of cold-blooded young woman who could easily ignore the fact that I had a Cyprian in keeping. What she is less likely to forgive, however, is the public humiliation that will reflect on her now that this story is known. And in order to avoid future misunderstandings, I reluctantly feel it is my duty to travel to Dillingham and ascertain exactly what the situation is.' His voice hardened. 'I am sure that, with the right inducement, Miss Kellaway can be impelled to see sense.'

Peter had never met Susanna Kellaway but suddenly, hearing the underlying anger in his brother's voice, he found himself feeling very sorry for her indeed. A thought occurred to him.

'I say, Nick, do you know Miss Kellaway at all?'

'Not in the sense you mean,' Seagrave said dryly. 'I've met her, of course.' His tone was unpleasant. 'A cheap little piece with a commercial mind—and the commodity she sells is herself.' He hesitated. 'Do you remember Miranda Lethbridge?'

'Cousin Sally Lethbridge's girl?' Peter frowned.

'Yes, of course—she was about fifteen when I went away in '12. Why do you ask?'

'Miranda made her come out a couple of years ago.' Seagrave sounded amused. 'You may remember her as a child in pinafores, Peter, but she had improved dramatically and there were plenty who fell at her feet.' The amusement fled from his tone. 'Amongst them was Justin Tatton, whom you may remember served with me in Spain. He was bowled over by Miranda and she was equally smitten. We all thought they'd make a match of it.' Seagrave's voice was suddenly savage. 'Miss Kellaway had other ideas, however. This was before Penscombe swam into view, and though Justin has no title, he was rich... Anyway, she made a dead set at him, and in a weak moment he succumbed.' Seagrave shrugged, a little uncomfortably. 'God knows, I am in no position to judge another man, but the unutterable folly... Justin said later that it had been a moment of madness, that after a single night he felt nothing but disgust and repulsion. But the damage was done. He begged Susanna Kellaway to tell no one, but she was furious that she could not hold him, and she made very sure that Miranda heard—and in the worst terms possible. Naturally the poor girl was devastated. She refused to even speak to Justin, and last year she made that hasty marriage to Wareham...' Seagrave shook his head.

'I am not a sentimentalist,' he added with a touch of humour, 'but I deplore the way Miss Kellaway takes whatever she wants with no concern for the destruction she causes! Even in my worst excesses I was never so careless of the feelings of others, and God knows, I have done some damnably stupid things in my time!'

Peter was silent. When Seagrave had first returned home from the Peninsula he had been possessed by a spirit of wildness which Peter suspected was the result of escaping the war with his life intact. He knew that as one of Wellington's most promising officers, his brother had been sent on some secret and highly dangerous missions and had brushed with death on more than one occasion. He had fought with the Portuguese militia, the *ordenanca*, as well as covering himself with glory in a more orthodox manner on the battlefield of Talavera. Seagrave's reaction to civilian life had been a very public and unrestrained year of hellraising that blazed a trail through the *ton* until it had burned itself out and he had changed into the deeply world-weary individual he was now.

Seagrave looked up to where the crescent moon was perched above the rooftops, fading from the summer sky as dawn approached. He sighed. 'No, with Miss Kellaway it is one excess after another! There will always be some poor fool who is besotted and will fall victim to an experienced woman preying on impressionable young men for their fortunes!'

Peter grimaced. 'I wonder what she wants with you, Nick,' he mused. 'You could scarcely be described as an inexperienced youth!'

His brother gave him a cynical glance. 'Come on, Peter, you're not an innocent either! She wants money—in one form or another! It's what she always wants! And I'm damned if she'll get any out of me!'

The reception which Seagrave met with the following morning at Lord Elliott's house in Grosvenor

Street was not auspicious. The butler had at first tried to turn him away with the news that Miss Elliott was not at home, but Seagrave greeted this information with well-bred disbelief. The butler, flustered, could not stand his ground and could only protest as the Earl swept past him into the drawing-room, where he found both Lady Elliott and her daughter. Seagrave's intended, a plumply pretty blonde with pale, slightly protruberant blue eyes, looked up from her embroidery frame at his entrance and uttered a small shriek.

'You!' she gasped, in tones of outrage. 'Seagrave! How *could* you! Oh, I wish I were dead!' She burst into noisy tears.

Lady Elliott was made of sterner stuff. She swelled with indignation. 'I am astounded that you see fit to show your face here, my lord! To come from the arms of that creature to my own, sweet, innocent Louise! It defies belief! The notice terminating the engagement has already been sent to the *Gazette*!'

Louise sobbed all the louder. Seagrave, who had as yet uttered not one word, found that there was no necessity for him to do so. His sense of humour, long buried, began to reassert itself. Giving the outraged matron and her snivelling daughter the full benefit of a wicked smile, he executed an immaculate bow, turned on his heel and left the room.

It was late when the stage pulled into the yard of the Lamb and Flag in Felixstowe and decanted its occupants onto the cobbles. Lucille Kellaway, stiff and sore from the discomforts of her journey, picked up her shabby portmanteau and looked about her.

There was no sign of her sister Susanna, despite the
agreement that the two had to meet there.

Lucille had found the journey from Oakham fascinating. She had travelled so little that each new
view was a delight to her and each new acquaintance
was a pleasure to meet. She now knew all about Miss
Grafton, a governess about to take up a new position
with a family in Ipswich, and Mr Burrows, a lawyer
visiting a client in Orford. She had looked out of the
coach window and admired the well-kept farmland
that stretched as far and as flat as the eye could see,
and had glimpsed the sea as they drew into the town.

She struggled towards the inn door, her heavy case
weighing her down. The smell of roast meat wafted
enticingly from the kitchen and light spilled from the
taproom onto the cobbles, accompanied by the sound
of male voices and laughter. Lucille shrank. Although
not of a timid disposition, she was too shy to march
into the public bar and demand attention. The landlady found her cowering in the passageway.

'I am looking for Miss Kellaway,' Lucille said, a
little shyly, and immediately saw an expression of
mingled prurience, curiosity and disgust flit across the
good lady's features.

'Miss Kellaway and the gentleman are in the pri-
vate parlour,' the landlady said, tight-lipped, nodding
in the direction of a closed door at the end of the
passage. She marched off to the kitchen, leaving
Lucille alone.

Lucille knocked a little hesitantly on the door of
the parlour. She could hear the intimate murmur of
voices, but no one answered her. She pushed the door
open and recoiled, almost turning on her heel to run

away. Susanna was reclining on the parlour sofa in much the same pose as she had held at the school, but with shocking differences. Her emerald green silk dress was cut very low and it had fallen off one shoulder completely, exposing one of Susanna's plump breasts. A portly, florid man with thinning sandy hair was leaning over her, fondling her with impatient hands whilst his mouth trailed wet kisses over her shoulder. He looked up, met Lucille's horrified gaze and straightened up, an unpleasantly challenging look in his eyes.

'Egad, what's this! My good woman—'

Susanna pushed him away much as one might repel a fractious child. She hoisted her dress back up without the least embarrassment.

'This is my sister, Eddie.' She turned to Lucille, a frown marring her brow. 'You're monstrously late, Lucille! I had quite given up hope of you! We sail with the tide tomorrow morning, so there isn't much time.' She did not ask whether Lucille had had a good journey, or if she was hungry, nor did she invite her to sit down.

'Now, my carriage will take you to Dillingham in the morning. I have left Felicity there—my housekeeper, Felicity Appleton,' she added irritably, seeing Lucille's look of incomprehension. 'She will help you choose your clothes appropriately. I have left a large wardrobe at Dillingham, but Eddie will buy me more in Paris, won't you, darling?' She touched his hand and fluttered her lashes at him.

The gentleman, whom Lucille assumed to be Sir Edwin Bolt, had been scrutinising her through his quizzing glass these few minutes past with what

Lucille considered a most ill-bred regard. Now he
guffawed.

'Take more than a parcel of clothes, Susie m'dear!
Why, the girl's as strait-laced as a nun, and as cold,
I'll wager!'

Lucille flushed and Susanna gave a flounce. 'Well,
she need not meet anyone in Dillingham! I am not
asking her to *be* me!' She saw his sulky, mulish expression and her tone softened. 'But I do see what
you mean, my love!' She giggled girlishly. 'I fear that
my prim little twin will never thrill to a man's touch!
The delights of love are not for her!'

Lucille was beginning to feel rather sick. An insight into Susanna's relationship with her lover was
something that repelled rather than interested her. Sir
Edwin, mollified, had started to paw Susanna's shoulder again as though he could not keep away from her.
His hot, blue gaze roved lustfully over her opulent
curves. The dress slipped a little.

'Send the girl away so we may pick up where we
left off,' he muttered, pressing avid, open-mouthed
kisses on Susanna's white skin. Lucille looked away,
her face flaming.

'If that is all——' she said, with constraint.

Susanna had tilted her head back to facilitate the
progress of Sir Edwin's lips down her neck. He was
already pulling at her dress again. She waved her sister away. 'Very well, Luce——' she sounded like someone dismissing her servant '——you may go now.
Unless you wish to join us, that is!'

Sir Edwin looked up, a lascivious look suddenly in
his eye. 'Now there's an idea! Introduce the priggish
virgin to fleshly delights, eh? What do you say, Miss

Kellaway? Why, we could show you a thing or two…'

Their mocking laughter followed Lucille from the room. She closed the door with exaggerated care and leant against the wall of the passage for a moment to recover herself. Her whole body was one burning blush, her mind revolted, a sick taste in her mouth. That Susanna should have sold herself for that, and not even appear to care… The stone wall was cool beneath her fingers and Lucille was glad of its chill and the darkness that surrounded her. As she straightened up, however, she realised to her horror that she was not alone. At the end of the passageway, hidden from view, two men were talking.

'…travel on to Dillingham tomorrow. Do you go to the Yoxleys' for a while?'

It was a mellow voice, the cadences smooth and pleasing to the ear. Lucille paused, her attention arrested despite herself. The other man's voice was less distinguishable.

'…a sen'night, perhaps…join you at the Court… A Seagrave…back at Dillingham, Nick…'

From being overheated, Lucille suddenly found herself icily chill. Surely she could not have misheard? Had the man not mentioned the names of Seagrave and Dillingham? She dropped her portmanteau from nerveless fingers.

The voices cut off abruptly at the crash. Lucille bent clumsily to pick her case up again, only to find that when she stood up her way was blocked by the tall figure of a man. The light was behind him and she could not see his face, but in the claustrophobi-

cally small passage, his physical presence was overwhelming.

'Can I be of assistance, ma'am? Are you unwell?'
His voice was very pleasing to the ear, smooth and
mellifluous, Lucille thought again, confused. His hand
had taken her elbow in a steadying grip which nevertheless felt as though it burned through the fabric
of her dress. She had not heard him speak on that
infamous occasion when they had seen each other in
Oakham, but she knew instinctively who he was.

'No...' Lucille's voice came out as a thread of a
whisper. She looked up into the dark face, into fierce,
gold-flecked eyes, and felt quite dizzy. 'I thank you,
sir, I am quite well... Excuse me.'

She had pushed past his astonished figure and was
already halfway up the stairs before she realised that
she had no notion of where she was going. She
paused in dread, hoping that the gentleman would not
follow her; a moment later, to her inexpressible relief,
she heard a door close softly below. She sat down
heavily on her portmanteau and almost cried. Had she
been able to return to Oakham at that very moment
she would not have hesitated. But Miss Pym had
closed the school for the summer, and had gone to
visit her good friend Fanny Burney for a few weeks.
Lucille realised that she had nowhere to go except
Cookes. She leant her head against the wall and
closed her eyes.

'Whatever is it, miss? You look proper moped and
no mistake!' The landlady's judgmental tone had softened as she considered the shabby, huddled figure.

This one was no Cyprian like that painted hussy downstairs! 'Come along, miss,' she added encouragingly. 'I'll show you to your room. Everything will look better in the morning!'

Chapter Two

'Miss Kellaway.' The voice was soft and smooth as warm honey. It spoke in Lucille's ear.

Lucille had been at Cookes for ten days and thought that she had stumbled into paradise. The house, converted from a charming jumble of medieval cottages, was crammed full of books, treatises and journals enough to keep her occupied for weeks. Her previous reading had been restricted to the books available from Miss Pym's limited collection and from the Oakham subscription library. At Cookes she could read until the print blurred and her head ached. And then there was the garden—a wilderness where one could wander for hours amidst the rioting roses, or sit in the cool shade of the orchard. It had all been like a blissful dream, a thousand miles away from the petty cares of the school regime and uninterrupted by callers from the outside world.

Lucille's conscience, originally troubled by the impersonation of Susanna, had grown quiescent as nobody disturbed her peace. The memory of that dreadful night in the inn at Felixstowe had faded away. She now thought it quite possible that she had misheard the snatches of conversation that had led her to believe that the Earl of Seagrave would be in Dillingham, and mistakenly believed him to be the gentleman who had offered her his help. Certainly she had seen neither hide nor hair of him since her arrival.

The other legacy of that evening had been the slow realisation of what an impersonation of Susanna might mean—the memory of the landlady's prurient scorn and Sir Edwin's lustful advances still made her shiver. That someone might think she was Susanna, and as such was fair game for such treatment, made her feel ill. In her innocence she had not even considered it before—ignorance, not innocence, she now chided herself bitterly. But while nobody called and she had no wish to go out, it was a matter that could be put to one side, if not ignored.

The warm, southern aspect of Cookes's drawing-room, with its delightful views across the lawn to the fishpond, had lulled Lucille into a sleepy state of relaxation that afternoon. Her copy of Walter Scott's *Waverley* had slid from her hand as her head rested against the panelling and her eyes closed irresistibly in the sunshine. She had removed her reading glasses, which rested on the window-seat beside her, and had drifted into a light doze.

The voice spoke again, this time with an inflection of impatience.

'Miss Kellaway?'

Lucille opened her eyes slowly, and thought that she was probably still dreaming. Eyes of the darkest bitter chocolate flecked with gold were about three inches away from her own. His face was all planes and angles, she thought, bemused, except for his mouth which, though firm, was sensuously curved and quite delicious… Her gaze lingered, transfixed, and then one of the pins holding her unaccustomed Grecian knot dug into her head painfully, and she realised she was awake.

With growing horror, Lucille removed her gaze hastily from the man's mouth and met the distinctly speculative look in those dark eyes. They were not friendly but piercingly appraising. He had been leaning on the seat beside her and now straightened up, moving away from her, and Lucille found to her relief that she could breathe again. She struggled upright, aware that the charming gown of rose pink crêpe— one of Susanna's more restrained dresses—had slipped off her shoulder as she dozed, and was revealing the upper curves of her breasts in a manner to which she was completely unaccustomed. The gentleman, on the other hand, was clearly the sort of man who was used to seeing women in *déshabillé*. Certainly he was not in the least embarrassed by her obvious discomposure and his gaze lingered with blatant consideration in a way she found completely disconcerting.

'Miss Kellaway?' he said for a third time, with the same deceptive gentleness. 'We have met before, but may I perhaps remind you? I am Nicholas, Earl of Seagrave and as such—' his voice became heavily ironic '—your landlord.'

Lucille already knew. She had recognised him almost at once. He was just as she remembered, only more so. He had a tall, athletic figure, immaculately clad in buff pantaloons and a coat of blue superfine, and the sort of brooding dark good looks that immediately made her feel completely out of her depth. It was the same voice that she remembered, mellow and distinctive. Fortunately he did not appear to have recognised her, but then, he thought she was her sister... Lucille jumped visibly. Oh Lord, Seagrave thought she was Susanna! The scorching heat which had suffused her body when she had first seen him faded abruptly to leave her feeling cold and shaken. She had to tell him at once! For a moment she wavered, within an inch of revealing her true identity. But he looked so authoritative, so forbidding, that her courage failed her. Surely, if she could just get rid of him quickly, he would not call again...

She sat up straighter with what she hoped was a fair imitation of her sister's elegance and tried to pull herself together. No doubt he already thought her a lackwit, first staring, then silent!

'Lord Seagrave! Excuse me, I was not attending! How kind of you to call, sir. May I offer you some refreshment, perhaps? A glass of wine?' Her attempt at Susanna's husky drawl came out a little strangely. She sounded as though she had a sore throat.

Seagrave's gaze, coolly assessing, remained focused on her with disconcerting intentness. 'No, thank you. This is not a social call, Miss Kellaway.' He strode over to the fireplace and turned back to face her, awesomely in control.

'When I first heard that you had moved into Dillingham I thought my informant must be in jest,' he said conversationally. 'You are hardly renowned for your interest in country living, are you, Miss Kellaway? I cannot see what conceivable attraction a house like this could hold for you. Why, it is not as though you even own it! Your position is tenuous, to say the least! You know, of course, that I can terminate the lease at any time?'

Lucille did not know. Susanna's brief instructions to her sister had not included any information on the lease on Cookes. Marshalling her scattered thoughts in the face of this sudden and unwelcome attack, Lucille tried desperately to work out how Susanna would deal with this situation. She plumped for a certainty.

'Lud, is that so?' She managed to sound quite careless. 'You'll understand, my lord, that I leave such matters to my man of business. But surely you are not about to evict me?' She attempted a melting look at him through her eyelashes. Seagrave seemed totally unmoved. Evidently, Lucille thought, the business of flirtation was more difficult than she had imagined.

'I prefer,' Seagrave said, with scrupulous politeness, 'that you see the error of your ways of your own accord, Miss Kellaway. I feel sure that when you have considered the matter, you will see that the country is not really the place for you. This house can hardly be to your taste, and the village…well, you will find it an uncomfortable place to live.' There was no hint of a threat in his tone, but Lucille felt a shiver go through her. She knew he was trying to intimidate her. There was something powerfully compelling about that tall figure dominating her shabby drawing-room.

She arched her eyebrows in delicate enquiry. 'Whatever can you mean, my lord?' Her tone was

provocatively innocent. 'This house is delightful and
Dillingham appears to be a charming village!'

Seagrave's dark eyes narrowed momentarily. He
had betrayed no temper or even irritation during their
exchange, yet Lucille had the unnerving feeling that
that was only because he was holding himself on a
tight rein. Now he thrust his hands into his jacket
pockets as if to restrain himself further, but his voice
remained level.

'It is indeed a delightful place, Miss Kellaway, but
I doubt that you will find it so. Like many villages it
can be insular and intolerant. You will find that the
arrival of such a gaudy bird of paradise as yourself
amongst the sparrows is not welcomed warmly.' He
frowned. 'It puzzles me why you wish to bury yourself in the country in the first place. Are you escaping
your creditors, perhaps? Or…' his tone took on a sar-
castic edge '…perhaps you have some quarry in your
sights and feel that absence will make the heart grow
fonder?'

Susanna would almost certainly have used the opportunity to make a push to engage his interest.
Lucille, however, momentarily forgot the part she was
supposed to be playing and forgot to be afraid of him.
How dare he treat her with such contemptuous disdain! 'I'm sure you do not expect me to answer that,
sir,' she snapped, and almost immediately realised she
had betrayed herself as his gaze sharpened on her with
acute interest. He was too quick. She would have to
be much more careful. Her gaze suddenly fell on the
copy of *Waverley*, lying carelessly on the window-
seat. Susanna would never even have had a book in
the house, let alone appeared to read one. Would

Seagrave know that? Would it be better to attempt to
hide it, or just to ignore it? She suddenly realised that
the Earl had asked her something else, and was waiting politely for her response. Her colour rose at his
steady regard with its edge of scorn. She gave him
Susanna's dazzling smile.

'I beg your pardon, sir?'

'I said that you did not strike me as a lady who
would enjoy social ostracism, Miss Kellaway,'
Seagrave was saying, with weary patience. 'No one
will call on you, everyone will cut you dead… Do
you really want that? Do not tell me that you do not
regard it, for I shall not believe you!'

There was so much repressed violence in his tone
that Lucille was suddenly frightened. He was taut
with tension. Surely there was more to this than a
simple desire to remove her from Cookes? But she
was supposed to be Susanna, who would probably be
less sensitive to the atmosphere and would no doubt
have tried to flirt her way out of trouble. She tried a
light, petulant shrug.

'Lud, my lord, you're monstrous serious! What
does one small house matter to you? Or perhaps—'
she gave him a saucy look over her shoulder '—you
have a more personal reason for wishing me off your
property?'

It was a shot in the dark but its effect was electric.
Seagrave spun round and caught her wrist in a grip
that hurt. Lucille looked up at him. His face was expressionless but there was a look in his eyes which
chilled her.

'I do, madam, and you know why! Oh, I have no
opinion of how you choose to earn a living—I make

no judgments. But I do not like you.' He spoke through his teeth. 'You had already brought enough trouble on my family before this latest escapade single-handedly sabotaged my betrothal! You are like a bird of ill omen rather than a bird of paradise!'

Lucille felt her lips twitch at this colourful metaphor. She did not understand his allusion to Susanna's previous entanglement with his family, but could see that he might be justifiably angry that her actions had resulted in a broken engagement. She tried to free her wrist and found herself held fast.

'I am sorry to have unwittingly caused you trouble, sir—'

'Unwittingly!' For a moment his fingers tightened even more cruelly before he dropped her wrist as though he could not bear to touch her. His tone was savage. 'There was nothing *unwitting* about your decision to claim this house, madam! Well, hear this! I shall do everything in my power to drive you out of Dillingham! You will be scorned and reviled at every turn! You will wish you had never come here!'

The slamming of the front door behind him echoed through Lucille's head, causing it to ache again. She rested it in her hands in despair. Oh, why had she not told him the truth when she had had the opportunity? To try to deceive such a man was a piece of complete folly! He was both too acute to be fooled for long, and too forceful to be manipulated with feminine wiles. Feminine wiles! Lucille grimaced. What did she know of such coquetry? Her attempt to impersonate Susanna had been hopeless and she detested the blend of sexual appraisal and contempt with which Seagrave, and no doubt many other men, contemplated her sister. Lucille groaned aloud.

Seagrave... The blood was still singing through her veins from his touch, which was a singularly unhelpful reaction to him, she told herself sternly. It seemed that his slightest glance addled her wits, which was the last thing she needed when she had to have those wits about her! There was no accounting for it. No scientific theory could explain the peculiar mixture of breathlessness and excitement which possessed her in his presence. She had read about romance, of course, but had considered it to be ephemeral and often painful, not something she wished to experience. Then there was physical love, of course—she shuddered, remembering Sir Edwin's licentious gaze and questing hands.

Lucille sighed. She thought of the uncharacteristic excitement with which she had hurried to ask Miss Pym for leave from the school, and her pleased surprise when that good lady had cautiously agreed. Her anticipation at visiting Cookes had reached fever pitch by the time Susanna's summons had arrived. On the day after the meeting at Felixstowe Lucille had rolled into Dillingham village in Susanna's carriage. A bevy of small children had run alongside the coach, chattering and laughing, but their elders had stood silently on the roadside, watching as she passed by. In her ignorance, Lucille had not considered that significant until this day.

But now...she was wearing borrowed plumes and impersonating a notorious woman who, if Seagrave was to be believed, was not at all welcome in the rural tranquillity of Dillingham. She did not doubt

that Seagrave had meant every word he had said when
he had threatened to drive her out of the village.
Lucille sighed again. Why had she given into the
cowardly impulse to play along with the masquerade
when it would have been so much more sensible to
tell him the truth? Now she really was starting to
weave a tangled web through her deception!

There was a tap at the door and Mrs Appleton stuck
her head around it. Felicity Appleton had accompanied Susanna to Dillingham when she first claimed
Cookes, in the hope, Mrs Appleton had said with a
wry smile, that the presence of a reputable older
woman might reassure the good villagers of
Susanna's own respectability. It had been an unsuc-
cessful attempt. The small resident staff at Cookes
had walked out in a spirit of righteous indignation as
soon as their new employer had arrived, and from
then onwards Mrs Appleton had had to run the house
single-handedly.

'I do apologise, Miss Kellaway,' Mrs Appleton said
now, her plump, motherly face creased with anxiety.
'I tried to tell his lordship that you were not receiving,
but he would not be gainsaid!'

Lucille laughed at the thought of Mrs Appleton trying to deter the Earl from his visit. Nicholas Seagrave
had hardly struck her as the sort of man to brook any
opposition.

'Pray do not concern yourself, Mrs Appleton! His
lordship is very forceful, is he not!'

'A man used to command,' Mrs Appleton agreed
with a twinkle in her eye. 'I saw him a few times
when I was on campaign in the Peninsula with my
husband's regiment. He was one of Wellington's

brightest officers, you know, and an inspirational leader of men!'

Lucille already knew that Mrs Appleton was the widow of an army sergeant killed at Vittoria, though how this pillar of rectitude had fallen in with Susanna was another matter. Lucille had not pried into their connection, and was only grateful that she had both Mrs Appleton's calm good sense and knowledge of fashion to call upon. The housekeeper had advised her on matters of dress and hairstyle with a patience which Susanna would never have shown, and the result had been surprising. Although Lucille would never achieve the high fashion of her sister, the simple elegance of her new appearance gave her an absurd pleasure that astonished her. She had never been concerned with her dress before, but then, she had not met the Earl of Seagrave before… She shook her head to drive the thought away.

'Well, would that Seagrave had left his military manners behind in Spain!' she said crossly, still smarting from the Earl's arrogant attitude. 'The man is overbearing to a fault!'

Mrs Appleton laughed. 'But prodigious attractive!' she said shrewdly, and did not miss Lucille's telltale blush. Her smile faded a little. 'I must own myself vastly surprised to see him,' she said thoughtfully. 'Your sister may have told you, Miss Kellaway, that Seagrave never spends time on his estates! I can only assume that the furore caused by Miss Susanna's arrival here has brought him from London! She will be most disappointed to have missed him!'

'A sorry business then, since I had no wish to meet him at all!' Lucille said, with a sigh. It was a half-truth, for whilst Seagrave held a mysteriously strong attraction for her, she certainly had no wish for him to think her Susanna. 'I realise now that I have been very naive about the whole situation!' She continued wryly, 'I truly believed that I would not need to meet anyone during my time here, and that Susanna would only be away a week or two.'

Her worried blue eyes met Mrs Appleton's kind brown ones. 'You must have wondered, ma'am, how I could ever have lent myself to such a deception! I agreed on impulse, you see, wanting a change from a routine that was becoming irksome, and now I am well served for my folly! I do not mind admitting that I almost confessed the whole to Lord Seagrave, and would have done so had he not appeared so terrifying!'

Mrs Appleton sat down, wiping her floury hands carefully on her apron. 'Miss Susanna explained to me her concerns about the lease, and that she had persuaded you to come here to represent her interests whilst she was away.' She shook her head slowly. 'She told me that you were a...' she hesitated, then smiled in a kindly fashion '...forgive me, a bluestocking, was her description of you! She said that you were looking for a rural idyll in which to walk and read! I must confess, Miss Kellaway, that I thought it a foolish scheme from the outset! How Miss Susanna ever thought that you could impersonate a courtesan, I cannot imagine! *You* may have had no notion of having to meet people here in Dillingham, but she has no excuse! She must always have known that there was a chance someone would seek her—you— out!'

Lucille raised a hand in rueful protest. 'Please do not exonerate me of blame entirely, Mrs Appleton! My conscience is happier if I admit to some responsibility! I may not be worldly, but I am not stupid. I should have guessed what might happen! Indeed,' she added thoughtfully, 'deep down I probably knew the risk I was taking, but I wanted to escape the school so much that I was prepared to do it!'

There was a silence whilst both of them contemplated the situation. After a moment, Mrs Appleton spoke a little tentatively. 'I suppose the Earl wants us out of Dillingham? I thought as much, for he has already begun a war of attrition! They will not serve me in the shops, Miss Kellaway, and some most unpleasant things are being said! I would counsel you not to go out into the village. Feeling is running very high!'

Lucille stared at her in growing disbelief. Until that morning it had not occurred to her that the inhabitants of Dillingham would react so badly to her presence among them, but this was all far worse than she could have imagined. She knew that the local gentry would not have condescended to acknowledge Susanna, but that had not worried her as she had had no interest in mixing in rural society. This malicious campaign, though, was another matter again. To be starved out of the village seemed a horrid fate. Mrs Appleton, somewhat shamefacedly, was retrieving something from her apron pocket.

'I had thought not to trouble you with this, Miss Kellaway,' she said a little awkwardly, 'but perhaps you should know... It arrived just like this, with no envelope. Of course, I immediately realised what it was and I will put it in the kitchen fire directly.'

Lucille realised with a sudden shock that it was a letter she was holding out, a letter printed with bold capitals which she could read quite easily, '…nothing but a shameless whore and we do not want your sort here…' She flushed scarlet and looked up at the housekeeper in horrified understanding.

'An anonymous letter! Oh, Mrs Appleton, how dreadful! But when did it arrive? Who could possibly…?' Her voice trailed away as she realised that any one of Dillingham's outraged inhabitants could have composed the missive. Mrs Appleton had not exaggerated when she had spoken of feelings running high.

The housekeeper's mouth was a grim line as she stuck the offending letter back in her pocket. 'I am so sorry that you have been exposed to this, Miss Kellaway! The only advice I can offer is that you return to Oakham at once, before matters become even more unpleasant. Can that be arranged?'

Lucille rested her chin thoughtfully on her hand. 'I cannot return to Oakham for another ten days,' she said dolefully, 'for Miss Pym has closed the school and gone to visit Fanny Burney, the authoress, whilst I am away! Only Mr Kingston, the music master, has been left to keep an eye on matters in her absence. It would not be appropriate for me to stay there alone with him—' She broke off, unable to repress a giggle. 'Gracious, that is tame stuff compared to what our anonymous author thinks of me!'

Mrs Appleton smiled. 'Even so, my dear, do you not have any friends you could go to visit for a little?

I do not wish to alarm you, but if you stay here you will not be able to show your face beyond the gates! I imagine Miss Susanna may return in a week or so, but there is no guarantee…' She let the sentence hang but Lucille understood what she meant. Susanna's timekeeping had never been of the most reliable, particularly if it suited her to be doing something else. She would not hesitate to stay with Sir Edwin for as long as it took to get what she wanted out of him.

For a moment, Lucille considered visiting Mrs Markham. Gilbert Markham's widow and daughter were always pleased to see her, but they were living with Mrs Markham's sister and Lucille knew she could not just arrive without warning. And there was no one else. She sighed.

'I am sorry, ma'am! It seems I must stay here another ten days or so. Perhaps it will not be so bad…' She knew she sounded unconvincing. The idea of having to impersonate Susanna for that time seemed suddenly intolerable. From being blissfully happy in her country retreat that morning, she suddenly felt unbearably trapped. After a moment Mrs Appleton sighed as well.

'Very well, Miss Kellaway! Perhaps matters will settle down once the village is over the initial shock of Miss Susanna's arrival.' She sounded as unpersuaded as Lucille herself. She sighed again. 'It is easier in London, where such matters are commonplace. The society in which your sister lives operates in much the same way as the *beau monde*. But here the community is insular and judgmental, and I do not doubt Miss Susanna would detest it!'

'Seagrave said he made no judgments on the way

in which Susanna chooses to make a living,' Lucille said slowly, 'yet he would not simply allow her to reside here quietly without interference!'

Mrs Appleton gave a wry smile. 'My dear Miss Kellaway, you will find that most gentlemen have no difficulty in preserving a dual attitude towards ladies such as your sister! They…enjoy their company but they would never marry them, nor even consider them fit company for their sisters! By the same token, I suspect Seagrave believes a Cyprian should stay in London and not cause a stir in his sleepy dovecote!'

Lucille frowned, remembering something else Seagrave had said. 'Does my sister know the Earl?' she asked, carefully. 'He made some reference to her causing trouble for his family before this…'

Mrs Appleton looked disapproving, though whether of Susanna's exploits or Lucille's enquiry was hard to judge. She fidgeted with the edge of her apron before looking up to meet Lucille's gaze. 'I collect he must be referring to Miranda Lethbridge,' she said with constraint. 'I believe she is some connection of the Seagraves. Last winter your sister…' she hesitated, seeing Lucille's innocent blue eyes fixed on her '…well, no point in prevaricating! Miss Susanna took it into her head to seduce Miranda Lethbridge's betrothed, who was also a war comrade of the Earl of Seagrave.

'She did it solely because he was rich, and she was bored! It was a shocking thing, and believe me, Miss Kellaway, I thought myself unshockable! After one night Mr Tatton—Justin Tatton was his name—realised that he had made a mistake and tried to disengage, and Miss Susanna was furious. She spread the rumour that they had been having a lengthy and passionate affair, and she made sure that Miss Lethbridge heard all about it. The poor girl was completely distraught and broke off the engagement immediately.'

Mrs Appleton shook her head. 'I do not condone the behaviour of men such as Mr Tatton, but he had made a mistake and did not deserve to be punished so cruelly. But I fear Miss Susanna detests rejection.'

'I hear very little of Susanna's exploits, tucked away as I am in Oakham,' Lucille said a little hesitantly, 'but I do remember hearing of a young man, the son of a duke, who was ruined—'

'You mean Adrian Crosby, I collect,' Mrs Appleton said expressionlessly. 'He was just one of many! He was infatuated with Miss Susanna and bought her costly gifts by the barrow load. Worse, she took him to dens—' she saw Lucille's puzzled frown '—gaming dens, Miss Kellaway, where he played deep and lost a fortune to the House who, of course, gave Miss Susanna her share of the pickings! The affair only ended when the boy's father realised the extent of his debt and sent him off to the country to rusticate!'

Mrs Appleton looked unhappy. 'I am in no position to criticise your sister, Miss Kellaway, for she pays my wages! But in my book, men such as Seagrave are fair game for a woman like Miss Susanna, for they know the rules of engagement! But Adrian Crosby was barely more than a boy... And Miranda Lethbridge did not deserve—'

She broke off. 'Forgive me, Miss Kellaway. I am not normally one to gossip, but I thought it only fair that you should know what kind of woman you are impersonating—and why the Earl of Seagrave dislikes your sister so much!'

Lucille's heart felt like lead. Although naive in the ways of the world, she had common sense enough to have realised a long time before that she knew nothing of her sister's way of life, nor did she want to know. She had already learned too much in the inn at Felixstowe. Any lover was good enough, it seemed, as long as he was rich enough to pay Susanna's price. No wonder Seagrave held her in such contempt! Lucille had no time for the double standards of men who kept mistresses and then denounced the very women they would have in keeping, but she had some sympathy with Seagrave's point of view over Miranda Lethbridge. The prospect of being obliged to meet him again, knowing what she did now, made her feel vaguely sick.

Mrs Appleton was watching her sympathetically. 'I thought it best to tell you, Miss Kellaway,' she said apologetically. 'Should you meet Seagrave again—'

'I cannot bear to meet him again!' Lucille said, in anguish. 'Mrs Appleton, forgive my curiosity, but however did you come to work for Susanna? I cannot imagine—' She broke off, aware that her comments could offend. But the housekeeper was smiling, albeit a little sadly.

'You are right in thinking that it was not what I might have chosen, Miss Kellaway, given different circumstances! After I was widowed I had very little money, you see, and no means of keeping myself, so I applied for a post as cook/housekeeper with Miss Susanna. I knew what sort of an establishment it was, of course, but without references I could not hope for a position elsewhere...'

She paused. 'As I said earlier, I am fairly unshock-able after ten years on campaign, and am in no way missish! And indeed I have very little to do with Miss Susanna's business, for she has a maid to attend to her.' She smiled suddenly. 'That is not to say that I haven't had my moments! A gentleman was once overly amorous to me, but I was able to dissuade him from his attentions with a saucepan! And believe me, Miss Kellaway, I could have done a great deal worse than work for Miss Susanna!'

Lucille was left shaking her head in disbelief. She knew that *she* was both missish and easily shocked, and yet she was the one who had so foolishly agreed to impersonate Susanna. She had not known the half of it—and now she was trapped by her own folly. Thinking of this led her thoughts inevitably back to the Earl of Seagrave.

'Apparently Susanna's arrival at Dillingham has caused Seagrave's betrothed to cry off,' she told Mrs Appleton solemnly, 'so he has another reason to dis-like her now!' Despite her feelings, she could not sup-press a smile. 'He seemed remarkably annoyed by the fact!'

'I doubt his emotions are involved, only his pride,' Mrs Appleton said calmly. 'Seagrave is notorious for having no feelings at all! No more than a month ago he got engaged to Louise Elliott, a hen-witted girl of absolutely no distinction other than in her lineage. If she has thrown him over he may one day come to thank your sister! They say girls become very like their mothers and Lady Elliott is an arrogant, overbearing woman! But enough of this gossiping!' She got to her feet. 'I must make shift to find us some dinner!' She cast a look at Lucille's unhappy face. 'Never fear, Miss Kellaway,' she said bracingly, 'I have found sustenance under far more adverse conditions than this! As for Seagrave, well, we will just have to keep you out of his way in future!'

Chapter Three

Lucille felt that the whole atmosphere of Cookes had changed after that one meeting with the Earl of Seagrave and her illuminating chat with Mrs Appleton. Instead of enjoying the tranquil silence, she began to feel oppressed and lonely. It was the greatest irony that when she had been in ignorance of the villagers' attitude towards her she had not felt the need to leave the house and grounds—now she knew of their hostility, she longed to go out but did not dare. No longer could she lose herself in the pages of a book, or concentrate on her father's esoteric research into eastern civilisations.

Fully awakened, her conscience nagged her and gave her no peace, calling her a stupid little fool for her thoughtless agreement to so damaging a plan as Susanna had suggested. Better by far to have stayed within the safe confines of Miss Pym's school than to perpetrate such a deception.

Then there was the unfortunate effect that the Earl himself appeared to have on her. It seemed that the confusion he had thrown her into that day in Oakham was nothing compared to encountering him at close quarters. Lucille had led a sheltered existence, but none of the fathers or brothers of her pupils had ever made her pulse race in the disconcerting way Seagrave had affected her. His face had a disquieting tendency of imposing itself between her and the written page; the cadences of that mellow voice haunted her thoughts.

None of her reading could help her to understand this peculiar chemistry between them. She even caught herself daydreaming, an indulgence which both puzzled and horrified her. But none of her dreams of him could be in any way encouraging. He thought she was Susanna, after all, and even if he had met her under her own identity she did not flatter herself that he would have any time for a frumpish bluestocking. As for what he would think of her if he discovered her impersonation... She refused to allow herself to even consider that.

Fortunately for Lucille's equilibrium, Seagrave did not appear again at Cookes, although his agent, Mr Josselyn, called with some long and convoluted legal papers for Lucille to sign. She perused these with intense concentration and made a list of points on which she required clarification. She then stopped dead, realising that it was not her place to query the lease, but Susanna's. That inevitably made her recall the masquerade and she found herself out of sorts again. Normally she would have walked off her low spirits, but now she felt she could not even venture outside the gate of Cookes.

On the second day of enforced inactivity, Lucille threw her book aside in despair. It was Sunday evening and the church bells had been calling across the green. The shadows were falling now and all was still in the dusk. It was such a beautiful evening that Lucille was suddenly determined to go out. She put on her bonnet and coat, and slipped out of the front door.

The green was deserted and it was indeed pleasant to be outside now that the heat of the day had gone and the air was full of birdsong. Lucille left the shelter of Cookes's gates and crossed to the duck pond, holding her breath lest anyone see her. But all was quiet. It felt astonishingly liberating to be in the open air. For a while she just stood and enjoyed the neat prettiness of the cottages about the green, their gardens bursting with verdant summer flowers, their white-painted walls reflecting the last rays of the sun. Then she walked slowly across to the ancient stone church, and paused with her hand on the iron gate, suddenly overwhelmed with the need to go inside.

The church, like the village, was deserted now that the evening service was over and the congregation dispersed. Lucille let herself into the green darkness of the interior, and sat in a worn wooden back pew, breathing in the mixture of flower scent and ancient dust. It was so evocative of her childhood with the Markhams that her breath caught in her throat. The familiarity was soothing in an existence that had become so unexpectedly difficult. She said a few heartfelt prayers before letting herself out of the door into the churchyard, which had become full of deep shadows.

The first intimation Lucille had that she was not alone came with the pattering of paws along the path, and then a magnificent chocolate-coloured retriever was before her, sniffing inquisitively at her skirts and pressing its damp nose into the palm of her hand. Lucille laughed at this shameless bid for attention, bent down, and fondled the creature's silky ears.

'What a beauty you are, aren't you! I wonder what your name is…?'

The dog snuffled softly, rubbing its head against her hand, before turning, suddenly alert, its ears pricking up.

'Her name is Sal, Miss Kellaway, short for Salamanca.'

The Earl of Seagrave had stepped out from the shadows of an ancient yew tree and was viewing Lucille with thoughtful interest. 'She is not usually so friendly to strangers.'

Lucille watched Sal return submissively to her master's heel, and smiled at the look of adoration in those limpid dark eyes. No doubt that was the type of gaze she should be perfecting in the interests of her impersonation. However, there was something about the clear evening, scented with herbs and yew, which made her rebel against the idea of acting a part. She looked up from the dog to see that Seagrave was still watching her.

'Were you at Salamanca, my lord?'

'I was.' He straightened, coming towards her down the path, the dog now close at his heels. 'It was my last battle, Miss Kellaway. I had been in the Peninsula for four years, first serving under General Sir John Moore and then under Wellington—Sir Arthur Wellesley, as he was to begin with. It was July when we came up against the French just south of Salamanca; July, just as it is now. I remember it well.'

Seagrave took a deep breath of cool, scented air. 'It was hot, with the kind of oppressive, airless heat you can get in Spain in the summer. The land around was arid, dry as dust. The dust was everywhere…in our mouths, in our noses, in our clothes… We sat on the flat top of our hill and watched the French lines to the south of us, on the higher ground.'

His voice had taken on a still, reflective quality. 'You may have read that the battle was a great triumph for Wellington. So it was. The French were cut to pieces with at least fourteen thousand casualties. It was carnage. I was wounded advancing across the valley between the two hills. We were in the range of the cannon and I fell with shrapnel in the chest and shoulder. So I was invalided out, and shortly after that I inherited the title and thought to stay at home.'

He stirred slightly and gave a short, bitter laugh. 'My apologies, Miss Kellaway! It is unforgivable to speak of such matters to a lady. You must forgive me.'

Lucille shook her head slightly. She had become caught up in the tale, could almost feel the heat of the Spanish sun and taste the dust. War was an experience so far removed from the lives of most people that it was almost impossible to begin to imagine it. Many did not want to try, finding the contrast with their own easy existence too uncomfortable to contemplate.

'I am sorry,' she began, unsure what she was really apologising for, but aware that the undercurrent of bitterness which had touched his voice briefly was present in that still, shadowed face. 'It must have been very difficult to adapt to civilian life after such experiences.'

Seagrave gave another harsh laugh. 'Indeed it was, Miss Kellaway! After the immediacies of life and death, the delights of the *ton*, whilst entertaining, seem damnably shallow! But it is hardly fashionable to speak so! No doubt you think me most singular!'

'No, sir.' Lucille caught herself just as she was about to express her own preferences for reading and studying over routs and parties. The shock of realising that she had almost betrayed herself caused her to fall silent, her mind suddenly blank. It was impossible to be forever remembering that she was supposed to be Susanna.

'I am glad to see you have overcome your aversion to dogs,' Seagrave observed suddenly, watching as Sal lay down with her head at Lucille's feet. 'I thought you once said that you hated them.'

Lucille froze. Did Susanna hate dogs? She had no idea. Seagrave was looking quite bland, but she suddenly had an unnerving feeling that he was deliberately testing her. She shrugged lightly.

'I do not recall...'

'When you were driving in the Park one day last summer...or was it two summers ago?' Seagrave mused. 'Harriette Wilson's dog bit your arm and I am sure I remember you saying you thought they were hateful creatures and should all be destroyed. You were quite vehement on the subject!'

Lucille mentally added another item to the list of things about Susanna which she found unattractive. The list was getting rather long and she was learning

far more about her sister than she had known from
the first seventeen years of their lives together. As for
Harriette Wilson, Lucille knew her to be a legendary
Cyprian in the same mould as Susanna, but her choice
in pets was beyond her. 'Oh, well...' she managed to
sound quite vague '...that dreadful little, yapping
creature—'

'Miss Wilson has a wolfhound, as I recall,'
Seagrave commented, with mild irony. 'Scarcely a
small creature, and one which left a scar on your
arm.'

Lucille glanced down instinctively, although she
was wearing a jacket whose sleeves covered her arms
from shoulder to wrist. Which arm would Susanna
have injured? How could she tell? This was getting
ridiculous. She cast about hastily for a change of
topic.

'And what do you call your horse, sir?'

'I beg your pardon?' Seagrave sounded mystified
at the sudden change of direction.

'Your horse—that magnificent creature I have
heard that you ride about your estate. Surely it must
have some equally magnificent name?'

Seagrave laughed. 'I named him after Alexander
the Great's steed, Miss Kellaway! A conceit, I suppose, though he is worthy of it!'

'Bucephalus,' Lucille said absently, then recollected herself again as Seagrave shifted slightly, giving her a look that was quizzical to say the least.

'You have an interest in classical history, Miss
Kellaway? I would never have suspected it! You must
have inherited some of your father's scholarly nature,
after all!'

What did he mean, 'after all'? Lucille bit her lip. She was bristling with indignation at the slur on her intelligence but since she knew Seagrave was actually criticising Susanna rather than herself, she realised she should not regard it. She reminded herself that Susanna would shudder to be thought a bluestocking. 'Lud, we were always being fed such tedious facts at school,' she said, as carelessly as she could. 'How tiresome to discover that some of it remains with me! I would rather die than become an intellectual!'

'No danger of that!' Seagrave said laconically. 'I imagine your talents must lie in other directions!'

The comprehensively assessing look he gave her made Lucille tingle suddenly with an awareness which was completely outside her experience. She shivered in the cool air. Strangely she felt no insult, as she had done with Sir Edwin. The shadows were deepening with every moment, creating a dangerously intimate atmosphere about them. The thin, sickle moon rising above the branches of the yew and the scent of honeysuckle on the breeze did nothing to dispel this illusion.

Seagrave took another step towards her. He was now so close that he could have reached out and touched her but as yet he made no move to do so. Lucille's pulse was racing, the blood singing quick and light through her veins. Her mouth was dry and she moistened her lips nervously, watching in fascination as Seagrave's gaze followed the movement of her tongue, the look in his eyes suddenly so sexually explicit that she caught her breath. Then Sal ran forward, barking at shadows and Lucille turned hastily towards the lych-gate.

'I'll bid you good evening, sir.' She hardly recognised her own voice, so shaken it sounded.

Seagrave caught up to her at the gate. 'I saw you coming out of the church, Miss Kellaway,' he said abruptly. 'Can this be some remarkable conversion to moral rectitude?'

The mocking undertone in his voice banished the magical spell his presence had cast on Lucille. She had read about physical attraction, she reminded herself sharply, and knew that it had nothing to do with loving, liking or respecting another person. No doubt she should just be grateful that Seagrave was indeed no Sir Edwin Bolt, with his insultingly lewd comments and disgusting mauling of Susanna's naked flesh. Only she, Lucille, in her inexperience, had for a moment confused that intense physical awareness with feelings of a deeper and more meaningful kind.

'Did you imagine that I was there to steal the candlesticks?' she snapped, angry with herself for her susceptibility and with him for his sarcasm. She gathered up her skirts in one hand to enable her to walk away from him more quickly. 'Do you exercise the right to decree whether your tenants attend church or not, my lord? Take care that you do not assume too many of the Almighty's own privileges!'

Seagrave's eyes narrowed at this before he unexpectedly burst out laughing. 'A well-judged reproof, Miss Kellaway! What a contradictory creature you are! Come, I shall escort you back to Cookes!'

Lucille preferred not to torment herself with his company. 'Thank you, but there is not the least need! Good night, sir!'

Seagrave, who was used to having his companionship actively sought by women rather than abruptly refused, found this rather amusing. He wished he had kissed her when he had had the chance. He watched with a rueful smile as her small, upright figure crossed the green and disappeared in at the gates of Cookes. Susanna Kellaway… He frowned abruptly, recalling what he knew of her. His wits must be a-begging to find her remotely attractive.

He knew she was supposed to exercise a powerful sexual sway over her conquests, but the attraction he had felt had been far more complex than mere lust. God alone knew what had prompted him to tell her about Salamanca. If he had not forcibly stopped himself, he imagined he would have blurted out all about his alienation from normal life, the driven madness which had possessed him when he had returned from the wars… Damnation! This sojourn in the country must be making him soft in the head! He called Sal sharply to heel and set off across the moonlit fields back to Dillingham Court.

The good weather broke the following day, and Lucille spent the morning curled up in the drawing-room with an ancient map of Dillingham that she had found in her father's study. Each lane and dwelling was carefully labelled; Cookes was there, though at that time it was still a row of individual timbered cottages, drawn with skill and precision by the cartographer's pen. On the other side of Dragon Hill, the only high land in the area, lay a beautifully stylised house named on the map as Dillingham Court and surrounded by its pleasure gardens. Lucille's curiosity was whetted, but she knew it was unlikely that she would ever see the Court in real life.

There had still been no word from Susanna, and two weeks had already passed. Lucille no longer really believed that her sister would return in the time she had promised, and she itched to be away from Cookes. Wearing Susanna's character, even without an audience, suddenly grated on her. If only Seagrave had not come to Dillingham! Lucille shifted uncomfortably in her chair, her conscience pricking her again.

Immediately after luncheon the rain ceased, driven away by a brisk wind that hurried the ragged clouds across the sky. Lucille was tired of being cooped up all day. She put on a pair of stout boots to protect her from the puddles and called for the carriage to be brought round.

'I wish to go to the seaside, John,' she told the startled coachman.

It was six miles to the sea at the nearest point, which was Shingle Street, and the journey was a slow one over rutted tracks. Clearly John thought that she was mad to attempt such an expedition, but Lucille did not care. Once out of the village environs, the lush green fields soon gave way to thick forest and heathland, flat, dark and empty to the horizons. On such a grey day it was both forbidding and desolate, but Lucille found it a fascinating place. When they finally reached the sea, she descended from the carriage to be met by the full force of the wind and was almost blown over. The fresh salty tang of the air was exhilarating.

Feeling much better, Lucille told John that she would walk along the shore for a little way and asked him to meet her at the gates of the only house she had seen in the vicinity. Scratching his head, the coachman watched her walk off along the shingle beach, a slight, lonely figure in her outmoded coat and boots. How could two sisters be so different? he wondered. Miss Susanna Kellaway never walked anywhere if she could ride; more fundamentally, she had never said please or thank you in all the time he had worked for her.

The walking was hard along the shingle, and the power of the waves was awesome at close quarters. The sea was gunmetal grey, a heaving, bad-tempered maelstrom as it hurled itself on the shore. Seabirds screamed and wheeled overhead. Here and there, sea wrack was scattered across the beach; flotsam and jetsam from ships, bent and misshapen after their time in the water. Lucille stooped to consider a few pieces and picked up a piece of wood that had been worn smooth by the force of the waves.

She had reached a point where there was a set of ancient, worn steps cut into the shingle and she turned away from the sea to follow them up the small cliff. On the headland the turf was smooth and springy, the path skirting an ancient fence which marked the boundary of the house Lucille had seen earlier. She paused, wondering who could have chosen to live in so desolate a spot. The house itself was hidden from her view by a well-established shrubbery and cluster of gnarled trees, but it looked a substantial dwelling. And as she considered it, leaning on the fence, a voice from near at hand said:

'Goddess! Excellently bright!'

Lucille jumped and spun around. The voice was of a rich, deep-velvet quality and would have carried from pit to gallery at a Drury Lane theatre. Emerging from the shrubbery was an extraordinary figure, a large woman of indeterminate age, wrapped in what seemed like endless scarves of blue chiffon and purple gauze in complete defiance of the climate. Over her arm was a basket full of roses and at her heels stalked a large fluffy white cat. The most worldly-wise, disillusioned pair of dark eyes that Lucille had ever seen were appraising her thoughtfully.

'That, Miss Kellaway,' the lady said impressively, 'was in tribute to your beauty and was—'

'Ben Jonson,' Lucille said, spontaneously. 'Yes, I know!'

The pessimistic dark eyes focussed on her more intently. 'Would you care to take tea with me, Miss Kellaway? I have so few visitors here for I am not recognised in the county!'

For a moment, Lucille wondered what on earth she meant. It seemed impossible that such a character would remain unrecognised wherever she went.

'I am Bessie Bellingham,' the lady continued, grandly. 'The Dowager Lady Bellingham! Bessie Bowles, as was!'

She paused, clearly expecting the recognition she deserved, and Lucille did not disappoint her.

'Of course! I have read of you, ma'am—your performance as Viola in *Twelfth Night* was accounted one of the best ever seen at Drury Lane, and the papers were forever arguing over whether comedy or melodrama was your forté!'

'Well, well, before your time, my child!' But Lady
Bellingham was smiling, well pleased, and the cat
was rubbing around Lucille's ankles and purring. 'My
own favourite was Priscilla Tomboy in *The Romp*, but
it was a long time ago, before I met dear Bellingham
and ended up in this mausoleum!'

She took Lucille's arm and steered her through the
shrubbery towards the house. 'You have no idea how
delighted I was when I saw you on the beach,' she
continued. 'Of course, I had heard that you were staying in Dillingham—my maid, Conchita, knows everything! And I thought that, as we two are the black
sheep of the neighbourhood, we could take tea and
talk of the London this provincial crowd will never
know!'

Lucille remembered, with a sudden uprush of
alarm, that Lady Bellingham, in common with the
whole of Suffolk, would think that she was Susanna.
But it was too late to cry off—the house had come
into view and Lady Bellingham was drawing her forward up the wide, shallow steps and onto the terrace.
It was, Lucille thought, a particularly ugly house,
foursquare and squat, brick-built and crouching low
to the ground as though sheltering from the wind off
the sea. And how such a character as Lady
Bellingham could choose to immure herself here,
Lucille could not imagine.

'I am seldom at home,' Lady Bellingham was saying as though she had read Lucille's thoughts, 'for I
travel a great deal on the continent—when the
European situation will allow! But for now you find
me all alone—' she gave a theatrical shrug '—and
happy for some distraction!'

They had gone into the drawing-room, which was stuffed full of furniture mostly in the French style. Lady Bellingham subsided on to the gilt-wood settee, and Lucille somewhat gingerly perched on one of the matching, silk-upholstered chairs, which proved a lot less spindly than it looked. The cat, graciously accepting the bonbon Lady Bellingham held out, curled up in a large *fauteuil* and fell instantly asleep. Lady Bellingham rang a small brass bell and ordered tea, then turned her world-weary gaze back to Lucille.

'So tell me how dear Bertie Penscombe is these days,' she invited, her dark eyes sparkling with malicious enjoyment. 'Is it really true that you have thrown him over for Seagrave? Not that I can fault you there, my dear! Seagrave has to be one of the most charismatic men that I have ever had the pleasure of meeting! Now, if I were thirty years younger...' She helped herself to another bonbon, her eyes never leaving Lucille's face.

Lucille found herself to be completely tongue-tied. She was unable to comment on the attributes of Susanna's former lover, and was all too aware of the attractions of the Earl of Seagrave. And as she hesitated fatally, Lady Bellingham clapped her hands together in a sudden, energetic gesture that made Lucille jump.

'No, no, no, no, no, no!' she said abruptly and melodramatically. 'I have puzzled over it since we first met, and I cannot account for it! *You* cannot be the Cyprian!'

To be unmasked so emphatically, in tones which would have riveted an entire audience, silenced

Lucille completely. Lady Bellingham, seeing her total confusion, smiled in kindly fashion.

'No need to look so shocked, my poor child! It is simply that I have played the Cyprian—oh, many and many times! You do not have the air, the style!' She got to her feet. 'A courtesan minces, so...' it was ludicrous to see that solid figure prancing across the drawing-room in such an accurate and cruel caricature of Susanna's provocatively swaying walk '...and she has the air...' Lady Bellingham stuck her nose in the air and raised a hand to her forehead in an exact parody of Susanna's delicate, die-away affectations. 'I vow,' she said in a languishing drawl, ''tis impossible to choose between Lord Rook and Lord Crow, but for their fortune!'

Lucille could not help herself. She gave a peal of laughter.

'And your dress, the hair...' Lady Bellingham was shaking her head sorrowfully. 'My dear Miss Kellaway, if Miss Kellaway you really are, it simply will not do!'

'I know I am very bad at it,' Lucille said regretfully. 'You see, Lady Bellingham, I had no idea...and Susanna had so little time... Oh dear, now I really am in the suds!'

'Tell me All!' Lady Bellingham said impressively, her dark eyes sparkling at Lucille over the rim of her teacup. 'Horace and I—' she eyed the sleeping cat with affection '—have so little excitement! Can you be Susanna Kellaway's sister?'

'I am Lucille Kellaway and I am her twin,' Lucille confirmed sadly, 'and lamentably poor at impersonating her!'

'Well,' Lady Bellingham said astringently, 'that is no bad thing! Why pretend to be a Cyprian when one is not? Lord knows, there's precious little amusement in it, whatever one might think!'

Lucille was beginning to feel better under this unsentimental assessment. Slowly, the whole story came out, of Susanna's request to her and her own foolish agreement. Lady Bellingham nodded and ate biscuits and stroked Horace absentmindedly.

'I only wanted to escape the confines of the school for a little, and visit the place where our father had lived,' Lucille finished ruefully. 'I had no idea that matters would get so complicated! But not only do the villagers detest having Susanna amongst them, but I have been obliged to deceive the Earl of Seagrave—something which I would have wished to avoid at all costs!'

Lady Bellingham put down her cup and brushed the biscuit crumbs absentmindedly from the folds of her scarves. 'Seagrave…yes…' she said thoughtfully. 'He is not the man to try to cozen! His father was another such—an honourable man, but most awe-inspiring! Not like your own dear papa, my dear—' her eyes twinkled at Lucille '—with whom I once flirted at a hunt breakfast! A gentleman and a scholar, George Kellaway, and quite, quite charming! But he had not an ounce of Seagrave's authority!'

'I plan to leave Dillingham as soon as I may,' Lucille said in a rush, 'and put an end to this imprudent charade! I have been very foolish and do not wish for matters to go any further!'

'A pity!' Lady Bellingham smiled warmly at her. 'I am persuaded that I could have taught you suffi-

cient tricks to pull it off! But if you would rather
not…' She shrugged her ample shoulders. 'Now, I see
your carriage is waiting and I should not delay you,
for it is a slow drive back to Dillingham! But come
and see me again, dear child, for I have enjoyed your
visit immensely!'

'You have been very kind to me, ma'am,' Lucille
said, slowly, 'and I am very glad to have met you! I
was quite blue-devilled today!'

Lady Bellingham enfolded Lucille in a warm embrace and insisted on coming with her to the front
door, where John the coachman was waiting, having
been summoned from his vigil at the gates by the
butler. They drove slowly away down the chestnut-
lined drive, and Lucille waved to the bulky, chiffon-
draped figure on the steps until they were out of sight.

The encounter with Lady Bellingham certainly
lifted Lucille's spirits. She now had even less sympathy for a society which could deny itself the pleasure of the company of such an idiosyncratic character through pure snobbery. It seemed that former
actresses, like Cyprians, were not to be received or
even acknowledged amongst the bigoted gentry of
Suffolk. The thought bred determination and bravado.
There was not the least need, Lucille told herself, to
spend her remaining time in Dillingham moping behind closed doors.

Accordingly she woke the next morning resolved
to take a walk, and follow one of the paths she had
seen marked on the map the previous day. Her only
difficulty lay in negotiating the village green, which
she knew was unlikely to be as empty as on the

Sunday evening. That was where the bravado came in. Lucille put on her bonnet and raised her chin defiantly. Let the villagers show their disapproval!

Cookes was set back from the road down a short drive, with a carriage sweep at the front and well-tended lawns bordering the gates. Lucille walked slowly down the drive and out on to the green. Despite her defiant thoughts of a few minutes before, she admitted to a large measure of apprehension when she realised that it was market day and the green was packed with stalls and hawkers. There was a wealth of seafood on offer: crab, eels, flounder and oysters tumbled from baskets and across trestles. Nearby were flower girls, and fruit-sellers with panniers of oranges, lemons and cherries. A pieman cheerfully shouted his wares. It was a vivid scene. It was also too late for her to retreat, for she had been noticed. Straightening her spine, she picked her way between the vendors and started to cross the green.

The change in atmosphere was both sudden and tangible. The hostility was all too real. As Lucille passed by a sudden silence fell. Men stared and women pulled their skirts aside as if she might contaminate them. Children were abruptly hushed and summoned to their parents' side. Lucille, who had expected to be able to cope with the animosity, was unprepared for the depth of feeling. It shook her. She actually felt unsafe. Stallholders watched in silence as she walked through the market; trade was suspended. People turned away. One man even spat on the ground at her feet. And behind her she was aware of the crescendo of sound.

'We don't want her sort here…no better than she

ought to be…the hussy! She should be driven out! Nothing but a common trollop!'

By the time she had reached the other side of the green and run the gauntlet of so many hostile faces, Lucille found the angry, unshed tears stinging her eyes and blocking her throat. She wanted to shout at them all for their stupid ignorance and intolerance, but equally she wanted to run away and hide, never to have to face them again. Even the curate had emerged from the door of the charming stone church and was watching her progress with hard, condemning eyes. She almost expected him to step forward and denounce her as a harlot before the assembled throng.

Lucille had reached the lane which led out of the village towards the Court, and was starting to feel marginally better, when a stout woman carrying a marketing basket full of vegetables stepped out from a nearby path and blocked her way. Her high colour suggested a choleric nature and her livid gaze made Lucille's heart sink. Behind her lounged a dark young man with a narrow, watchful face, whose bold gaze was appraising Lucille in the presumptuous way that she hated. Her heart started to beat faster.

'Miss Kellaway! I am Serena Mutch, George Kellaway's sister! I had to see with my own eyes if you could really be his daughter!'

Lucille took a deep breath. 'I am delighted to meet you, Aunt,' she said, carefully. 'It is a pleasure to meet the family I have never known—'

Mrs Mutch snorted with disgust. 'Pleasure! It's a disgrace! You have brought nothing but dishonour on the name of Kellaway, and you should be ashamed to show your face here! You shameless trollop!'

There was a grin on the young man's face now as he leant back against the fence and enjoyed her discomfiture. Lucille itched to slap his arrogance away. If this was Mrs Mutch, the young man could only be her cousin Walter, who had been cut out of his inheritance by Susanna's unexpected claim to Cookes.

'She may be anybody's to ride, but she looks nothing like Farmer Trudgeon's mare!' he said, in a rich country drawl which seemed only to accentuate the insult in the words. Mrs Mutch's face flamed, but whether in anger or embarrassment at her son's coarseness, it was difficult to gauge. She turned to Lucille in a sudden fury.

'Well, what are you waiting for? Get out of this village! Get out, I say!' Her fingers closed around the large cauliflower she had in the basket, and Lucille realised with incredulity that she was about to throw it at her. The insane idea of the villagers pelting her with rotten fruit and vegetables flashed across her mind even as Mrs Mutch raised her arm. It would be messy, Lucille thought hysterically, but not as bad as stoning…

'Good day, Mrs Mutch, Walter…'

The mellow tones, utterly expressionless, cut right across them. Preoccupied in the confrontation, neither Lucille nor her relatives had heard the approaching hoofbeats and Lucille turned in amazement to see the Earl of Seagrave reining in Bucephalus and summing up the entire scene with one swift, assessing glance. He swung down from the saddle and stood next to her. Extraordinarily, there was something so reassuring about his presence that Lucille could feel herself relaxing, despite the fact that her conscious mind was telling her that Seagrave was more likely to join in the denunciation than to defend her.

Mrs Mutch lowered the cauliflower slowly and dropped an embarrassed curtsy. Walter straightened up and threw away the piece of straw he had been chewing.

'Good day, my lord!' Mrs Mutch sounded flustered. 'I was just…greeting my niece!'

Seagrave's gaze rested thoughtfully on the vegetables. 'So I see. A charming family reunion.' He looked at Walter for a moment, and the man's thin face flushed slightly. 'I am loath to interrupt,' Seagrave continued smoothly, 'but I feel Miss Kellaway must be fatigued in this heat. Miss Kellaway, I shall escort you back to Cookes now. Good day, Mrs Mutch.'

His tone brooked no refusal. He looped the horse's reins over his arm and took Lucille's elbow in his other hand, turning back towards the green and walking between her and the avid villagers, effectively shielding her from their view. He steered her down the lane towards Cookes and did not pause or speak until a bend in the road cut them off from sight.

'I did warn you how it would be, Miss Kellaway.' There was no pity in his tone or sympathy in his gaze as he looked down at her. Lucille, shaking with anger and reaction, was so incensed that she looked him straight in the eye.

'You did indeed, Lord Seagrave! I see that you have already been extremely busy putting your threat into practice! A pity you could not have warned me about it the last time we met, instead of making a pretence of civility!'

For some reason her furious comment seemed to touch Seagrave on the raw. The black stallion, a magnificent and highly bred beast, jibbed as he jerked its rein in an involuntary movement.

'It is none of my doing, Miss Kellaway.' The mellow tones were unusually harsh.

Lucille's voice caught on a sob. 'Then it seems you may spare yourself the trouble, my lord! I am already scorned as a scarlet woman and my housekeeper is refused provisions by every stallholder and shopowner in the place! Anyone, it seems, may insult me as they please! Even I am not so brass faced as to stay in a place where I am so clearly despised!'

To her horror, Lucille felt the scalding tears about to overflow. She turned away in anger and distress, covering her face with her hands.

Seagrave's hand tightened on her arm. 'Do not let that old harridan put you out of countenance, Miss Kellaway!' he said, urgently, in her ear. 'Serena Mutch's bad temper springs more from the disappointment and anger of seeing her son disinherited than her disapproval of you!'

Lucille swallowed hard. The insults might have been intended for Susanna, not her, but they were wounding nevertheless. She had never experienced such bitter animosity in her life. 'Whatever her reasons, Mrs Mutch said only what the whole village was thinking!' She took a gulp of air and managed to overcome her tears with an immense effort, even summoning up a wan smile as she remembered the cauliflower.

'At the least, I must thank you for your prompt rescue, sir. I believe I was about to be pilloried with my aunt's vegetables! And on the subject of reputation, I fear that it will scarce do either of us any good for you to be seen in converse with me! You may leave me here, I think. I shall be quite safe!'

'My reputation can stand it,' Seagrave said, with a hint of amusement in his tone, 'and yours, Miss Kellaway—'

'Was lost long since!' Lucille finished for him. She gave a tired shrug. 'As you wish, sir!'

Seagrave, again brought up short by her reluctant toleration of his company, discovered that he wished to prolong the encounter very much. He looked at her, his gaze suddenly intent. She was not beautiful, he thought judiciously, but there was a formidable appeal about her looks which probably in some part explained her success. She was not in the common style, with her oval face set with those magnificent cornflower blue eyes, the small retroussé nose, and the soft pink mouth made for smiling—or to be kissed. Then there was the unconscious challenge of that pert, determined chin and the graceful line of her neck…he could not argue with those who called her looks striking.

Her figure was less voluptuous than he remembered from seeing her in Town, but it showed to advantage in the tight-fitting blue jacket worn over her high-waisted jonquil dress. Less obvious, less easy to explain though, was the clear intelligence in that flashing blue gaze, a very different matter from the cupidity and opportunism that he had seen and despised when he knew her before. Finally, and even more confusingly, she had an air of fragility and innocence which aroused powerful feelings of protectiveness in him. What else could have sent him to her aid when he could have turned the situation to his own benefit and completed her humiliation? Cursing himself for a susceptible fool, he deliberately tried to distance himself.

'It was foolish of you to venture out in the daylight, all the same,' he drawled. 'I had thought you only dared to flit about the village in the dark!'

'Like a bat, perhaps?' Lucille asked sweetly, and earned herself a quizzical look.

She tried to get a grip on herself, knowing she was in grave danger of giving away the entire masquerade. Susanna would never have spoken thus. But her feelings had swung from misery to a heady relief that she had escaped so unpleasant a scene, and the presence of the Earl of Seagrave added some indefinable element of excitement that was in danger of making her almost too reckless. At that moment she would not even have cared very much had the whole deception come tumbling about her ears, were it not for the thought of Seagrave's inevitable disgust and disapproval. That, on top of her recent humiliation, was more than she could bear.

They continued to walk slowly down the lane that skirted Cookes's orchards, with the mighty Bucephalus trotting along behind in complete disgust. Lucille was finding, disconcertingly, that Seagrave's powerful effect on her had not waned. She was almost unbearably aware of his physical presence, the brush of his sleeve against her arm, the strength of the hand that had held her arm and was now clasping

Bucephalus's reins lightly between tanned fingers… For a moment she imagined those same hands sliding over her skin and was transfixed by the image, both dismayed and confused by whatever was happening to her. She did not understand it and could not explain it away. To distract herself, she reminded herself that she was supposed to be Susanna, who would not be thrown into confusion by a staid summer stroll with a charismatic Earl.

'So how do you find Cookes now that you have had time to get to know it a little?' the Earl asked a few moments later.

'Oh, it is a charming little house,' Lucille said, attempting Susanna's condescending drawl, 'though no doubt your lordship would prefer that I thought otherwise!' She looked at him through her eyelashes and saw the slight, cynical smile on his lips. Encouraged, she continued archly, 'Be warned, sir, I may give up Dillingham but I shall not give up the lease so easily!'

She saw that sardonic smile grow. 'I never doubted it for a moment, Miss Kellaway,' Seagrave said smoothly. 'You must be feeling more the thing now, I think, for you have reverted to form! How slow I was in not realising that all I had to do to get you to leave was to offer you enough money!'

Lucille smiled to herself. He certainly had Susanna's measure! 'I would consider any reasonable offer,' she said virtuously. 'After all, a young lady must make shift to take care of herself!' She saw his lip curl in barely concealed distaste and tried not to laugh. She must be a more accomplished actress than she had imagined, to ape Susanna so accurately! She was almost beginning to enjoy herself! Perhaps she should have taken Lady Bellingham up on her offer after all... Half appalled, half exhilarated, Lucille wondered how she had the audacity to further the impersonation.

'I will think about paying you off,' Seagrave said coolly. 'I am not sure how much the lease of Cookes is really worth to me!'

Lucille cast him a coy look. 'Ah, but it is not merely the lease, is it, my lord! I imagine you would pay a great deal to remove my presence from your estate, but I warn you, my price is high!'

'So I have heard,' Seagrave said, with a searing look sideways at her that made his meaning quite clear. Those dark eyes considered her body with insulting thoroughness, dwelling thoughtfully on the curve of her breasts before moving downwards. Lucille felt as though his gaze stripped every item of clothing from her. She willed herself not to blush. She could hardly complain, after all, if he treated her as the Cyprian she had set herself up to be! And strangely, once again his look evoked none of the squirming disgust she had felt with Sir Edwin, or the outrage provoked by Walter Mutch...

'However,' the Earl continued without interest after a moment, 'it is not a cost I would wish to incur, though I shall offer you a fair price for the lease.'

It was a humiliating setdown, Lucille felt. She remembered Mrs Appleton saying that the one thing Susanna could not bear was rejection. She had never been able to bear the thought that she was not irresistibly attractive, even when a small girl. Accordingly, Lucille set her lips in a mutinous line and pretended to sulk. They walked on a little way in silence. The road was skirting the edge of Cookes's orchards and briar roses tumbled over the ancient wall. Lucille had to stop herself from pausing to breathe in their scent—Susanna had never really appreciated the beauties of nature.

'I am glad that the lease of Cookes prevents you from evicting me as you threatened that first time,' she said, emulating the spite she had sometimes seen Susanna display when crossed. 'At least matters are not made *that* easy for your lordship!'

Seagrave merely looked amused. 'No,' he agreed affably, 'unfortunately I am not to be rid of you so easily, Miss Kellaway! I am afraid I lied at that first encounter! But you see, it might have worked—and spared me a lot of trouble!'

He was not the only one who lied, Lucille thought, with a sudden and inconvenient return of her guilty conscience. She had done nothing but lie to him since they first met. And here she was parodying her sister to the extent of almost creating a caricature! The enormity of it all rendered her temporarily speechless.

They had reached the wooden gate into Cookes. Bucephalus started to help himself to the hedge. Seagrave turned to Lucille, smiling politely. 'I am glad that your experience in the village has not overset you, Miss Kellaway. You are feeling quite recovered, I hope?'

Lucille managed an artistic shiver. 'Well, I'll own it was most unpleasant, but—simple people…what can one expect but a small-minded, illiterate intolerance!'

'These simple country people often have a very well-developed sense of morality, Miss Kellaway,'

Seagrave said dryly, 'which is something I doubt you ever had, or perhaps lost a long time ago! Where did your foster father go wrong, I wonder?'

Lucille tried a delicate yawn, the type of reaction Susanna would most certainly have shown to such moralising. She followed it up with a pert toss of the head.

'Lud, I don't doubt Mr Markham has been spinning in his grave these nine years past! But what a prosy bore you have turned out to be, my lord! I would never have guessed it! You sound just like my foster mother, forever exhorting us to marry well and settle down! I had no taste for respectable, genteel poverty! I declare, if I must give myself to an old man I might as well be paid for it!'

'A most practical attitude, Miss Kellaway,' Seagrave agreed, his face expressionless. 'And your sister, the schoolmistress—I collect she took a different approach to earning a living! How did she feel at being left at the mercy of the world, with Markham dead and Kellaway abroad?'

With a shock, Lucille remembered that *she* was the schoolmistress to whom he was referring. 'La, I do not know! I never asked her!' That, at least was true. 'She spends all her time immured in Miss Pym's school teaching those tiresome little girls! I vow, it's enough to make one run quite mad!' And that, she thought, was quite enough of Susanna for one day. She felt empty and guilt ridden at the things she had said. It was time to make an end.

She turned to Seagrave and held out her hand. 'It seems we may not meet again, so I shall bid you farewell, my lord. I plan to remove from here shortly.'

Seagrave looked down at the small hand in his own, then up again at her face. 'Truly, Miss Kellaway? I did not realise you were in earnest when you said that earlier.'

Lucille tried to free her hand but he was holding on to it. She dropped her gaze from his intent one. 'La, sir, Dillingham is too slow for me!' She gave him one last dazzling smile and tried again to free herself. He had still not let her go and the warm clasp of his fingers was sending small, exquisite sensations trembling along her nerve endings.

'If it is the matter of provisions that is worrying you, I will see that you are sent all that you need,' Seagrave said abruptly, 'and will undertake that you do not have such problems again. And if your house-keeper needs help in running Cookes, I am sure that Josselyn can arrange something. After all, it is in my interests that the upkeep of the house and gardens is maintained.'

Lucille hesitated. This sudden generosity seemed odd and out of character. What new approach was this? Could he be trying to lull her suspicions, pretend to stand her friend, whilst he tried to find a new way to break the lease? No doubt, were she really Susanna, she would be thinking that he had proved susceptible to her charm after all!

'It's monstrous good of you, sir,' she said, giving him a melting look from under her lashes. 'I knew you would relent. I am so grateful…'

'Keep your gratitude within bounds, Miss Kellaway,' Seagrave said coolly. He let go of her at last. 'Make no mistake of it, I want you out of Cookes. But the lease of the property is yours by right

of inheritance. I shall not have it said that I have
driven you from the house with no recompense. Good
day, Miss Kellaway.'

Arrogant man! Lucille let out a huge sigh as she
watched him mount a very disgruntled Bucephalus
and canter off up the track towards Dillingham Court.
She never wanted to have to go through such an encounter again. She felt exhausted, and overcome with
remorse. She had behaved in a truly disgraceful way,
and if Seagrave had called her bluff and offered her
carte blanche it would have served her right!
Dangling her bonnet from its strings, she made her
way slowly through the dappled shade of the orchard
towards the house, her mind still full of the charismatic Earl and his quixotic generosity.

Had she but known it, Seagrave's own reaction was
just as complicated as her own. Once clear of the
village he set the stallion to a gallop across the fields
to the Court. The speed was exhilarating, but did
nothing to help him clarify his thoughts. He was both
puzzled and annoyed by his response to Susanna
Kellaway. He was not an inexperienced youth, nor
was he willing to delude himself. He was therefore
obliged to accept that he was attracted to her, and had
been ever since their first encounter. He had lied when
he had said that he was not interested in her—he was
beginning to want her like a fever in the blood. His
feelings prevented him from driving her out of the
village with the ruthlessness the situation clearly demanded. It was a completely unexpected reaction and
one that was as unwelcome as it was surprising.

Worse, he could not make up his mind about her.

She was so contradictory, so unpredictable! One moment she was truly the Susanna he remembered, then a moment later she would reveal unexpected depths before retreating behind that superficial façade once more. It was infuriating, but it was fascinating as well. There was something else, too, that did not fit the case—something at the back of his mind, troubling him…something that his agent had mentioned about the Kellaway sisters when he had first arrived at the Court. He handed over the sweating horse to a stablehand with a word of thanks and strode into the house, calling for Josselyn as he went. He was so wrapped up in his own thoughts that it escaped his notice that his habitual boredom had vanished like mist in the summer sun.

Chapter Four

There were five days left before Lucille could depart for Oakham, and she felt sometimes as though she were counting the hours. She had not ventured beyond Cookes's boundaries again, contenting herself with strolling through the orchard or sitting beside the pond and watching the brown trout basking in the sun. Lucille had always considered herself to be a solitary soul by choice, with plenty of resources to help her occupy her time, and she was surprised and depressed to find her self-imposed solitude lonely. Since she could not go out, her only companion was Mrs Appleton, and the housekeeper had made it plain in the most pleasant of ways that Lucille's position as her employer's sister precluded a closer friendship between them.

Lucille understood this, but found herself wishing for someone in whom to confide. Over the years Miss Pym had fulfilled this role admirably, and Lucille missed her mentor's advice. She considered going to see Lady Bellingham again, but did not want to impose, and that left only her books for distraction. In an effort to immerse herself once more she turned to Miss Austen's *Mansfield Park*, hoping that the wittily observed social conventions would divert her from her feeling of isolation.

She had been sitting on the rustic bench beneath the apple tree when she heard the sound of footsteps on the gravel path. For a moment her heart began to race in the absurd hope and conviction that it might be Seagrave, but the man who appeared around the side of the house was a complete stranger to her. Excitement was replaced by apprehension, but she had little time to wonder about his identity as he hurried forward across the grass.

'*Suzanne! Ma belle! Enfin!*' Then, breaking into English: 'You little minx, I have scoured this so-dull countryside just to find you!'

He took her hand and covered it with moist kisses, then held her at arm's length, his berry-black eyes twinkling suggestively. 'But you have lost weight, *mon ange*! Whatever can 'ave 'appened to you?'

'I am very well, I thank you, sir.' Lucille knew she sounded ludicrously formal after his fulsome greeting, but she could not help herself. In the first place she did not have the least idea who he was and she was repelled by his moist breath on her face. She tried surreptitiously to wipe his kisses off her hand.

The gentleman was looking comically crestfallen. 'So cold, *ma belle*? You were not so cruel to your *petit* Charles last spring! Why, we made a fine time of it, you and I, did we not, Suzanne!'

Lucille was fairly certain that she could now place the gentleman as one of Susanna's ex-lovers. And at least she knew his name now. She wished she had been inside when he had called; wished Mrs Appleton had been on hand to help her; wished even that the ground could open up beneath her feet and swallow her up before she had to attempt this difficult conversation. But there was no help on hand. It was a beautiful day, perfect for a romantic tête-à-tête beneath the spreading branches of the apple tree. A turtle dove began to coo above their heads.

She looked at her unexpected visitor thoughtfully. He looked very Gallic, with long black locks, heavily pomaded, and impressive side-whiskers. He was wearing a gaudy purple coat with huge gold buttons, and there was excessive lace at his wrists and throat. There was also a twinkle in his black eyes which Lucille, inexperienced as she was, recognised with misgiving. So far, none of the men who had cast covetous eyes on her in her role as Susanna had actually taken any action, but there was the same lascivious gleam in this man's eyes as she had seen from the occasional father, delivering his daughter back to school, and she had once had to fight off the goaty advances of a repellent geography master. A suspicion that the Frenchman might wish to rekindle his relationship with her sister took shape in her mind.

Lucille gave him a cool smile, moving away to sit down gracefully on the bench. 'My dear Charles, that was then and this is now.' She gave Susanna's light shrug. 'You know how fickle I am, my dear!'

The gentleman seemed to take this in good part, smiling a little cynically as his familiar gaze continued to rove over her. Lucille found this presumptuous but knew by now that Susanna must be used to such attentions. Under his scrutiny the mauve silk and lace dress, another of Susanna's most modest confections, felt as though it was both far too low cut and too transparent. He took a seat at the opposite end of the bench, which was too close to Lucille for comfort, and allowed his arm to lie along the back of the seat, just touching her shoulder. Lucille found she had to steel herself not to flinch away.

'I am *aux anges* to see you again, *mon amour*,' he murmured seductively. 'I have missed you so much!' Lust flared suddenly in his eyes. 'Ah, Suzanne, there is no one quite like you—so warm, so skilful! Do you remember—?'

Lucille broke in rather desperately. 'So how did you find me, Charles?' she asked, certain that Susanna would not have told anyone of her address in Suffolk.

The gentleman rolled his eyes. '*Mon Dieu*, Suzanne, you put me to a lot of trouble! No one at your London house would give your direction—in the end I had to bribe a kitchen maid for the information I wanted! Why are you hiding in this tedious place, *ma belle*?' He raised an interrogative eyebrow.

Lucille shrugged evasively. 'There were reasons, Charles…'

He laughed. 'Reasons? That I understand very well! After all, I have my own reasons for seeking you out, *ma chère*!'

Lucille gave him what she hoped passed for a look of languid enquiry. At least she seemed to have successfully distracted his thoughts from seduction—for the time being. 'Money, my dear?'

Charles looked a little chagrined. '*Alors*, you have no delicacy, you English! I admit to a temporary embarrassment only… If you could see your way clear to advancing me a small loan…'

'My dear…' Lucille hesitated. How difficult it was to achieve the casual intimacy of old lovers! Never having had a lover, old or new, she had no idea.

But the gentleman was on his feet and speaking again. 'A paltry sum, *mon ange*, only my card debts are becoming pressing…'

Lucille felt uncomfortable with him looming over her and stood up. They were of a height and his pleading black eyes, so like a puppy's, gazed melodramatically into hers. She was hard put to it not to laugh.

'My dear Charles,' she began again, 'I would truly love to help you, but I fear I have with me here nowhere near the amount you need. Now, if you were to apply to me in a few weeks' time in London, I might be able to be more forthcoming.'

'You wish to get rid of me,' the gentleman said, hangdog. '*Alors*, Suzanne, be kind to me! I have come all this way—'

Before Lucille had realised it, he had caught her to him and was trying to kiss her. She turned her head just in time and his wet lips landed on her cheek rather than her mouth. She pushed hard but ineffectually against his chest. He was a lot stronger than he appeared and Lucille suddenly wished Mrs Appleton were there with her saucepan.

'Suzanne!' This time there was reproach in his voice. He really was a consummate actor, Lucille thought. Perhaps he could mend his fortunes with a career on the stage. 'To deny a man a little comfort when he has travelled all this way to see you—'

'To borrow money from me, you mean!' Lucille

snapped, twisting her head away again to avoid him. 'Let me go at once!' She had no idea how Susanna would have handled this and did not really care. Her only concern was to get away from him. She looked round a little desperately, but there were no suitable objects within reach. If only they had been inside she could have used one of her father's Chinese souvenirs, although it would have been a pity to treat a Ming vase in such a way...

She felt his lips trail wet kisses down her neck and his insinuating hands slipping from her waist to knead her breast. It was disgusting. Freeing one hand at last, she delivered a stinging blow to the side of his face. He let her go with an oath, and at the same time an amused voice from just behind them drawled: 'A very true and proper hit, Miss Kellaway!'

Both Lucille and the gentleman, now nursing his jaw, turned to see the Earl of Seagrave saunter across the path towards them. His muscular height dwarfed the other man and beside Seagrave's severe elegance the gentleman's fussy tailoring suddenly looked completely ridiculous.

Seagrave fixed him with his most quelling look. 'My dear Comte De Vigny, can you not take a hint? I believe the lady expressed a disinclination for your company! You will oblige me by removing yourself at once!'

'*Parbleu!*' De Vigny's gaze moved from Seagrave to Lucille with sudden comprehension. 'So that is how it is, *hein*!'

Lucille opened her mouth to dispel his illusions but Seagrave was before her.

'Precisely so,' he said easily, sliding a proprietorial

arm around Lucille's waist, 'so you see how damnably *de trop* you are, do you not, sir?'

There was suddenly an ugly look on De Vigny's face. 'Not your usual style, is it, Seagrave, to deal in such shop-soiled goods? *Merde*, I can tell you all the tricks this one will turn—if you pay her enough—'

'But you will do no such thing!' Seagrave's voice cut across him like a whiplash. The hostility between the two men was suddenly almost tangible. 'Take yourself off my land, De Vigny, before I call you out!'

De Vigny knew when he was beaten. He muttered a epithet which Lucille, for all her extensive knowledge of French, did not recognise, and sketched a mocking bow. '*Au 'voir* then, Suzanne! I congratulate you on your conquest! *Monsieur...*'

Lucille sat down rather suddenly on the bench, afraid she might faint. Of all her recent insights into Susanna's lifestyle, this had been the most shocking because it had touched her so closely. De Vigny's ugly words had spilled corrosively across the bright beauty of the summer day. Seagrave, who clearly expected her—Susanna—to be inured to such coarseness as De Vigny had shown, was watching the retreating figure with some satisfaction.

'He will not trouble you again,' he said carelessly. He took a closer look at Lucille's white face and gave a quick frown of concern. 'Are you all right, Miss Kellaway? You look a trifle pale. I will fetch you a brandy...'

Lucille closed her eyes, turning her face up to the soothing warmth of the sun and allowing the shock to drain out of her mind. It was absurd to be so affected by an attack which was not really aimed at her, but she had been shaken in the same way as when she was exposed to the malice of the villagers. Yet again the effects of her masquerade had come home to roost in an unexpectedly unpleasant way…

'Your father always kept an excellent brandy. You will find it most restorative.' Seagrave's voice broke into her thoughts and Lucille opened her eyes. He took the seat beside her and handed her the glass.

'The spite of old lovers must be a hazard of your profession,' he said commiseratingly.

Lucille, who had just taken a mouthful of liquid, choked as the fiery spirit caught in her throat.

'That's better,' Seagrave continued approvingly, as the colour returned to her face. 'I had not imagined the encounter would shake you so. I must say, that was a very accurate shot you delivered, Miss Kellaway! One might almost believe that you had learnt cricket, to be so on target!'

'We play rounders at school,' Lucille began thoughtlessly, then caught herself. 'That is, I played when I was at school…'

Seagrave's dark eyes dwelt thoughtfully on her face. 'An unexpected talent, Miss Kellaway.' His voice hardened. 'And no doubt a useful one for a lady in your position. There must be times… But I doubt the Comte was truly dangerous. From what I have heard, I would judge he believes himself more a Lothario than he really is! But, of course—' he inclined his head '—you are the only one who knows the truth of that!'

Lucille was beginning to feel much better. The brandy had restored her natural resilience and added something besides but, unaccustomed to strong liquor, she was in ignorance of its effect on her. She looked at Seagrave pugnaciously. 'You could have intervened to help me, sir! To stand by and do nothing—well, upon my word!'

Seagrave gave her a lopsided grin which seemed to do strange things to Lucille's equilibrium. 'But you might have been wanting to encourage him, ma'am! How was I to judge? Besides, you coped very well on your own, did you not?'

Lucille gave him a fulminating look which met nothing but his unrepentant smile. Another thought occurred to her. 'And now you have led him to believe I'm—' She broke off in confusion.

'My mistress,' Seagrave supplied, with a smile. 'I am not flattered by your aghast expression, Miss Kellaway! Am I then so unattractive that you cannot stomach the idea?'

Lucille blushed. Her fertile imagination, inflamed by the brandy, presented her with the image of herself held close in Seagrave's arms. For a moment she could even feel the hard lines of his body against her own pliancy. Heat suffused her. There was nothing unattractive about the Earl of Seagrave. Those dark, gold-flecked eyes, fringed with thick black lashes, were holding hers with a hint of mockery in their depths that suggested he could read her mind.

Lucille's bemused gaze considered his face thoughtfully. Its delineations were very pleasing, with those high cheekbones, straight nose and firm jaw, and that mouth... Lucille removed her gaze hastily, remembering the fire that had overcome her the last time she had dwelt on its firmly sensuous lines... Yet there was more to Seagrave's face than a mere collection of features. It was the humour and vitality that gave it its character... Lucille suddenly realised that she had not answered his question and blushed even more.

'I...yes...no!' She made a grab for her self-control. 'You are pleased to jest, sir!'

'I assure you, I was never more serious in my life.' Seagrave's gaze was unfaltering. 'We should deal admirably together.' He took the empty glass from her hand and put it gently on one side. Lucille, suddenly gripped by the most terrifying of premonitions, found that the power of movement had temporarily deserted her. She watched, mesmerised, as he leant closer, and closed her eyes when he was too near to be in focus any more. His lips brushed hers in the lightest of kisses, shockingly sweet and piercingly intense. He had already started to withdraw as Lucille gasped with surprise, her eyes opening wide.

'Think about it,' Seagrave said softly, persuasively. He sat back, his tone changing to one of brisk practicality. 'In the meantime, I have another proposal for you to consider. I have a house in Chelsea, which I am willing to offer you on the same terms as this— provided that you give up all claim to the lease of Cookes.'

The kiss completed Lucille's confusion. She struggled to regain some small semblance of control over her wayward reactions. Her whole body was trembling with what she realised was a deep and disturbing sense of anticipation. All that, from one light touch of his lips! There could be no scientific explanation for such a phenomenon. The reassuring thought of the laws of science served to steady her. This could only be a temporary lapse and soon her own innate good sense would be restored.

Then she realised her next dilemma—whilst Susanna might well be thrilled to exchange Cookes for the more appealing prospect of a fashionable London house, Lucille could not make that decision for her.

'Thank you for your offer of the house, sir,' she said, careful to distinguish just which offer she was contemplating. 'I shall let you know my answer as soon as possible.'

She saw his swift frown. 'Can you not give it your consideration now, Miss Kellaway?'

Lucille avoided his eyes. 'I cannot…it is not my—' She broke off, adding carefully, 'It requires much thought, sir.'

Seagrave was still frowning. 'You sound as though you need to consult the wishes of someone else,' he said acutely, and did not miss the sudden rush of colour to her cheeks.

'My lawyer—' Lucille said, constrainedly, and saw his face harden again.

'Of course,' he said politely. 'You will wish to ascertain whether the properties are of equal value. I shall have Josselyn send the details to your man immediately, if you will furnish me with his name and direction.' He raised a questioning eyebrow.

Lucille racked her brains to remember what Susanna had said. She knew Barnes was her sister's man of business, but could not for the life of her remember his address. She said evasively, 'I will send them to Mr Josselyn, sir. Thank you.'

She stood up, suddenly wanting him to leave. Her nerves were distinctly on edge. Worse, she knew that he knew she felt uncomfortable. It was clear in the mocking smile he gave her as he took her hand and bowed over it with grave formality.

'I forgot to thank you,' Lucille added suddenly. 'We were overwhelmed by your generosity, sir! Poultry, game and meat from your own herds; vegetables from your allotments and fruit from your own hothouses!'

Seagrave grinned down at her. 'It was nothing, Miss Kellaway! And I understand that you now have help in the gardens and the house?'

'Yes,' Lucille looked away uncomfortably. 'I am glad your agent was able to find two villagers whose curiosity outweighed their moral scruples! No doubt they find us a sad disappointment, so quietly do we live!'

'Never mind,' Seagrave said comfortingly. 'Today they will be able to report that you have had a visit from both myself and a dashing French Count! Plenty of scandal to suffice for one day, although plain fare for such as yourself, Miss Kellaway! But perhaps...' he glanced around '...we can do better than that! After all, I have yet to demand payment of the heriot!'

Lucille, who had just started to feel a little calmer, looked up in trepidation to meet the speculative look in Seagrave's eyes. 'My lord?'

'The heriot,' Seagrave repeated, a little satirically, 'is the price, if you like, that I exact for your succession to the lease of Cookes!'

Lucille's heart had begun to beat fast and erratically. 'The price, my lord? I assume you mean a financial transaction?'

The mockery on Seagrave's face deepened. 'Sometimes, Miss Kellaway—but not always.' He moved closer to her. 'In your case, I am tempted to set another payment...this, perhaps...'

This time it was more like Lucille's fevered imaginings. She had no clear idea how she came to be in Seagrave's arms, but as she felt them close around her she started to tremble with the same mixture of apprehension and anticipation that had seized her earlier. The material of his coat was smooth beneath her fingers as her hands came up hard against his chest, as though she were uncertain whether to push him away or draw him closer. And Seagrave seemed in no hurry, determined to prolong the moment of expectation.

'I am inclined to show you how pleasurable you would find it to accept my offer, Miss Kellaway,' he murmured, lowering his head until his mouth barely touched hers and Lucille's lips parted on a gasp of mingled shock and delight. She would not have believed that such a gentle contact could create such an exquisite reaction. That molten heat swept through her again, leaving her weak with longing. This time he did not let her go, but took advantage of her parted lips to deepen the kiss with quite shattering effects.

The seductive warmth of the sun combined with this sensual onslaught went straight to Lucille's head. Her arms slid around Seagrave's neck without any conscious thought on her part. She pulled him closer, a deep shiver running right through her. She was achingly aware of all the points at which his body touched hers and wanted to be closer still. The mingled male scent of his skin and the fresh air filled her senses, intoxicating and heady. The silk dress, made for Susanna's more opulent curves, slid off one shoulder and Lucille felt Seagrave's fingers brush across her bare skin before tracing the edging of the lace that had slipped halfway down her breasts.

Then, to Lucille's immense frustration and disappointment, he had put her gently from him, smiling down into her dazed blue eyes.

'And that is only the start,' he said enigmatically. 'I warn you, I shall exact a heavy price! I'll bid you good day, Miss Kellaway.'

Further up the garden, the boy whom Josselyn had engaged to help keep Cookes's grounds tidy, leant on his hoe, his mouth wide open. So all he had heard about that Miss Kellaway was true after all, and her such a refined and quietly spoken lady as well! Not that anyone could blame the Earl, he thought regretfully. There were plenty who would wish to be in his shoes!

The second poison-pen letter arrived the next morning. Lucille had spent a miserable night. Before she had gone to bed she had stood before her mirror, critically examining her face and figure for any hint as to why the Earl of Seagrave had undergone this strange transformation and suddenly found her so attractive. She could see none. Her soft, fair hair was too straight and too pale, her complexion was positively pallid and her figure was too thin to be at all pleasing. The Earl could only be amusing himself at her expense. Or perhaps he was acting out of a need

for revenge, hoping to engage her feelings and, when
he had done so, taking great delight in rejecting her?
With a heavy sigh, she got into bed, only to be tor-
mented by erotic dreams which caused her to toss and
turn all night in a fever of unsatisfied desire.

She felt tired at breakfast time, and the dark
smudges beneath her eyes did little to persuade her
that her appearance was anything other than old and
grey. She was too preoccupied to question the arrival
of the neat, white envelope which she found resting
on the hall floor, having evidently been pushed under
the door. It bore Susanna's name in bold capitals, and
after a moment's hesitation Lucille opened it. She was
totally unprepared for its contents. In the same bold
print as before, the author gave a vindictive and
wholly unpleasant opinion of Susanna's character and
morals, and ended with the threat that she should remove her vile presence from the neighbourhood or
suffer the consequences.

Lucille felt shocked and disgusted in equal measure, horrified once again at the spite and malice rep-
resented there. Had the fires been lit, she would have
thrust it into the grate with no second thought, but
she had to make do with tearing it into little shreds
instead. She promised herself that she would not think
about it any more, and sat down with her book.
Almost immediately she found her mind wandering
from the page as she dwelt on the letter's sender instead, and she put her book down in despair, deciding
to take a stroll in the garden instead.

It was early, and the garden was shady and cool.
Lucille sat down on the little bench in the orchard
and reflected once more on the hatred which someone

bore towards her sister. Could it be their cousin? she wondered. Walter Mutch had made his contempt very clear that day in the village and since he had the lease of Cookes snatched from beneath his nose he would be bound to bear a grudge. It would be in his interests to drive her out of the village, for the lease might then be settled in his favour. Remembering Seagrave's comments on Serena Mutch's resentment, Lucille supposed that she must also consider her aunt as the anonymous author.

Seagrave... A horrible thought took hold in her mind and refused to be dislodged. Could the Earl have written the letters, or perhaps have instigated their writing as part of his campaign to make her leave Dillingham? The idea made her feel sick. Surely he would not stoop so low? And yet, what did she know of him, after all? For her own peace of mind, Lucille knew she had to avoid seeing Seagrave any more. She had already found herself hoping that he would call, dwelling romantically on their encounters like the veriest schoolgirl! She knew she was close to committing the unutterable folly of falling in love with him.

Lucille plucked a stray leaf from her hair and regarded it rather sadly. She knew she should not be too hard on herself. After all, she had lived almost a nun's life at Miss Pym's, rarely going out into company and never meeting any eligible men. It would have been a rare woman indeed who could have gone from so sequestered an existence into the company of a man as attractive as the Earl of Seagrave, without feeling at least a small pang of the heart. The knowledge did nothing to comfort her, nor could it help her put him from her mind. The thought that she would never see him again once she returned to Oakham made her feel even more unhappy.

Another two days limped past without word from Susanna. Lucille began to pack her small trunk in preparation for the journey back home, no longer prepared to sustain the impersonation just for Susanna's sake. Now that she was close to leaving Cookes she felt relieved and disappointed in almost equal measure, sorry that she had not had more opportunity to explore the countryside and discover more about the county for herself. It had been an educational visit to Suffolk, she thought, a little sadly, but not perhaps in the way that she had intended.

She was just considering whether she dared to take a short walk, and remembering the threats of the anonymous letter-writer, regretfully rejecting the idea, when there was the peal of the front door bell. Hurrying down Cookes's elegantly sweeping stairs, she found Lady Bellingham in the hall, swathed in imperial purple and fur this time, and with a dashing feather-trimmed shako perched on her head. Her ladyship kissed her warmly.

'Dear child! How glad I am to find you still at Cookes!' She scrutinised Lucille closely. 'But you are so wan, my love! How lucky, then, that I am come to take you into Woodbridge!'

Lucille began to say that she did not think this a good idea, but was overruled in the kindest possible way.

'Nonsense!' Lady Bellingham was bracing. 'It is a sadly provincial little place, 'tis true, but it has a certain charm! The outing will do you good!' Her pessimistic, dark gaze took in Lucille's apprehensive face and she smiled a little. 'My poor Miss Kellaway, have they been so cruel to you?' The dark eyes sparkled. 'You must not worry, my love! The gentry may scorn us, but you may be sure that the shopkeepers will welcome us with open arms, for I am so very rich they have no choice!'

And she swept Lucille out of the front door without further ado.

The Bellingham carriage was a remarkable sight: massive, ancient, and unquestionably luxurious. Lucille was not in the least surprised to see Horace curled up asleep inside on a scarlet cushion.

'I cannot abide these modern contraptions,' Lady Bellingham confided, as she settled herself on the thick velvet seat. 'Curricles, phaetons...pah! They may be fast but the workmanship cannot match my barouche! Now, tell me, child, how have you fared since we last met?'

Her tone was so kindly that Lucille almost dissolved into tears. 'It has not been too bad if one has a taste for insults, anonymous letters and *carte blanche*!' she said, aware that in her misery she had probably been losing her sense of proportion. One day, perhaps, she would laugh at this preposterous masquerade and the trouble it had brought her...

Lady Bellingham looked sympathetic. 'Nasty things, poison- pen letters,' she said gruffly. 'You must disregard them, Miss Kellaway! As for the insults, it is no comfort to think that they are directed at your sister rather than you... Small-minded, intolerant people!' She gave a Gallic shrug. 'But the offer of *carte blanche*—now, that sounds far more exciting!'

Lucille found herself smiling, in spite of everything.

'The Comte De Vigny, perhaps?' Lady Bellingham continued. 'Conchita told me that he was in the neighbourhood. He is an old lover of your sister's, is he not? Was he minded to rekindle their *affaire*?'

'I believe he might have been, given the slightest encouragement,' Lucille admitted.

'Not De Vigny, then,' Lady Bellingham said, thoughtfully, watching her face, 'but some more... attractive proposition, perhaps, Miss Kellaway? The Earl of Seagrave, for instance?'

Lucille felt the pink colour stain her cheeks. 'You must be clairvoyant, Lady Bellingham!' she said involuntarily.

'Now, I find that *most* interesting,' Lady Bellingham said, amused. 'Seagrave is always most particular in his choice, and your sister, Miss Kellaway...' she paused delicately '...well, her reputation would normally be too much for such a man to stomach! Which can only mean that either he knows you are not Susanna Kellaway, or he is much drawn to you personally!' she finished triumphantly.

'Neither conclusion gives me much comfort, ma'am!' Lucille said, shifting uncomfortably on her seat. 'I have to tell you that on one of the occasions we met, I gave Lord Seagrave the impression that I was indeed prepared to be bought off, and so cannot be surprised that he treats me like the Cyprian I set out to play!'

Lady Bellingham was much diverted. 'But you

would not accept him, would you, my child,' she said, shrewdly, 'for all that you are as drawn to him as he is to you!'

The hot colour flooded Lucille's face again. 'I...could not do such a thing,' she said, her voice stifled. 'Now, if you please, Lady Bellingham, can we not *please* speak of other matters?'

They were rumbling into the outskirts of the town now, past a working windmill and through narrow streets with their charmingly painted villas set in leafy gardens. The Deben estuary could be seen glinting distantly in the sun. The coach entered the cobbled streets of the centre, where the pavements were crowded with ladies in their summer dresses, their parasols warding off the sun, and the gentlemen were strolling and chatting on the street corners. Lucille and Lady Bellingham descended, her ladyship instructing the coachman to wait for them down by the harbour.

Lucille, made self-conscious by her recent experiences, was sensitive to every curious glance and whispered comment that was being cast their way. Lady Bellingham, on the other hand, ignored the interest of the passers-by with a superb indifference.

'This is a very fine musical instrument makers,' she declared, pausing before a shop where the bow windows displayed a harpsichord and reclining double bass. 'Bellingham bought me a piano from Mr Fenton the second year of our marriage, declaring that it would complement my pretty singing.' She looked most indulgent as she remembered her late spouse. 'Of course,' she continued, 'it is *young* Mr Fenton who keeps the shop now, though he must be all of five and forty! But if you require a guitar to take back to play for those schoolchildren of yours, my dear Lucille, this is the place to buy one!'

Lucille declined the invitation regretfully, explaining that she had neither the money nor the talent for such a purchase. Lady Bellingham was not cast down.

'No instruments, then…' She took Lucille's arm and guided her to the next shopfront. 'Now, how about a gown, my dear?' She wrinkled up her nose. 'I know it says French modes, but the sad truth is that the Misses Browne have not set foot abroad these twenty years or more! No, all their fashions come from London via Ipswich, and it takes several years at that!' She saw the hopeful face of one of the Misses Browne peering from behind the curtains, and hurried on. 'Now, the milliners…'

At last, it seemed, they could make a purchase. A bowing Monsieur Gaston Deneuve was there to greet his noble client almost before Lady Bellingham had reached for the door handle. He tenderly relieved her of the dashing shako, one of his earlier creations, before bringing out a whole range of other hats for them to try.

Lady Bellingham considered them all, gave a blunt opinion on each, and finally settled for a truly outrageous creation with an upstanding poke-front lined with crimson silk, and a high crown adorned with ostrich feathers. Monsieur Gaston, Lucille thought, might well have designed it precisely with Lady Bellingham in mind. Feeling rather tame in comparison, Lucille chose a rose pink bonnet trimmed with coquelicot ribbons, and was bowed out of the shop by the smiling milliner, hatbox in hand.

The next stop was the drapers for several pairs of embroidered gloves and silk stockings. Lady Bellingham spent copiously, Lucille rather more carefully, for she was aware that she had already parted with a good deal more money than she had intended.

'Now, my love,' Lady Bellingham said, with the satisfaction of one who has already made several desirable purchases, 'I have a small errand to run. I know that you have been surreptitiously eyeing the booksellers this age, so I shall not feel the smallest guilt for deserting you for a little! I will meet you at the carriage within the half hour!'

The time went swiftly for Lucille, browsing amidst the musty interior of the shop, finding old friends on the bookshelves and sighing over the prohibitive cost of new works. By the time she had emerged, with a copy of Fanny Burney's *Evelina* tucked under her arm, the town clock was chiming the half hour and she had almost forgotten that she was supposed to be Susanna Kellaway. She crossed Market Street and turned towards the river.

Remembrance returned swiftly and unpleasantly. The cobbled streets were crowded and Lucille stepped out into the road to avoid a flower seller whose wide panniers threatened to knock her off the pavement. A group of people were moving towards her, and with a slight shock Lucille recognised the Earl of Seagrave, for there was no mistaking his height and breadth of shoulder.

Accompanying him were a young lady and a gentleman whose facial resemblance both to each other and to a horse was striking. The lady, dressed in the first stare of fashion, was hanging on Seagrave's arm

in a proprietorial manner as she spoke intimately
close in his ear. Her brother, a rather foppish young
man who looked as though he were about to impale
himself on his shirt points, raised his quizzing glass
and gave Lucille the comprehensive stare that she was
beginning to recognise as well as resent.

'Gad, if it isn't the Cyprian! How damnably awkward! Who would have thought to meet such a barque
of frailty in Woodbridge, of all places! Come away,
Thalia, my dear! Were the two of you to meet, Mama
would never let me hear the end of it!'

His high-pitched tones carried to Lucille and a
number of other curious passers-by. The young lady
stared, tittered, and reluctantly allowed herself to be
steered in the opposite direction by the Earl, who
seemed in a great hurry to depart, and had not acknowledged Lucille by either look or word. Lucille
dropped her book. A mixture of fury and anguish rose
in her. So he thought nothing of offering her *carte
blanche*, but she was not good enough to be introduced to his friends! Although Lucille knew that this
was the way of the world, the blatant hypocrisy made
her fume. She realised suddenly that she was standing
stock-still in the middle of the thoroughfare and that
a carter was shouting at her to make way.

'Can I be of assistance, madam?' A gentleman was
beside her, handing her parcel back to her and taking
her arm to guide her onto the pavement. He removed
his curly-brimmed beaver hat and bowed slightly.
'Charles Farrant, at your service, ma'am. Can I escort
you anywhere?'

'I...yes, I thank you, sir.' Lucille pulled herself together. 'The carriage is waiting down by the harbour. If you would be so good…'

'Of course.' He put her hand reassuringly through his arm and turned down Quay Street. 'A fine day, is it not, ma'am, although I believe there will be a strong breeze down on the river.'

Lucille realised that he was talking to give her time to recover herself, and felt a rush of gratitude. She looked at him properly for the first time. He was tall and fair, with a pleasant, open face and kind blue eyes that smiled down at hers. His dress was sober rather than elegant—a country gentleman of modest estate, perhaps, or a professional man… She gave him a tremulous smile. The gentleman blinked.

'Indeed, I do thank you, sir, for rescuing me! For a moment I…' Her voice trailed away.

'I saw what happened,' Mr Farrant said, a little abruptly. 'Mr Ditton is unpardonable.'

'Mr Ditton?' Lucille suddenly realised that he must be referring to the fop. 'Oh, I beg your pardon, sir, I did not know the gentleman…'

A slight frown touched Mr Farrant's brow. 'Oh, but I thought—' He broke off, a little self-consciously. 'As you say, madam.'

Clarification burst upon Lucille with a blinding flash. At the time she had been so overcome by the Earl of Seagrave cutting her dead that she had hardly given the other man a thought, but now she understood Mr Farrant's embarrassment. So Mr Ditton was another of them! Well, she had had enough of Susanna and her lovers! Surely there could be no danger in revealing her true identity now that she was on the verge of leaving Suffolk! She stopped dead and turned to her companion.

'Mr Farrant, I believe there must have been some misunderstanding, and largely of my own making. I have not introduced myself.' She stressed the name. 'I am Lucille Kellaway.'

Mr Farrant's open features cleared. He was very easy to read, Lucille thought, amused, for all that he must be at least seven and thirty years old!

'Oh! Miss Kellaway! I thought—' He broke off again, clearly mortified.

'That I was my sister,' Lucille finished for him, without embarrassment. 'An understandable mistake, sir. We are twins and very like in appearance.'

'Yes, although now I come to look at you I can easily see the difference,' Farrant said, loquacious in his attempts to gloss over the difficult moment. 'You are much fairer, Miss Kellaway, and...a most modest style of dress...and the book...I do apologise!' He flushed bright red.

'Not at all,' Lucille said, smiling in spite of herself. 'I collect that you have met my sister, Mr Farrant?' Which gentleman has not? she wondered.

'I've *seen* her, of course,' Farrant said, as though referring to an exotic circus animal, 'and I had heard that she was staying in the neighbourhood, though now I see that it must be you instead!' He frowned. 'But I had heard rumours that your sister was under the protection of the Earl of Seagrave, and I am sure that that cannot be true of you, Miss Kellaway! One has only to look at you to see that you are a woman of unimpeachable virtue! Oh, your pardon, ma'am—' Once again, he broke off in complete confusion.

'Pray do stop apologising, sir,' Lucille said, a little
wearily. 'This is all my fault. I should have known
that to appear in public would give rise to this inevitable confusion. I *have* been staying in the neighbourhood, though the rest of your tale is mere gossip!'

Farrant started trying to apologise once again and
Lucille could only be grateful that the river was in
sight, and beside the harbour wall Lady Bellingham's
imposing carriage was waiting. The tide was in on the
river and a profusion of craft bobbed at anchor.
Seabirds wheeled and soared and the air had a fresh,
cutting salty edge. Lucille wished she could have
paused to appreciate the scene, but she was anxious
to be away. She turned to thank her companion for
his escort. Mr Farrant seemed a pleasant enough gentleman, she supposed, though he had nothing of the
compulsive attraction of the Earl of Seagrave—

'Your servant, Farrant. Miss Kellaway.'

The last person Lucille wanted to speak to at that
moment was Seagrave himself, for her feelings were
still very raw. He had evidently parted from the odious Mr Ditton and his sister, and was strolling along
the path towards them quite alone.

Farrant bowed awkwardly, clearly at a social disadvantage. Lucille's greeting was cool to the point of
frigidity.

'Good day, my lord.' She turned back to Mr Farrant
with a warm smile. 'Thank you for your kindness this
day, sir. Had you not been so good as to befriend me
when others were less amiable, I have no notion how
I might have managed!'

Seagrave's eyes narrowed as this point went home
and Farrant, acutely uncomfortable, began to stammer

that it was a pleasure and that he was always at her disposal. Seagrave watched in sardonic amusement as this flow of words finally dried up and Farrant swallowed convulsively before excusing himself and hurrying off.

'To what do I owe that pretty piece of play-acting?' Seagrave demanded, turning back to Lucille, who was caught between gratitude that Mr Farrant had not inadvertently revealed her identity and annoyance at his inopportune departure. She had no wish for a tête-à-tête with the Earl—or for any conversation with him at all, she told herself fiercely.

'I do not understand you, sir,' Lucille said. There was no need to try to imitate Susanna—she knew she sounded sulky and irritable, and for once it was entirely genuine. She turned towards the carriage, but Seagrave prevented her from moving away by the simple expedient of catching hold of her arm.

'You are being devilishly awkward this afternoon, Susanna!' he said pleasantly. 'All I wanted to know was whether you had considered my offer!'

'The Chelsea house?' Lucille freed herself from his grip and turned to look out over the river so that she did not have to look at him. 'I will let you know as soon as I may, sir.'

'I meant my other offer,' Seagrave said gently.

Lucille turned to stare at him. The sea breeze was ruffling his thick dark hair and she felt a sudden, frighteningly strong urge to reach up and touch it. So he had been serious. He was asking her—Susanna— to become his mistress. For a moment she considered it. Did he really want her, or Susanna? Perhaps the trophy of Susanna hanging on his arm was all that mattered?

If so, how would he react when he discovered it was Lucille he had seduced rather than her sister… She gave herself an appalled shake. Whatever was she doing, seriously considering this? Fifteen minutes previously, this man had cut her dead, refused to even acknowledge that he knew her. He had no respect for her.

As she hesitated, he took a small blue box out of his pocket. Horrified, Lucille realised that it was a jewellery case. So that was part of the bargain, was it? Some necklace, or bracelet, perhaps, to buy her favours? Perhaps he had just bought it in the town, and now the whole of Woodbridge would know what he intended… She began to feel quite ill with disgust.

'You may keep your bribery, sir!' she snapped, restraining herself from knocking it out of his hand. 'I do not care to be distinguished by your attentions only when it suits you!' Suddenly she did not give a damn about the way Susanna would have treated him. Soon she would be leaving forever, and it made her reckless. Let her sister pick up the threads of the masquerade if she chose! Let Susanna blame her for whistling an Earl down the wind if she dared! Lucille was not about to compromise her own principles just to emulate her sister.

'You are angry that I did not speak to you just now,' Seagrave observed calmly, 'but I thought it best to take the Dittons away as quickly as possible! After all, I understood that your…' he hesitated '…intimate relationship with Mr Ditton ended on less than amicable terms. And as for his sister, even you must surely see that you are not a suitable person to be introduced to Miss Ditton?'

Seagrave sounded so infuriatingly reasonable that Lucille could have slapped him. He had put the box away and was watching her with a degree of cynical humour which suggested that he had assumed she wished to play a scene, but would come around in the end.

'I have no wish to meet that Friday-faced female,' Lucille said scathingly. The cold air and her own anger had brought the pink colour into her face. Her blue eyes were very bright. 'Nor do I wish for a liaison with a man who has no respect for me. Good day, sir!'

She would have walked past him, but he barred her way with one arm on the harbour wall. Lucille was delighted to see that he had stopped smiling.

'Respect? A singular notion, Miss Kellaway! When did you become so fastidious? I dare swear it was not when you allowed Ditton into your bed!' His eyes were almost black with fury but he kept his voice discreetly low. 'Yet you see with what respect he treats you now!'

Lucille knew she was well out of her depth but she was now as angry as he. 'Perhaps I liked Mr Ditton more!' she said, with unforgivable provocation.

Seagrave caught both her arms above the elbow and gave her a shake. 'I see! Perhaps he pandered to your particular tastes? And Farrant?' he added, through his teeth. 'Do you have him lined up as a diversion? A little game to help you pass your time in the country? The poor man is enslaved already! One glance from those limpid blue eyes, one smile, and he is yours! He will be easy meat for you, poor fool!'

At last, too late and with total incredulity, Lucille realised that it was jealousy she could read in his face. Sexual jealousy, certainly, for surely he could have no deep feelings for her. Yet he seemed to resent that Tristan Ditton—and no doubt many others—had apparently taken what she was now refusing him. Lucille suddenly realised how ill-equipped she was to deal with this. She could hardly explain that Charles Farrant knew her to be Lucille Kellaway and not Susanna, and that she had no designs on him of any nature.

'I have the claim to you, Miss Kellaway,' Seagrave said with a soft insistence under which the anger ran hot, 'not Farrant, or any other! Remember that!'

'I think not, sir!' Lucille responded furiously. 'Upon my word, you have a strange concept of possession! What gives you that right?'

'Those who put themselves up for sale, Miss Kellaway—' Seagrave began, only to break off as she interrupted him with no thought for courtesy.

'I am not to be bought, sir, nor have I ever been! You may take your insulting suggestions elsewhere!'

Lucille's bright blue gaze clashed with his own angry one. She found to her amazement that she could not break the contact. The tension between them was almost tangible. The anger drained from Seagrave's eyes as they travelled over her face almost caressingly, as if memorising every detail. His breath stirred a tendril of her hair. Lucille felt as though she were drowning, melting in a sensation completely new to her and dangerously seductive.

She wanted to put her hand up to trace the unyielding line of his jaw, to run her fingers into his hair and bring his head down so that she could touch that firm mouth with her own. Seagrave must have read something of her feelings in her face, for the expression in his eyes changed again to a potent demand, darkening in response to her own need, and he bent his head...

There was a cough, very loud and very deliberate, just behind them. Seagrave released Lucille and stood aside.

'I beg your pardon, Miss Kellaway, for keeping you waiting,' Lady Bellingham said calmly. She held out a hand to the Earl. 'Good day, Lord Seagrave.'

Seagrave wrenched his gaze and his attention away from Lucille. He took Lady Bellingham's hand and gave her a reluctant smile, appreciative of her tactics. 'How do you do, Lady Bellingham? It is a pleasure to see you forsaking your coastal retreat to be amongst us again!'

Lady Bellingham had her head on one side, considering him with an openly appraising look. She smiled a little regretfully. Then her gaze fell on Lucille, who was so mortified that she had not been able to look at Seagrave for several minutes. Lady Bellingham took her arm gently.

'You look done up, my poor child,' she said gently. 'Come along—we shall go home to Cookes for tea!'

She nodded to Seagrave and steered Lucille like a sleepwalker towards the jetty where the carriage was drawn up. Seagrave, watching their departure, found that he was still breathing hard, as though he had run a mile. He leant on the harbour wall and stared out across the river, where a barge was attempting to navigate the corner called Troublesome Reach.

He knew all that he needed now, had known even before Lady Bellingham had hurried her protégée away with a concern quite misplaced had her charge truly been Susanna Kellaway. And no doubt Josselyn would have the answers to the questions he had posed earlier in the week, but it was unnecessary. He knew that this could not be Susanna. Amidst all the deception and artifice, the one thing that had rung true was her assertion that she was not for sale. He remembered again the blazing honesty of those blue eyes and shifted slightly.

No, Miss Kellaway—if that was her name—had been telling the truth at that moment. And it made sense of all the other matters that had puzzled him: the wit and intelligence that had added spice to their encounters, her shock at De Vigny's behaviour, the way that she had trembled in his arms as he had kissed her, with an innocence that could not have been affectation...

And there was the rub... Seagrave let his breath out on a rueful sigh. He wanted her, whoever she was. He had previously been accustomed to conducting his affairs of the heart as business transactions where emotion never intruded; so, at first, when he had found himself so strongly attracted to the woman he thought was Susanna Kellaway, he had come to the obvious conclusion that his need for her would slake itself if only he could set her up as his mistress.

Now matters were not so simple. His own code of conduct did not permit him to try to seduce an innocent, no matter how much she richly deserved it.

Unfortunately that meant that his desire for her was doomed to be unfulfilled and the very idea put him back in a very bad mood indeed.

Seagrave picked up a handful of pebbles and moodily tossed them down into the swirling waters below. Because he was no green youth, he was forced to admit that there was another, more serious aspect to the case. He could no longer dismiss his own feelings as simple physical desire. In a strange way he found he actually *liked* her, enjoyed her company, wanted to be with her, which was far more insidiously dangerous than a mere attraction. Even the fact that she had deceived him, which made a part of him furious with her, could not, it seemed, destroy the feelings he was beginning to have for her.

If he could only sort out this infuriating matter of her masquerade. He groaned aloud, startling a nearby seagull. He could see precisely where his train of thought was leading and it could not be. But one way and another, the arrival of Miss Kellaway in Dillingham was proving far more costly and complicated than he had ever imagined.

Lucille and Lady Bellingham had travelled for a couple of miles in silence before her ladyship ventured a comment.

'Forgive my intrusion, Miss Kellaway,' she said carefully, making a play of adjusting her new embroidered gloves, 'but I thought that you were perhaps in some danger...'

Lucille sighed. 'You were right, ma'am! I was in danger of just about everything! I was in danger of betraying my impersonation of Susanna by stepping completely out of character, I was in danger of either slapping Lord Seagrave's face or kissing him—I am not sure which is worse—and most of all I am in the most serious danger of losing my heart! Now if that is not a sad testament to my folly, I know not what is!'

'Do not reproach yourself, Miss Kellaway,' Lady Bellingham said, so authoritatively that Lucille almost jumped. 'Seagrave is a man of considerable experience, yet judging by your recent encounter, he finds it as difficult as you do to resist the attraction that draws the two of you together. It will do him no harm,' she added, with satisfaction.

Lucille shook her head a little sadly. 'It is of no consequence, Lady Bellingham! I still intend to return to Oakham next week. Mrs Appleton will keep the house open against my sister's return.' She gazed out of the window at the lush Suffolk farmland. 'It will be far better for me to go away,' she finished sadly. 'I can contend with a broken heart only if the cause of it is a long way away from me!'

'Do not be too hard on yourself, Miss Kellaway,' Lady Bellingham said again, with a rueful smile. 'Seagrave is a remarkably attractive man! You are not the first—'

'Nor indeed the last!' Lucille said, bitterly, and Lady Bellingham wisely left it at that as they completed the journey home in silence.

But as her coach pulled out of the drive of Cookes a couple of hours later, she addressed the sleeping cat thoughtfully. 'You know, Horace, unless I miss my guess, Miss Lucille Kellaway will be Countess of Seagrave within six months!'

Horace stretched and yawned widely, showing a very pink mouth and sharp incisors. 'Three months, then!' Lady Bellingham corrected herself, reaching for the bonbon dish.

'I must have been seven sorts of idiot not to have seen it from the first.' The Earl of Seagrave frowned moodily down at his mud-spattered boots. He was sprawled in an armchair on one side of the fireplace, his long legs stretched out in front of him, whilst his brother, who had joined him at the Court a few days previously, had taken the chair opposite. It was almost full dark outside. Inside the room the lamps burned, turning the brandy in the balloon-shaped glasses to a rich amber glow.

Peter Seagrave looked up from the draughtsboard. He had already won two games that evening, a circumstance which only occurred when the Earl was deeply preoccupied. Now, he sat back in his chair and viewed Seagrave with amusement.

'You could scarcely be expected to have to contend with twins!' he said, mildly.

Seagrave looked up, impatiently pushing a hand through his disordered dark hair. 'No, but it only needed a little thought! Josselyn had told me at the outset that there were two daughters—I just didn't realise…' He was shaking his head in patent disbelief. 'And if you had met her, Peter—' His eyes met those of his brother. 'An innocent abroad! Devil take it, how could I have been such a fool! She was like a little girl dressed up in her big sister's clothes—and her sister's personality! She kept forgetting her part: good God, she knew who Bucephalus was; she was even reading *Waverley*!' He finished on a note of total incredulity.

Peter took a mouthful of brandy, savouring the taste. 'The Cyprian and the bluestocking!' he said thoughtfully. 'So whilst Susanna Kellaway has been making a notorious living in London, her twin has been quietly teaching schoolgirls in Oakham! It's an extraordinary idea! But can a woman who lends herself to such a masquerade be the innocent you seem to think her, Nick? Maybe she is really of the same stamp as Susanna Kellaway!'

That went straight to the crux of the matter. Peter saw a flash of expression in his brother's eyes, too quick to be read, before Seagrave said expressionlessly, 'I think not, Peter. Miss Kellaway may be deceitful, but she is not experienced. I may have been taken in on all other matters, but on that I am convinced.'

Peter raised his eyebrows. He considered Seagrave's judgment to be sound, this latest incident notwithstanding. And he knew his brother well enough to suspect that he was not entirely indifferent to Miss Lucille Kellaway, which was very interesting. Why else this determination to believe her virtuous when all the evidence suggested, at the very least, a rather adaptable attitude towards right and wrong?

'You seem very sure,' he said coolly.

'I am.' Seagrave met his eyes directly. 'I offered her *carte blanche*, Peter!'

His brother almost choked. This was even more interesting! For Seagrave to have been so attracted to the woman he thought was Susanna Kellaway was remarkable! And since she had been proved to be no Cyprian, what now?

'She refused you, I infer?' he said, when he had recovered himself.

'She did,' Seagrave said, a little grimly. 'In no uncertain terms! Miss Lucille Kellaway cannot be bought at any price!'

'Then I wonder why she is playing such a trick,' Peter mused quietly. 'Do you intend to challenge her about it, Nick?'

Seagrave shook his head slowly. There was a wicked glint in his eyes. 'Not just yet! No, I shall play along with this masquerade and see what I can learn! Miss Kellaway deserves to be taught a lesson, Peter!' He reached for his glass and raised it in silent toast. 'It should provide some sport!'

Chapter Five

'You cannot really refuse to see him,' Mrs Appleton said, in an agitated whisper. Her arms were full of hothouse flowers as she hovered in the bedroom doorway. Lucille stared at her, completely at a loss, her headache all but forgotten.

'But Mrs Appleton, he cannot possibly expect to come up to my bedroom—'

'When I told him that you had a sick headache and were resting, he assured me that he knew just the cure, and I do not imagine that he was referring to Dr James' Antimonial Powders!' the housekeeper said, grimly. 'Now we are undone, Miss Kellaway! If the Earl of Seagrave is intent on setting you up as his mistress—'

'I must get up at once,' Lucille said, throwing back the covers only to dive back under them again in horror, as she heard the sound of footsteps on the stair. Her horrified gaze met Mrs Appleton's. 'Oh no, he would not—' she began, breaking off as the Earl of Seagrave himself strolled casually into the bedroom as though he was accustomed to being there every day. He perched on the end of the bed, one booted foot swinging, and viewed Mrs Appleton's outraged consternation with amusement.

'Go and put those flowers in water, ma'am, and leave me to cure Miss Kellaway! I know you are reputed to be a dragon of respectability, but Miss Kellaway is, after all, accustomed to receiving gentlemen in her bedchamber and does not need your chaperonage!' The wicked dark gaze swung back to Lucille, who was shrinking as far beneath the bedclothes as she was able. 'Come, my dear! Such modesty! I am persuaded that you will soon be much more comfortable with me when we are intimate together!'

'My lord!' Mrs Appleton was doing her best. 'Miss Kellaway really is very unwell today! Perhaps it would be better—'

'Nonsense,' Seagrave said bracingly, his assessing gaze resting warmly on Lucille's flushed face. 'A fit of the blue devils, that is all! Perhaps I could take you for a drive later, Miss Kellaway—the fresh air will do you good! But first, we have a small matter to discuss, do we not?'

'I do not understand your lordship.' Lucille's voice, very small, came muffled from even further beneath the blankets. 'It was my belief that we had no more to say to each other and I would be obliged if you would leave immediately!'

'A lovers' tiff, perhaps!' Seagrave shrugged casually. He gave Mrs Appleton a conspiratorial smile. 'The necklace was a little paltry, I'll own, but it was the best that a provincial jeweller could muster! Miss Kellaway was quite right to draw my attention to its deficiencies!' He turned back to Lucille. 'I will make up for it, I swear!'

There was an outraged squeak from beneath the covers. Seagrave's smile grew. He got up and strolled towards the window, admiring the view across the orchards to the open country beyond. 'This is a charming house, and most conveniently placed for our liaison,' he observed thoughtfully. He turned to consider the room. 'The bed is perhaps a trifle small, but we shall see!' He raised his eyebrows questioningly as Lucille's red, outraged face appeared.

'I wish that you would go and leave me alone! At once!' Lucille had abandoned finesse in her anxiety to be rid of him. She was thoroughly confused by this ludicrously out-of-character behaviour on Seagrave's part, this burlesque, but she was so much at a disadvantage that all she wanted to do was make him go away. Now was not the moment to challenge him on his behaviour, when she was half-naked and he had that particularly mischievous look in his eye.

Surely, she thought in horrified disbelief, he could not have misread their encounter of the previous day so profoundly as to believe that it was an attempt on her part to exact a higher price from him? He was far too astute to believe that! But Seagrave was sitting back down on the bed, far too close for comfort, and Lucille abandoned her attempt to puzzle out his motives given the overwhelming need to preserve her own modesty.

'I feel sick,' she said plaintively. 'No!' It came out as a small shriek as she realised that Mrs Appleton was about to hurry off to fetch a bowl. 'Do not leave me, dear ma'am! I shall be quite better directly!'

'That's the spirit!' Seagrave said approvingly, patting her thigh through the blankets. 'I have been thinking,' he added reflectively, 'that it might be a good idea for you to invite your sister to spend some time with you here! It might improve your humour and also give her the opportunity of a change of scene. What do you think, Susanna?'

Lucille did not know what to think. She had never seen him in so carefree a mood. And for him to suggest that she should invite herself to visit Cookes... She gave a faint moan. Seagrave took her hand comfortingly.

'Well, perhaps not. If we are to be spending a great deal of time together it would not be convenient...and no doubt she is one of those tiresomely puritanical and dry spinsters who thinks of nothing but her books!' He stood up, stretching with a lithe movement that drew Lucille's attention to his rippling muscles. She looked hastily away, the colour flooding her face again.

'I will leave you to recover,' Seagrave was saying, the devils dancing in his eyes. 'But do not keep me waiting long to taste your delights, Susanna!' He leant forward and placed a lingering kiss on Lucille's round, outraged mouth. 'That cambric nightgown will have to go,' he added thoughtfully. 'It is far too concealing!'

'He knows the truth!' Lucille averred, her face no longer red with affront but ashen pale. As soon as her unwanted visitor had left she had thrown back the covers and leapt out of bed, her headache quite forgotten. She paced the room in her reviled nightdress, thankful only that it was as all-concealing as Seagrave had said.

Mrs Appleton put down the flowers she was still clutching and sat down on the end of the bed.

'I agree it was most singular behaviour,' she said worriedly. 'Are you sure that there was nothing in your conversation yesterday, Miss Kellaway, that might have led him to believe—?'

Lucille shook her head stubbornly, wrapping her arms about her for comfort. 'At first I wondered, but as an explanation it will not serve. No, he has some-how divined the truth and is intent on making me suffer! I know it!' she finished fiercely. 'Seagrave would never normally behave thus! It was a parody, a caricature! Oh, that I had never started this! I must go away at once!'

She stared blindly out of the window. As soon as the idea that Seagrave might know the truth had taken hold, Lucille was convinced that it was the right one. Not only did it explain his ridiculous behaviour, but some deeper instinct told her that he knew; that he was making a game of her as small recompense for what she had done.

The idea threw her into a panic. What would his next step be? To attempt wholesale seduction, per-haps, still pretending that he thought she was Susanna? And she had only two alternatives—to play along with the charade, or to tell him the truth. Three alternatives, she corrected herself. She had been in-tending to leave on the morrow—why not now in-stead? She started to pull her half-filled trunk from under the bed, only to be stayed by Mrs Appleton's calm voice.

'Forgive me, Miss Kellaway, but is this hasty departure really the best thing to do? In the first place, Seagrave is quite capable of stopping you if he really wanted to, and John has the wheel off the carriage, as he did not think you would be going until tomorrow!'

Seeing Lucille's look of despair, she came across and laid a comforting hand on her arm. 'Do nothing precipitate,' she counselled in kindly fashion. 'Think about whether you wish to tell him the truth, and if you decide that you cannot, go tomorrow, as you had intended.'

Lucille nodded slowly. Her emotions were so jumbled that all she could think of was her overwhelming need to escape. 'But it must be tomorrow,' she said miserably. 'I have to go! Nothing must stop me!'

A sudden and violent summer storm kept Lucille indoors that afternoon, and she tried to while away the hours with a copy of Samuel Richardson's *Clarissa Harlowe*, which she had found on one of her father's bookshelves. It had proved quite impossible to concentrate, for her mind was occupied solely by the thought of the Earl, and fruitless speculation on how he could have realised her impersonation, and what he intended to do about it. She felt as though her customary good sense had completely deserted her, leaving her feeling hopelessly vulnerable.

The late morning had brought another huge bunch of flowers, this time from Charles Farrant, and a note expressing the hope that he might call upon her the following day. As Lucille planned to start her journey back to Oakham at first light, she knew this was not possible and felt a vague regret. She would have liked to have had the opportunity to thank him properly for his assistance. Charles Farrant had none of Seagrave's dash and brilliance, but he also lacked the Earl's arrogance and was, Lucille told herself severely, a very pleasant gentleman. Unfortunately, that seemed to weigh little with her. Lucille gave a little despairing sigh.

The thunder was retreating by the time four o'clock struck, and Mrs Appleton had just brought in some afternoon tea and cakes, when there was the sound of carriage wheels on the gravel outside, and a sudden and imperative knock on the front door. Lucille put her book down quickly, wondering if Susanna could have chosen this moment to return at last, but a moment later she heard a man's voice, followed swiftly by an exclamation from Mrs Appleton. Lucille hurried across to the drawing-room door and out into the hall.

The scene that met her gaze was a startling one. The gentleman in the hall was sufficiently like the Earl of Seagrave to make identification immediate, and to make Lucille's heart turn over, but he was more slender than his brother and had an open, youthful, boyish look that was very appealing. He carried in his arms a very slight young lady who appeared to have fainted. Her face was very pale and her soaking wet curls just brushed his chin as he held her with her head resting against his shoulder. Her clothing, the demure sprigged muslin gown of a schoolroom miss under her cloak, was also drenched and dripping onto the floor. She did not stir at all. In complete astonishment, Lucille recognised her to be Henrietta Markham, her adoptive sister.

'Hetty! Good God!' Lucille forgot her own preoccupations and hurried forward. 'Whatever can have happened?'

Mrs Appleton turned to her. 'This gentleman—the Honourable Peter Seagrave—says that he found the young lady on the road from Woodbridge, madam. She must have been caught in the thunderstorm. Shall I prepare a bedroom, ma'am? She looks as though she may have taken a chill!'

'We will put her in my room, I think, Mrs Appleton.' Lucille touched Hetty's cold cheek tentatively. 'Could you prepare a hot posset whilst I show this gentleman the way? Oh, and please bring some smelling salts if you can find any!' Lucille turned to Peter Seagrave. 'If you would be so good as to carry her upstairs, sir? I will show you to the room.'

Peter carried Hetty up Cookes's sweeping stairway and put her down very gently on Lucille's bed. He stood back, looking down at her with an anxiety that drew Lucille's attention even though her main concern was to try to rouse her sister. She sat down on the side of the bed and took Hetty's cold hands in hers.

'Hetty? Wake up, my love! You are quite safe!' She looked up at Peter. 'She was not injured when you found her, was she, sir?'

He heard the fear in her voice and was quick to reassure her.

'No, ma'am. Miss Markham was wet and tired, and I believe she had not eaten for some time, but she was not injured.'

At the sound of his voice, Hetty stirred. Her eyelids fluttered, then lifted.

'Lucille! Oh, thank goodness!' Her voice was a thread of a whisper and it caught on a sob. 'I was so afraid that I was wrong and I would not find you here…' Her gaze went past Lucille to Peter Seagrave and a little colour came into her cheeks. She struggled to sit up. Lucille pressed her back firmly against the pillows.

'You had better rest now, my love. Mrs Appleton will come up to help you. Can you manage a little food?' Then, seeing that Hetty's gaze was still riveted on Peter, she said: 'I will say all that is proper to Mr Seagrave. Perhaps, sir—'

Peter Seagrave took the hint. 'I will wait for you downstairs, Miss Kellaway.' The smile he gave Hetty had so much tenderness in it that Lucille blinked in shock. 'I shall hope to see you again soon and in better health, Miss Markham,' he said, and reluctantly made for the door.

Thirty minutes later, Hetty had been washed, fed and put to bed wearing one of Lucille's nightdresses. Lucille went slowly back downstairs to find Peter Seagrave standing by the drawing- room window, his hands deep in his pockets as he gazed out across the wilderness garden. He turned swiftly at her entrance.

'Miss Kellaway! Will Miss Markham be all right?'

Lucille smiled reassuringly. 'With a little rest and some care I am sure she will be perfectly all right, sir! And I have not yet had a chance to thank you for bringing her to us—I cannot bear to think what might have happened had you not rescued her!'

She took a seat, and gestured to him to do the same.

'Did Hetty explain how she came to be wandering so far from home? I did not like to press her just now, but I am rather concerned...'

Peter Seagrave's warm brown eyes rested on her thoughtfully. 'I cannot throw much light on the circumstances, I fear, ma'am! I found Miss Markham on the Dillingham road just outside Woodbridge. At first she would not consent to speak to me...' a reminiscent smile touched his lips '...for she claimed she had no need of help from strange gentlemen, although a more bedraggled and woebegone sight would have been difficult to find! Eventually I persuaded her to let me take her up, and she unbent sufficiently to confide that she had run away from home and was seeking out a relative with whom she hoped to find shelter.'

Peter got to his feet again restlessly, moving back to the window. 'Miss Kellaway, there is no easy way for me to say this. When Miss Markham told me that she was seeking Miss Kellaway of Cookes, I was horrified. I was convinced she must be mistaken, but she was adamant. Good God, an innocent like Miss Markham asking to be escorted to the house of a notorious Cyprian! At first I thought I had mistaken Miss Markham's quality, but it only takes one look to ascertain that she is a schoolroom miss!' He turned back to look at her, a deep frown on his brow. 'I knew Miss Markham's reputation was compromised the moment she was over this threshold, but I had no choice! I could not take her to Dillingham Court with only myself and my brother there and I did not know of anyone else nearby who could give her shelter. But devil take it, I cannot stand by and see her ruined by association with—' He broke off. 'I beg your pardon,' he said with constraint.

Lucille looked down at her clasped hands. The same thoughts had been preoccupying her ever since Hetty had arrived so unexpectedly. Given her state of health, it was clearly impossible to send her adoptive sister straight home, and it sounded as though there had been serious reasons that had driven Hetty to run away in the first place. Until she had had the chance to find out what had happened, Lucille did not want to upset Hetty by trying to explain why she could not stay at Cookes.

But Peter was right—news of Hetty's arrival at the house would inevitably leak out and her reputation would be ruined. Suddenly Lucille felt close to tears. It was bad enough that by her foolish masquerade she had landed herself in so much trouble, but that Hetty should now be compromised was utterly unfair!

Lucille, whose thoughts on her own circumstances had gone quite out of her mind, suddenly realised that she could not possibly remove from Cookes the following day as she had planned. Now all her problems were compounding themselves with a vengeance!

'Forgive me, Miss Kellaway, but there is more,' Peter Seagrave said suddenly. His fair, open face flushed. 'As I am being so frank, I may as well go further. I think that you should know that Nick—my brother, Lord Seagrave—knows that you are not Susanna Kellaway, although I understand that you have been using her identity…'

Lucille, who had been pondering how on earth Hetty had managed to trace her to Cookes, was all at sea for a moment. In her concern for Hetty she had

given no thought to the fact that her adoptive sister
had called her by her name—or that Hetty might well
have referred to her as Lucille when talking to Peter
on the journey. Yet now it seemed that it did not
matter anyway! Peter knew that she was not Susanna!
Seagrave knew, just as she had suspected…

The mortification overcame her in a huge wave.
She felt ready to sink with embarrassment now that
she had received this confirmation. How did he
know? How long had he known for? Why had he not
spoken? The thoughts tumbled over themselves inside
her head.

'You have been using her identity…' It sounded so
cheap, so deceitful! And so it was, Lucille told herself
fiercely, blinking back the hot tears which threatened
to overwhelm her. She had known all along that if
unmasked she would appear both dishonest and immoral.

'Forgive me, ma'am,' Peter said again, a note of
real concern in his voice. 'I had no wish to upset you.
It was anxiety for Miss Markham that prompted me
to speak.' He moved swiftly across to the desk, where
the bottle of brandy reposed. 'Drink this…' He
pressed the glass into her hand. 'It will make you feel
better.'

'More brandy!' Lucille thought ruefully, taking a
mouthful. The Seagrave family seemed intent on turning her into a toper! She felt the strong spirit burn her
throat and realised that she had needed it.

'Mr Seagrave—I should explain…'

Peter ran a hand through his dishevelled dark hair.
'I have no wish to pry, ma'am,' he said, with constraint. 'I understand that there must be reasons…'

His gaze swept over her comprehensively and he could not contain himself. 'But devil take it, Nick must be a slow-top not to have seen it from the start! I have never met your sister, Miss Kellaway, but it doesn't take much to see that *you* are no bird of paradise!'

Lucille could not help laughing, in spite of everything. 'Do not be too hard on your brother, sir! Susanna and I are identical twins, and as you have correctly stated, I deliberately deceived him as to my identity!' Her laughter died as she reflected on this. 'Indeed,' she added softly, 'unlike Hetty, I deserve the opprobrium of the world! I came to Cookes in the full knowledge that it belonged to my sister who is considered—let us not boggle at it—to be a fallen woman. Worse, I pretended to be that very woman! Hetty is an innocent who has been compromised through no fault of her own. I do not have her excuse.'

'You are too harsh on yourself, ma'am,' Peter Seagrave said, slowly. 'I do not pretend to understand why you should choose to perpetrate such a fraud on my brother, but no one who has spent any time in your company would think you other than a gentlewoman and,' he added in a rush of gallantry, 'I can understand why Miss Markham sought you out when she needed help!'

Lucille smiled a little sadly. 'Thank you, sir! I do not deserve your good opinion. But none of this helps Hetty,' she added quietly. 'Since the world believes me to be Susanna and this is indubitably her house...'

'Yes,' Peter agreed thoughtfully. 'Miss Markham's reputation is damaged just the same.' He squared his

shoulders. 'Miss Kellaway, I really feel we should ask
Nick's help in this. But that will inevitably entail
bringing your…masquerade…into the open. Can
you—are you prepared to talk to him about this?'

Lucille bit her lip. 'For Hetty's sake I am prepared
to face your brother and explain,' she agreed quietly.
She saw his swift nod of approval and said quickly,
'Mr Seagrave, I would account for my actions to you
if I could, but I must talk to your brother first. All I
ask is that you believe that my main concern is to
spare Miss Markham distress, and in that, I believe,
we are one.'

'Very well, Miss Kellaway.' Peter stood up. 'I must
go now, for Nick will be wondering if I've had an
accident on the road!' He took her hand. 'Thank you
for your frankness. I am sure we can resolve this predicament one way or another.' He flashed a grin, so
like his brother's sudden smile that Lucille's heart
missed a beat. 'Please give Miss Markham my best
wishes for her recovery,' he added. 'I shall call in a
day or two to see how she progresses.'

Lucille was sure that he would. As Peter Seagrave
went out to his cold and patient horses, Lucille wondered how such a youthful innocent as Hetty
Markham could possibly have caught him in her toils.
There was no doubt of it though. Peter Seagrave was
already fathoms deep in love with her.

When the Earl of Seagrave called the following
morning, Lucille was in such a state of pent-up ner-
vousness that she almost refused to see him. She had
lain awake for what had seemed like many long, dark
hours, reflecting in equal measure on the coil in which

Hetty was caught and on the frightening prospect of confessing to Seagrave. Neither situation provided a single comforting thought, and in the end she had fallen into a light doze from which she had awakened unrefreshed as soon as the sky began to lighten.

Hetty was still sleeping soundly by mid-morning and Lucille did not have the heart to wake her. She spent a lonely breakfast staring blankly into space over her coffee cup, then trailed off to the drawing-room to continue her reading of *Clarissa*, only to find that her thoughts distracted her so much that she did not take in a single word. Far from spending time at Cookes pursuing her favourite hobby of reading, she seemed to have done little but cast her books to one side! In a fit of annoyance she went out into the garden, but it was a grey day with a chill breeze. It seemed to suit her mood. She went back inside and tried to compose a letter to Mrs Markham.

Twenty minutes later, Lucille finished her carefully worded letter, acquainting Mrs Markham of her daughter's whereabouts, and blotted it thoughtfully. She had left out all reference to Cookes being Susanna's house now, simply informing that good matron that she was taking a short break in the house that had been her father's and that Hetty, having presumably gained her direction from the school, had sought her out there. That at least, she thought, should allay Mrs Markham's maternal fears and prevent her from descending on the neighbourhood in a fit of moralistic fury.

How to keep Hetty's presence a secret from the village was another matter, and one which Lucille considered a hopeless task. She was still frowning over this problem when Mrs Appleton announced the Earl of Seagrave. It was almost a relief to know that he had come. Lucille drew herself up a little straighter, stilled her shaking hands by putting them behind her back, and faced the door.

Seagrave came into the room with all the careless assurance which Lucille had come to expect of him. He accepted her offer of refreshments and sat down, allowing his dark gaze to travel over her very deliberately. Lucille found this distinctly disconcerting. She had chosen a gown of Susanna's in palest blue, from which she had ruthlessly removed all the yards of tulle and lace, and the result had been simple and pleasing. The appreciation in Seagrave's eyes suggested he considered it very flattering.

'Good morning, Miss Kellaway,' he murmured. 'You look entirely delightful. Now...' the observant gaze appeared to be fixed on her face '...how may I help you?'

'I beg your pardon, sir?' Lucille tried to get a grip on herself.

'My brother told me that you had something most particular to say to me.' Seagrave raised his eyebrows. 'I came as soon as I was able. So...what is it all about, Miss Kellaway?'

To her horror, Lucille found that she could not speak. She had keyed herself up to such a state of pent-up tension that the words simply would not come out.

After a moment, Seagrave said patiently, 'You appear to be in some difficulty, Miss Kellaway. Am I to understand that the problem involves Miss Markham? Peter told me a little of his meeting with her yesterday.' He studied the high gloss of his boots with sudden intensity. 'Certainly her situation appears most irregular. She is, I collect, a vicar's daughter fresh out of school—your adoptive parents' child, as I understand it! What desperate set of circumstances could have forced her to seek refuge with you?'

Lucille winced. Reflecting ruefully on the difference between Peter Seagrave's diffident courtesy and his brother's high-handed arrogance, she realised that every word he spoke made it more difficult for her to summon up the courage to explain her pretence. She had to do it. Sitting there, knowing that he knew her to be Lucille not Susanna, but with the fact unspoken between them, was extraordinary. And there was no possible way to help Hetty without touching on her own situation, but her courage almost failed her. She cleared her throat.

'My lord—'

'Miss Kellaway?' He was waiting for her to speak, a look of ironic patience on his face. Lucille took a deep breath.

The door opened and Hetty Markham skipped into the room, demure in her freshly laundered sprigged muslin gown.

'Good morning, Lucille! I feel so much better! I was never so glad as when I found you here—' She stopped dead on seeing Seagrave, then dropped a neat curtsy. 'I beg your pardon, sir, I had not realised that my sister was not alone!'

Lucille felt the ground give way beneath her feet. She pinned on the best semblance of a smile that she could muster. Why could Hetty not have recovered half an hour later? However, all was not lost if she could only manoeuvre her from the room.

'Good morning, Hetty,' she said rapidly. 'I am glad to see you so much improved this morning. Mrs Appleton will help you to breakfast in the parlour—'

'Oh, I have had my breakfast in bed!' Miss Markham announced insouciantly. She caught Lucille's eye. 'Oh! But I will wait for you in the parlour, of course!' She turned impulsively to Seagrave. 'Excuse me, sir—'

'Do not leave on my account, ma'am,' Seagrave said, getting to his feet and giving Hetty a smile so full of charm that she looked quite dazzled. 'I imagine that you must be Miss Markham. I am Nicholas Seagrave—I believe that you met my brother Peter yesterday?'

'Oh…yes, sir…how do you do!' Hetty blushed adorably. 'I am so grateful to Mr Seagrave for rescuing me!' She opened her huge blue eyes even wider. 'I am so very sorry that I was not able to thank him properly! Please could you convey my gratitude to your brother, sir, for the service he rendered me yesterday?'

Lucille saw Seagrave's lips twitch slightly. 'Certainly, Miss Markham! But I believe my brother is hoping to call on you himself. He was only waiting until you were well enough to receive him. He will be delighted when I tell him that you are so much recovered!'

'Oh!' Hetty turned to Lucille, her eyes shining. 'Please say that I may see him, dearest Lucille!'

Two pairs of eyes, one blue, one dark, were fixed on Lucille, although the expression in Seagrave's was somewhat more sardonic than Hetty's. Lucille could feel matters slipping beyond her control.

'I am sure it would be perfectly proper for you to see Mr Seagrave later and thank him for his help,' she said weakly. 'But for the time being, would you not prefer to rest? We must be sure that you did not take a chill yesterday.'

Hetty's glowing peaches and cream complexion could not have looked less feverish, and she gave a little laugh. 'Oh, no, I feel wonderful!' She sat down beside Seagrave with a confiding smile. 'I cannot tell you, sir, how glad I was to have Lucille here to turn to when I needed help! She has always been the best of sisters to me—why, she always used to write to me every month when I was at school, and even came to visit me sometimes when she was not needed at Miss Pym's!'

Across her glossy chestnut curls, Seagrave's eyes met Lucille's. His expression was quite unreadable. 'The best of sisters indeed,' he murmured smoothly. 'Tell me, Miss Markham, how did you find Miss Kellaway's direction, now that she is no longer at the school?'

'Oh, it was the easiest thing!' Hetty said, artlessly. 'I wrote to the school, of course, expecting Lucille to be there, but a gentleman—the music master or some such—returned my letter immediately, with a note explaining that Lucille had been here at Cookes for the past month! So I took the stage to Woodbridge and it was only by the worst chance that I got caught in the rain and could not find anyone to bring me to Dillingham! But, of course, it was not so bad at all, for then your brother came along and saved me! He seemed most surprised when I asked to be taken to Miss Kellaway's house, and I feared that there had been some misunderstanding, but all was resolved when I saw Lucille—' She broke off. 'I do beg your pardon, sir! I am always running on, and Mama says it is very bad of me!'

Seagrave smiled. 'Do not apologise, Miss Markham, you interest me vastly!' Again, his eyes met Lucille's. She put a hand to her head in despair and saw his smile deepen. Seagrave got to his feet. 'But you must have a hundred and one things to discuss with Miss Kellaway, so I shall leave you for now. It was a pleasure to meet you, Miss Markham! Miss Kellaway—' There was wicked amusement deep in his eyes, but to Lucille it was no laughing matter. She could have cried.

'I am sorry that you have not had the chance to discuss whatever you wished with me, Miss Kellaway,' Seagrave said pleasantly. He took her hand and drew her to one side. 'Tell me, did you learn your amateur dramatics at Miss Pym's school?' He pressed a kiss on her hand. 'I will call again tomorrow, when perhaps we may talk. Until then…' The amusement was still in his eyes, but beneath it Lucille thought she could sense anger—and the promise of retribution.

'Well!' Hetty said, when Seagrave had been shown out. 'He is a vastly handsome man, but somehow rather frightening! Do you like him, dearest Lucille?'

Lucille hesitated. At that precise moment, her feelings for Nick Seagrave defied description. 'He is charming enough,' she said as casually as she was able. 'But he is vastly above me, my dear! Why, Lord Seagrave is an Earl and his family owns most of the land hereabouts! Cookes is merely one of his tenant properties!'

Hetty drooped. 'I see,' she said despondently. 'Then I suppose Mr Seagrave is far too important to think of me!'

Lucille patted her hand bracingly. It was far too late to counsel Hetty not to fall in love with Peter Seagrave, for the damage was already done. 'The Earl said that his brother would call and I am sure that you may believe him. But Hetty, there are other more important things I need to discuss with you.'

Hetty looked as though she thought nothing could be more important than Peter Seagrave, but obligingly sat down to listen. Lucille looked her over carefully. It was no wonder that Peter was smitten. Henrietta Markham had blossomed into a remarkably pretty girl. She had a sweet, round face, dominated by the huge blue eyes, and complemented by her mass of soft, curly brown hair.

'Now, Hetty,' Lucille said severely, 'what is all this about? I understand from Mr Seagrave that you told him you had run away from home!'

Miss Markham blushed. 'Oh, Lucy, please don't send me back! It's all Aunt Dorinda's fault!' She looked at Lucille with desperation. 'She plans to marry me off to that dreadful curate, Mr Gillies! Did you ever meet him, Lucy? He is the most dreadful bore! His clothes smell of mothballs and his breath smells even worse! I'd rather die than marry him!'

Lucille was beginning to feel rather more than nine years older than her youthful relative. She sighed.

'I'm sure it will not come to that, my dear! Mrs Pledgeley will surely not force you into marriage against your will! And what does your mother have to say to this?'

Hetty looked up at Lucille's severe face, her own expression tragic. 'Oh, Mother would be glad to see me safely settled! She thinks I'm too wild—she says it's the Kellaway connection! And you've no idea how ruthless Aunt Dorinda can be! I know she looks fat and fluffy and indolent, but she has a heart of steel underneath and Mother is no match for her! And Mr Gillies is always calling and paying me unctuous compliments—I knew what they were at! I couldn't think what else to do except come to you!' She was determined to make a clean breast of it and hurried on. 'You know how I found out your direction! Then I waited until Aunt had gone into Ipswich with Mrs Berry, then I took out my valise—I had already packed it in preparation—and walked to the King's Arms. It's at least a mile, you know! I knew the stage passed through there at ten, for John, the gardener's boy, had mentioned it once to me. So I waited, and they took me up as far as Woodbridge, and the rest you know!'

She finished, and looked as though she were about to burst into tears. 'I'm s-s-sorry, Lucy! I didn't know what else to do! And now if you send me back they will make me marry Mr Gillies and I'll never see Peter again!' She stifled a sob and reached up her sleeve for a cambric handkerchief.

Lucille sighed again. 'Well, my love, you have been most resourceful in finding me, and I suppose you will have to stay at least until you are fit to travel!' She saw Hetty's blue eyes peeking at her hopefully above the handkerchief. 'I have written to your mother already to let her know that you are safe. There is, however, one other thing that you should know.' She drew a deep breath. 'This is in fact Susanna's house, not mine.'

Hetty, for all her youthful innocence, was not slow to grasp the significance of this. Although Mrs Markham disapproved of Susanna to the point of never mentioning her name, it had not been possible to keep the truth of Susanna's occupation from Hetty, particularly when it was deplored so loudly and avidly by all and sundry. She quite forgot her tears, her eyes growing huge as saucers.

'But I thought this was your house! Oh glory, Mama will be furious! You did not tell her in your letter?'

'I left that bit out,' Lucille said austerely, and frowned as Hetty stifled a giggle.

'Hetty, it's more serious than just your mama's disapproval! The very fact of your coming to Susanna's house—well, it's bound to reflect on your own reputation in a most unfortunate way. It is not your fault, for you did not know, but you know how unpleasant people can be—'

Lucille broke off, for Hetty had paled visibly as she realised what Lucille meant. 'Mr Seagrave!' she whispered through white lips. 'He seemed shocked when I asked for Cookes and now I see why! Oh, what must he think of me!' Her huge blue eyes filled with tears and overflowed. 'Oh, I cannot bear it! He must think me a loose woman!'

Lucille thought that this was most unlikely. She

moved swiftly to Hetty's side and took both her hands. 'I can assure you that he thinks no such thing!' she said briskly. 'He and I spoke last night, and he is perfectly aware that you are a young lady of impeccable reputation! He is as concerned as I to prevent any scandal touching your name, and has pledged himself to help us! Now, dry your eyes, my love! It will not do for you to look woebegone when he arrives!'

Hetty brightened immediately, with the adaptability of the young. 'Oh, Lucy! Do you think he really does like me?'

'I'm sure he does! Now, I shall get Mrs Appleton to bring you in some tea and pastries whilst I arrange to send the letter to your mama.'

Lucille went out feeling exhausted. She supposed that it was not so strange for Hetty to fall head over heels in love with Peter Seagrave on the strength of one meeting. He was, after all, a personable man and he had come to her rescue like a knight from the romances. When contrasted with the odious Mr Gillies, his charm would have bowled her over.

Lucille sighed. She had little doubt that Henrietta was right in thinking that her aunt planned to marry her off, although whether she would have forced the match was another matter. With two daughters of her own approaching marriageable age, Dorinda Pledgeley would have wanted to get so pretty a rival off her hands as soon as possible. Mrs Pledgeley was an overbearing woman, Lucille reflected, and had made the Markhams feel like poor relations ever since she had provided them with a home after the death of the Reverend Gilbert Markham. Just for a moment,

Lucille permitted herself to imagine the flutter in the Pledgeley dovecote were Hetty to catch herself an Earl's younger brother. Then she told herself severely not to count her—or in this case Hetty's—chickens before they were hatched.

The thought of an Earl brought her thoughts inevitably on to Seagrave. Hetty's artless confidences had wrecked all possible chance of her explaining the situation to him before he heard of it from anyone else. Lucille shivered as she remembered the look in his eyes as he had left her. The tension of waiting until the following day to see him was almost intolerable. Oh lord, how had she ever got herself into this knot? With hindsight she could see that Seagrave was the last possible person to try to hoodwink. She knew she was a fool to have got herself so entangled. Worse, she knew she would not emerge unscathed.

Peter Seagrave called that afternoon, bringing a huge bunch of flowers for Hetty which made her eyes open to their fullest extent. Lucille, reflecting that the house would soon look like a horticultural show, took them away to put in water whilst Peter took Hetty off for a sedate tour of the garden. Mrs Appleton, looking more indulgent than Lucille had ever seen her, strolled along with them as Hetty's chaperon.

Lucille stood in the scullery, half-heartedly trying to arrange the flowers in one of George Kellaway's more outlandish china vases, and watching as Peter settled both Hetty and Mrs Appleton on the seat beneath the apple tree and proceeded to charm them both. Lucille knew that she was in danger of envying Hetty Markham. Hetty had fallen madly in love in the most unexpected way and it seemed her feelings were returned.

Lucille pushed one unfortunate rosebud forcibly into the vase and stabbed herself painfully on the thorns. Her own situation, she reflected miserably, could hardly have been more different. She too, had fallen hopelessly in love, for in her own way she was as inexperienced in the ways of the world as Hetty. Her nine years' seniority counted for nothing. She had gone from the confines of Miss Pym's school and met the Earl of Seagrave, who had somehow been the personification of all her ideals. And now she had been exposed to him as a liar and a cheat. He had never had any respect for her when he thought she was Susanna, but this was worse, for now he knew her true identity and could have nothing but contempt for her.

Chapter Six

Lucille slept surprisingly well that night. She had been convinced that the combination of dread and a guilty conscience would keep her awake, but in the event she was too tired to be troubled by either. She awoke to a bright, sunny day, and decided to take a walk before the house was astir. No doubt the fresh air would make her feel more cheerful. She slipped through the garden and orchard, where the dew was fresh on the grass, and took a path that set off across the fields.

The sky was already bright blue, and the air had that fresh, keen edge that came straight from the sea. Skylarks were already singing high above. Lucille's spirits began to lift. She came to a stile and crossed another field. A hay wain rumbled down the gentle hill towards the village, but nothing else moved in the still landscape. Reaching the next lane, Lucille rested on a gate and considered the view.

'Good morning, Miss Kellaway. A beautiful day, is it not?'

How quietly he moved! Lucille had already recognised those distinctive tones when she turned her head to confront the Earl of Seagrave, who was clearly on a morning constitutional about his estate. It was now too late to deplore the fact that Susanna had no clothes remotely suited for a walk in the country, and that she had chosen to wear her own drab brown jacket and skirt, and sturdy boots. Very likely it would make no difference to Seagrave's opinion of her anyway, but he had obviously noticed, for he was looking at her with unconcealed interest.

'I had no idea your wardrobe contained anything so unflattering,' he observed with amusement.

Lucille, her heart beating suddenly in her throat as a result of his unexpected appearance, could think of no suitable rejoinder. Surely now that he knew she was not Susanna he would not expect her to be forever appearing in her borrowed plumes?

'It seemed sensible for a walk across fields,' she said after a moment, noting that his riding boots were liberally spattered with mud and that he was wearing what were obviously old trousers and a casual jacket. The neckerchief carelessly knotted at his throat completed an ensemble which had an informal elegance that did nothing to detract from his air of authority.

'Indeed it is,' Seagrave said, with a glimmer of an approving smile. 'But what a surprise to find you out walking at this hour, Miss Kellaway! Evidently a dislike of early hours is not something which you have in common with your sister! Unless, of course,' he gave her a speculative look, 'it is simply a bad conscience which has kept you awake!'

There it was, out in the open between them! Seeing Lucille blush, Seagrave continued kindly, 'Shall we continue walking whilst you tell me about it? I often find that it is easier to talk on delicate matters if one has some other occupation on which to concentrate as well!'

He fell into step beside her, shortening his stride to match her steps. 'My route back to the Court takes me past Clockhouse Woods—will you accompany me? Let me help you over this stile.'

Lucille knew she really had no choice. She put her hand reluctantly into his as she stepped up on to the stile. His touch was quite impersonal but Lucille felt a deep shiver go through her which she tried to pretend was the effect of the summer breeze. As though she did not have enough to contend with, without the added distraction of this disturbing physical attraction!

The path climbed slightly up a small hill, and Lucille preserved her breath to cope with the incline. She knew it was only a small stay of execution. At the top she paused for a rest and considered the view across to the River Deben and the silver sea beyond.

'This is one of the highest points in the county,' Seagrave commented, as Lucille gradually turned to look across the patchwork fields inland, momentarily diverted from the matter at hand. 'I had forgotten, in fact, what a beautiful county Suffolk is. It is a landscape made for artists, I think. Do you draw, Miss Kellaway?'

'Indifferently, my lord.'

'Ah, a pity. But perhaps you will try your skill? Such a view can only encourage you.'

Lucille had to agree. 'I can understand why John Constable finds it so inspirational,' she said, spontaneously. 'The light and the colour…the limitless space—why the sky seems to go on forever…' She turned a glowing face to Seagrave and almost immediately recollected the barrier between them. She fell silent and the silence seemed to last several hours.

At last he said, a little drily, 'It does not surprise me that you evidently know Constable's work well, Miss Kellaway. You must come to Dillingham Court some time and see the work I have commissioned from him, if that would please you.'

'I…yes, that would be delightful.' All animation had gone out of Lucille's manner.

'My lord, I must tell you…explain…'

Seagrave drove his hands into his jacket pockets. 'Indeed you must, Miss Kellaway. Why not start with the most important point, which is why it was necessary for you to impersonate your sister in the first place? For it was an impersonation, was it not? You had plenty of opportunities to tell me the truth, yet you deliberately chose not to avail yourself of them!'

His tone was quite gentle but with an underlying thread of steel which made refusal quite impossible. Lucille was aware of nothing except her misery. She had always prided herself on her integrity and could not bear him to think her deceitful. The regard she had for him just made matters worse. Plain, prim Miss Kellaway, playing a role in a masquerade and meeting her handsome Earl…

She shrugged away the fanciful idea. Practical Miss Kellaway did not believe in fairy stories. Soon, after all, she would have to return to her dull existence— very soon, now that the truth had come out. There could be no point in remaining in Dillingham and carrying on the charade. While she hesitated, he spoke again.

'Of course, I may be doing your sister an injustice, for I assumed her to be involved in this deception! But perhaps you claimed Cookes in her name and she is unaware of the impersonation?'

That got through to Lucille, as it had been intended to do. Her chin jerked up and she eyed him furiously.

'There is no need to represent matters in a worse light than they are, sir!' she said, hotly. 'Susanna claimed Cookes, as was her right by inheritance. But she found she had to go away for a short time and was anxious that her absence should not give your lawyers a lever to break the lease. And judging by your words to me when first we met, my lord, her fears were justified!'

Seagrave inclined his head with a slight smile. 'Touché, Miss Kellaway! That at least explains her motive in asking you to impersonate her. But what of your own motives?' He stopped walking and turned towards her. 'What did she offer you to make it worth your while, Miss Kellaway? You told me that you could not be bought, but it seems that is not true! So what is your price?'

Lucille bit her lip. Her throat was as dry and stiff as paper, and tears of strain and unhappiness were not far away. Suddenly all she wanted to do was go home and indulge in a hearty cry. The one man in all her twenty-seven years with whom she had fallen disastrously in love regarded her as nothing more than a mercenary adventuress!

'My price, as you put it, my lord, was the peace I believed I could find at Cookes, more fool I!' she said bitterly, pushing back the tendrils of silver hair which the breeze was tugging free from her bonnet. She faced him out stormily. 'I would not expect your lordship to understand—or pity—the restrictions of a proscribed existence, day in, day out, with no thought of change! When Susanna came to me I agreed to her proposal in a moment of weakness, wanting nothing but to escape! I never thought that I would have to meet anyone, or sustain the masquerade! Well, I am well served for my folly now, am I not!' She swallowed the lump in her throat. 'I had better go, I think. Your lordship must be wanting me from Cookes immediately!'

She turned aside, but Seagrave put a hand on her arm, restraining her. 'A moment, Miss Kellaway.' His face wore its customary inscrutable expression and there was no way of telling what he had thought of her words. He ran his hand through his dishevelled dark hair. 'There is no immediate necessity for you to leave Cookes.'

Lucille could not meet his eyes. 'Indeed, I think I must, sir.'

'And I say you shall not.' There was steel in his tone now. 'Be so good as to walk with me a little further, Miss Kellaway. There is something which you should know, I think.'

Lucille fell into step beside him, wondering what else he could possibly have to say to her. Seagrave did not look at her as they continued the downward path, which was now skirting the wall of the field and the woods beyond.

'This morning,' he said conversationally, 'I received word that a lady reliably identified as Miss

Susanna Kellaway was in Paris and would shortly be leaving for Vienna in the company of Sir Edwin Bolt.' He swung round to look at Lucille. 'I do not believe your sister will be returning to Cookes for a while, Miss Kellaway.'

Lucille's heart sank at the news but a moment's reflection told her that it made no difference. She would have to leave Cookes, and if that meant that Susanna lost the lease then so be it. At least her hopes of Sir Edwin had not as yet been dashed if Seagrave's intelligence of them was correct.

They had reached the point where the path to Dillingham Court struck off at right angles beneath the spreading canopy of oak trees. Lucille paused in the shadows.

'I cannot allow that to weigh with me, I think, sir,' she said carefully. 'I promised Susanna that I would stay at Cookes until she returned, but now my circumstances have changed, have they not? Nothing remains but for me to apologise to you for the pretence, and take myself back to Oakham.'

Seagrave was watching her with a slightly mocking smile. 'You are very certain that I will let you go, Miss Kellaway! What if I should choose to press charges to punish you for your duplicity? Obtaining property by deception…false representation…I am sure that I could make the crime fit the charge!'

Lucille felt the earth rock beneath her feet. She had not even thought of that. 'Surely you would not—' she gasped.

'Wouldn't I?' Seagrave looked thoughtful. 'I have a great dislike of being duped, Miss Kellaway! Am I to let you get away so easily?' He leant against the trunk of one vast oak and viewed her with amusement. 'You look horrified, Miss Kellaway! Did you never think of this when you and your sister hatched your plot? Were you so sure of remaining undetected?' He straightened up and Lucille took an instinctive step backwards and he followed. She could sense some force at work in him which she did not understand. It was comparatively dark beneath the trees and his face was in shadow.

'Just how far would you have gone to emulate your sister, I wonder?' Seagrave said slowly. 'I remember you now, of course, Miss Kellaway. We met in the inn at Felixstowe. No wonder you were so discomposed to overhear that I was intending to travel to Dillingham! And now that I know you are from Oakham I remember that I once caught sight of you during a brief stop there.' His inexorable gaze lingered on the strands of silver hair escaping from her bonnet, the sudden wild rose colour which had flooded her face. 'It was a revelatory moment, one might say,' he observed, in a caressing tone that made Lucille shiver, 'and I imagine you remember it too, do you not, Miss Kellaway? How charming you looked at that window—' His hand came up to touch her cheek with feather-light fingers and she felt herself tremble. She knew he could feel it too.

'How charming and how virginal,' Seagrave repeated, with sudden predatory intensity. 'As you do now. But is it possible for a woman who can play the Cyprian to be virtuous herself? I doubt it!'

Lucille tried to speak, but found she could not. She moistened her lips with the tip of her tongue. 'I do not—' She broke off, realising how husky her voice was. His proximity was having a disastrous effect on her, turning her knees to water and her mind to a morass of fevered thought, none of it intelligible. 'I do not understand you, sir,' she managed, and saw his eyes narrow with a mixture of exasperation and a less easily defined emotion. She took another step back, only to find that her back was against another of the broad oaks. Seagrave followed her without apparent hurry, placing one hand on each side of her head against the trunk of the tree so that she could not escape.

'I think you do, Lucille,' he said harshly. 'How far were you prepared to go to further your charade? Would you have eventually accepted my offer of *carte blanche*? Do I really have to take you here and now, against this tree, to discover the truth? Because, believe me, I will do so if I must!' He held her wide, horrified eyes with his very deliberately as he straightened and stepped even closer to her. Lucille instinctively closed her eyes and a moment later she felt his mouth on hers.

A small corner of Lucille's mind acknowledged that she had wanted this ever since he had first kissed her in the garden, then all conscious thought was lost in the sensations that he aroused in her. His anger apparently forgotten, Seagrave's mouth explored hers with a searching but gentle expertise which created such acute excitement that Lucille was lost in a maze of tactile pleasure. She became almost unbearably aware of the hard strength of Seagrave's body pressing her backwards against the unyielding tree trunk, the softness of her own curves as they moulded themselves to the taut lines of his.

The kiss deepened, intoxicatingly sweet. She wanted it to go on forever. Nothing in her experience could explain this delicious torment. And then she felt his fingers at the neck of her jacket, slowly undoing the tiny pearl buttons. The rush of cool air against her heated flesh was utterly delightful. Lucille moaned softly with pleasure. Half of her mind was telling her that she should make him stop, that he would think her as free with her favours as her sister was; the other half was shamelessly telling her that it did not care what he thought as long as he carried on arousing these pleasurable sensations within her...

All buttons unfastened, Seagrave parted the lapels of her jacket to reveal the fine lawn of her petticoat beneath. He traced the delicate line of her neck, her jaw, then her collarbone, with the lightest, most tantalising touch of his lips. Lucille's head fell back, the silver-gilt hair spilling from its pins to tumble down her back in a pale waterfall.

She no longer had any inclination to break off their encounter. Equally, she was so innocent, she had no real idea of what was happening to her, other than that it was wonderful. Above them, the breeze stirred the thick green canopy of leaves and the shifting shadows played over them. Though her eyes were still closed, Lucille, all senses fully alert, could feel Seagrave slide the soft material of her chemise away from her skin so smoothly, so seductively, every touch only serving to inflame her further. And when his lips continued their path downwards from her collarbone over the exposed curves of her upper breasts, she gasped aloud, arching against him, digging her fingers into his shoulders.

'Is that far enough, Miss Kellaway, or will you take more?' That mocking voice was so slurred that she scarcely recognised it. Lucille thought she would melt from sheer devastating pleasure. Here was a side of her nature which she had never even suspected, a side which even now was demanding that she take this much further and grant it the ultimate satisfaction.

'Well, Miss Lucille Kellaway? What a surprising girl you have turned out to be!' Seagrave's mouth was now an inch from her own, though his fingers had moved inside her jacket to torment the over-sensitised tips of her breasts. His tongue teased the corners of her mouth before returning fully to cover it again, drinking deeply. When at last he paused for breath, Lucille opened her eyes for the first time and saw the intensity of desire in those narrowed dark eyes so close to her own. She reached out to pull him closer.

His hands circled her waist, holding her against him. The linen of his shirt was rough against her skin as she slid her hands beneath his coat and over the firm muscles of his back, making him gasp in turn. He bit gently at the side of her neck until Lucille arched her head back once more, allowing his questing mouth to return to its teasing assault upon her heated skin. She felt his hands move to unfasten her chemise and she wanted nothing more in the whole world. But—

'No, oh no!' Lucille did not want sanity to return, but it was already there at the edges of her mind, persistent, telling her what unbelievable liberties she had permitted him, what was the next logical step... She had not cared that he had kissed her out of anger; that he thought her a cheap deceiver. She knew that she loved him, and that had been enough for her. But now! This time the touch of the cool breath of summer breeze on her skin brought reality back and Lucille struggled to free herself. She was instantly released.

'Thus far and no farther?' Seagrave said. His voice was rougher than usual and he was breathing hard. 'You would need to take matters much further, I fear, to imitate your sister!'

Lucille was desperately trying to regain control of her disordered senses. She knew he had only intended to punish her and in a strange way this helped to steady her. It could not be expected that an experience which had had such a cataclysmic effect on her would leave him similarly moved. She straightened her bodice, fastening the buttons of her jacket with fingers that shook and slipped. She could not look at Seagrave.

As her mind slowly assimilated what had happened to her she felt more and more horrified, desperately shocked at her own behaviour. Prudish, priggish Miss Lucille Kellaway, who lived life vicariously through her books, had turned out to be a flesh-and-blood creature whose passionate nature, whose needs and desires, could have been her own undoing. So before, Seagrave had thought her a cheat. Now he would think her of easy virtue as well!

The scalding tears which had threatened before welled up in her eyes.

'I have no ambition to emulate Susanna, sir.' Her voice wavered and she pressed her hand to her mouth in a desperate attempt to regain her self-control. She heard Seagrave swear softly under his breath, but

whether his anger was directed at her or at himself,
she could not tell. Nor did she care. Her sole attention
now was focussed on getting herself back to Cookes
in one piece. She turned aside from him, but he
caught her arm to restrain her.

'Miss Kellaway—'

It was too much. Lucille burst into tears.

Her eyes felt gritty and swollen with crying, her
cheeks were burning hot and her nose felt as though
it were twice its normal size. However, the greatest
shock to Lucille was that the Earl of Seagrave was
suddenly behaving as though she were his sister, and
had enfolded her in arms that were tenderly protective
but not remotely loverlike. Gentle fingers were brushing the damp hair away from her face whilst he
pressed his own laundered handkerchief into her
hand. His lips brushed her cheek and she heard him
murmur gentle words of comfort in her ear. She was
astounded.

Seagrave let her go. She felt bereft. 'Forgive me,
Miss Kellaway,' he said, with less assurance than she
had ever heard from him before. 'I have behaved ap-
pallingly and I must apologise.'

'No, sir,' Lucille said unsteadily, scrupulously fair,
even through her misery, 'it was all entirely my fault!
I am the one who should be apologising—'

'Oh, to hell with apologies!' Seagrave said, with
uncharacteristic irritation. 'Miss Kellaway, this is no
time for polite prevarication. You are in no state to
go back to Cookes on your own—you must allow me
to escort you to Dillingham Court. My housekeeper

will look after you until you are well enough to return home.'

Lucille almost argued with him, but she had no energy left to do so. Instead, she allowed him to place her unresisting hand on his arm and lead her back on to the path to the Court. She was amazed to see that the sun still shone and to feel the gentle breeze on her hot face. She could not begin to understand all that had just passed between them.

'You need not worry that you will meet anyone at the Court,' Seagrave said abruptly. 'Peter will not be rising before lunch, for he spent the night at the gaming tables, no doubt trying to win enough money to enable him to support a wife!' He slanted a look down at her and sighed as he took in the look of blank incomprehension on her face. Lucille Kellaway had had a tremendous shock and he was entirely responsible for it. He took a deep breath.

'Miss Kellaway...' his voice was very gentle '...forgive the necessity of referring to what has happened, which I know no gentleman should do. You are a lady of considerable intellect. What happened between us just now is what is termed, I believe, a chemical reaction. I imagine that you have studied the physical sciences and understand the concept. It was unpardonable of me to act in such a manner and it will not happen again. Do not regard it.'

Do not regard it! So that was how he considered an encounter which had left her shaken to the core! A part of Lucille was more miserable than she had ever been in her life, but for her own sake she could not allow it ascendancy. It was far better to be angry than to be humiliated. She turned on him furiously.

'I certainly understand your intention to punish and shame me, sir! It is a lesson I shall never forget!'

'Such was not my intention, Miss Kellaway,' Seagrave said quietly. 'Oh, it may have started that way, but I was as much a victim of my desires as you were! The only difference was that I knew what I was about, which you did not!'

Lucille knew that she could not allow herself to feel this insidious sense of empathy which was threatening to draw them together. There was no future for her with him, and to believe so only to be disappointed would destroy her completely. She tried to whip up her fury further. 'And to offer me *carte blanche* when you must already have guessed that I was not Susanna! That was not the action of a gentleman!'

'No.' Seagrave had followed her lead and sounded his inscrutable self once more. The brief flash of tenderness she had seen in him might never have been. 'It was not. But *that* you brought on yourself, Miss Kellaway! If you choose to play the Cyprian, you cannot complain when people treat you thus!'

Lucille knew that he was right and it made her even more furious. Anger with herself mingled with the hurt he had inflicted. Her feelings for him were mocking her and goaded her even further.

'I have explained my reasons, I have apologised for my actions and I can do no more,' she said in a voice which shook. 'And now I am going home! I would rather walk across coals of fire than spend another moment in your company, my lord!'

'You forget Miss Markham's situation.' Seagrave's voice halted her when she had taken only three steps away from him. There was no expression in his face to indicate his reaction to her impulsive words.

Lucille hesitated. She had indeed forgotten Hetty's predicament in the tumult of emotions that surrounded her own relationship with Seagrave. And now, reminded, she closed her eyes briefly for a moment in complete despair.

'Miss Kellaway.' There was a real determination in Seagrave's voice now, and for once the habitual mockery was absent. 'If we are to help Miss Markham, we must, I think, bury our own differences.' He rested one booted foot on a fallen log and looked at her thoughtfully. 'You should know that once I realised your true identity, I never for one moment suspected you to be a courtesan. There is a transparent innocence about you that makes such an idea nonsense! In fact, our recent passage of arms would never have happened had you truly been such a woman. It is only your inexperience which—' He broke off, seeing the colour flood her cheeks. 'But we will never speak of it again! As for the rest, I've heard and understood what you have said about coming to Cookes and—' he shrugged '—am willing to forget about it. Now are you also willing to put the past behind us?'

Lucille was filled with desolation. She understood that this was all she could expect of him; understood that he was being more generous than she might have expected. It was her own feelings that made it so difficult for her to accept this. Loving him as she did, she would always want more than this, more than he was prepared to give. At all costs she must keep him from discovering her true feelings. That would be the ultimate humiliation.

'Very well,' she said hesitantly, 'for Hetty's sake, I suppose…'

'Thank you. I believe I may have a solution to the problem. Now…' his dark eyes scrutinised her face carefully '…do you feel strong enough at present to cope with this, or are you quite overset?'

His words had the desired effect. Lucille's chin came up and a little colour crept back into her face. 'Of course I am! I am not an invalid! I have not had an accident!'

Seagrave's lips twitched at this. 'Just so,' he said, noncommittally. They began to walk once more, out of the edge of the shady woods and into the parkland that was the start of the Court's grounds. Dillingham Court itself could be seen in the hollow of the hill, its golden stone glowing in the summer sun. Normally Lucille would have paused to admire such a charming aspect, but now she did not feel like stopping to appreciate the view. At least it made it easier to forget what had happened between them when she had another more pressing problem on which to concentrate.

'If you have thought of a way of saving Hetty I shall be forever in your debt, sir!' she admitted honestly. 'I could never have foreseen that she would seek me out here and unwittingly embroil herself in this! I could not bear for her reputation to be ruined as a result!'

'A tangled web indeed, Miss Kellaway,' Seagrave said, gently. 'Society's rules are very harsh sometimes, and I agree that Miss Markham should not suffer as a result of the sins of others!'

For Hetty's sake Lucille swallowed her anger and mortification. It seemed that, despite his previous words, Seagrave would be forever reminding her of her folly and deceit, but who could blame him? And if she had to bear that for Hetty it seemed the least she could do.

They were descending to the house now, through groves of late rhododendron and glades of wild flowers. It was an enchanting place, but Lucille's spirits were lower than they had ever been. As they reached the gravel of the forecourt, Seagrave gave an exclamation.

'Good God, my mother is here!' Lucille followed his gaze to where a smart travelling coach with the family crest was disgorging what seemed like vast quantities of luggage onto the front steps. Seagrave swung round on her and caught both her hands. She met his imperative dark gaze.

'Listen to me, Miss Kellaway. You can save Miss Markham's reputation, but only if you are prepared to save your own in the process. You must stay at Cookes, and you *must* assume your own identity. Now, are you prepared to do so?'

He was so close. Lucille's bemused blue gaze was trapped by the intensity of those dark eyes. Once again, that peculiar empathy seemed to draw them together. She found that she could not look away.

'Yes, but I do not understand—'

To Lucille's astonishment he gave her hands a reassuring squeeze before letting her go. 'Trust me! Everything will be all right!'

Lucille gave up the attempt to think straight. In the course of one brief hour they appeared to have gone from opposition through a dangerous, if transient, physical intimacy, and were now united for the sake of Hetty's cause. She shook her head in disbelief.

Seagrave hurried her across the gravel sweep and into the entrance hall, which was an impressive room with its waxed flagstone floor and porphyry scagliola pillars. It seemed to be full of portmanteaux and harassed servants. A pregnant silence fell as they entered. One unfortunate footman was so startled to see Lucille that he dropped the bags he was carrying. Seagrave ignored him.

'Medlyn,' he addressed the butler, 'I see my mother has arrived! Where is she, please?'

'Lady Seagrave and Mr Peter are in the blue drawing-room, sir,' the butler said, expressionless. 'Her ladyship is partaking of refreshment. Lady Polly is currently in her room.' His thoughtful gaze swept over Lucille. 'Would the young lady wish to have a moment to compose herself before going through, my lord?'

Seagrave's gaze contemplated Lucille, taking in the twigs in her tumbled hair and the creased clothes. He smiled slightly. 'A good idea, Medlyn! Do ask Mrs Hazeldine to look after Miss Kellaway, whilst I have a word with my mother!' He turned to Lucille. 'Join us when you are ready, Miss Kellaway!' He bent closer. 'And don't run away!'

For some reason, his words and the warmth of his smile made Lucille feel marginally better. She went docilely with the housekeeper to a nearby cloakroom, and allowed herself to be led back to the drawing-room when once she had tidied her appearance and washed her hands and face. Her courage did not fail her until the door of the room swung open.

The drawing-room looked out across the park to the lake and Peter Seagrave and the Dowager Countess were sitting by the long windows, drinking tea. It was, Lucille thought, a particularly elegantly furnished room, with a pair of rosewood card tables and matching rosewood sofa and chairs. Seagrave, who had been speaking as she came in, broke off in the middle of his sentence and came swiftly across to her, ushering her into the room as Peter jumped to his feet.

'How do you do, ma'am? May we make you known to our mother?'

There was a pause. The diminutive, dark-haired lady put down her teacup and rose to her feet. Her lack of inches did not detract from her air of authority. She was impeccably elegant, her hair immaculately coiffed and her dress the epitome of understated good taste. Lucille immediately felt that her hasty preparations had been insufficient and was hideously aware of her own shabby state. She would not have been surprised to discover that she had done up all her buttons in the wrong holes.

Lady Seagrave raised one eyebrow. Her eyes were as dark as those of her sons, and just as inscrutable. They swept over Lucille appraisingly. Then the Countess gave an exclamation and hurried forward, enfolding Lucille in a warm and scented embrace.

'Miss Kellaway! When Nicholas said that he had brought you here I was hoping—! Thank goodness I've found you at last!'

Chapter Seven

The Earl of Seagrave was seldom put out of countenance, but even he could feel his composure slipping in the face of this unexpected and totally inexplicable welcome. He shot Peter a quizzical glance, but his brother's jaw had dropped so far that it was obvious he could not throw any light on the situation.

'Mama,' Seagrave began, 'I did not have time to explain fully—' He stopped and started again. 'This is Miss Kellaway—'

The Countess let Lucille go. 'Of course it is! I told you, I've been looking for her for several months!'

'Miss *Lucille* Kellaway,' Seagrave stressed, 'not Susanna Kellaway—'

The Dowager Countess looked scandalised. 'Why should I be looking for Susanna Kellaway? What an extraordinary idea!'

Seagrave, realising that the servants were providing them with a large and fascinated audience, closed the drawing-room door. 'You must tell us all about it, Mama!' he said smoothly. 'I am amazed you had not mentioned your…ah…mission to find Miss Kellaway to either of us before!'

The Countess had the grace to look a little embarrassed. 'Lord, Nicholas, I never see you or Peter at Everden from one year to the next!' She viewed her recalcitrant sons with exasperation. 'Both your sister and I would have been happy to tell you of our quest for Lucille had you put in an appearance!'

'So Polly is involved in this as well, is she?' Seagrave marvelled. 'You perceive me positively agog, Mama…'

'Your sister will join us later, I am sure,' Lady Seagrave said. 'She has gone upstairs to rest for a little. She has the headache.' She turned a glowing face to Lucille. 'Oh, she will be so pleased when I tell her! We had quite given up hope of ever finding you!'

Peter was shaking his head in disbelief. Seagrave looked as though he was trying not to laugh. He opened the door briefly to order some more refreshments, then closed it again very firmly.

Lady Seagrave subsided on to the couch in a sussuration of silks and laces, and patted the seat beside her to encourage Lucille to sit down. Seagrave took an armchair opposite, crossing his long legs at the ankle, and Peter moved across to the window and propped himself against the sill. The Countess gave Lucille her enchanting smile.

'You look completely bowled over, my poor child, and no wonder! What a splendid coincidence that Nicholas should have brought you here this morning! But…' she turned her enquiring gaze on her elder son

'…I understood you to be saying that there was a particular purpose to Miss Kellaway's visit?'

'That can wait, Mama,' Seagrave interposed swiftly, with a warning glance at Lucille. 'As it turns out, we need your help, but for now we are all on tenterhooks to hear your story!'

Lucille, sitting where the Countess directed, was completely confused by the turn of events. She had steeled herself to expect hostility from Lady Seagrave, if not direct rudeness. This dazzling warmth was so completely unexpected that she was almost afraid she was dreaming. The events of the entire morning now seemed strangely unreal. Any moment she would awaken in her bed at Cookes—or perhaps in her bed at Miss Pym's school, to find that it had all been an impossible dream…

'You are all kindness, ma'am,' she stammered. 'I had not expected such a welcome.'

Lady Seagrave touched her hand lightly. 'I have long been hoping to meet you, my dear. I have been shockingly remiss towards you in the past, I know, but I hope you will forgive me!' She saw that Lucille's look of perplexity had deepened and added, 'You see, Miss Kellaway—may I call you Lucille?— I am your godmother!'

'Godmother!' Both Seagrave brothers spoke simultaneously. Lady Seagrave frowned at them. 'Now, how am I to explain matters when you keep interrupting me? I do wish you would both be quiet!'

There was silence in the room. Lady Seagrave settled herself more comfortably, and addressed Lucille.

'Just as background, my dear, I wonder how well you know your parents' family situation?'

'Not at all well, ma'am,' Lucille said, even more confused than she had been before. Surely the Countess could not be her godmother? She had thought that the Markhams were godparents to both herself and Susanna, as well as being their guardians.

'Well,' Lady Seagrave said with a sigh, 'I suppose I should tell you a little, for it is pertinent to the situation. The Kellaways were once a respected county family—very wild, of course, and when that odious girl Serena ran off and married beneath her there were plenty to say it was no more than they expected...' She heard Seagrave give an exaggerated sigh at this digression and gave him a quelling look. 'Anyway, your father, my dear, inherited a tidy estate over at Westwell, and promptly sold it to finance his travels! He had been a contemporary of my dear husband's at Oxford, and Gerald offered him the lease of Cookes so that he at least had a roof over his head! Not that he was often in Dillingham, for he travelled nearly all the time.' She paused for breath and smiled to see that she had the rapt attention of her audience.

'It was on one of his tours of Italy that he met your mother, Lucille. Oh, Grace Kellaway was a lovely girl! So fair, so delicate! You have a great look of her, you know! She was distantly related to the Hampshire Fordhams, I believe, but her branch of the family never had any money and so she was acting as companion to a rich old woman. The Fordhams are so high in the instep as to be ridiculous, given that—' She broke off, having caught Seagrave's eye. 'Well, that's nothing to the purpose! But George swept Grace off her feet, married her and brought her back to Dillingham.'

Her gaze, misty eyed for a moment, rested on Lucille, who had propped her chin on her hand as she listened, absorbed, to the tale of her parents' romance. 'A year later Grace gave birth to you and your sister,' the Countess said, a little gruffly. 'You were beautiful babies! And at first all was well with her. George asked his cousins, the Markhams, to stand as godparents for your sister, but he asked Gerald and myself to sponsor you. ''The elder always has all the advantages,'' he said to me, ''so it seems only fair for the younger to have you.'' Of course, we agreed.' Lady Seagrave paused to wipe away a surreptitious tear. 'After that, it all went wrong! Grace was taken ill with childbed fever and George was devastated.'

She sniffed away the tears and this time it was Lucille who put a hand out to comfort her.

'Oh, dear ma'am, please do not distress yourself!'

'No, no, my child, it's all right.' The Countess took out her lacy handkerchief. 'It was just a terrible tragedy, for George Kellaway was so deep in love with his bride! I think the only way he could cope with his loss was to go travelling again, and after that he was seldom at home. And then there were the Markhams, so anxious to have a family that they offered to take you and your sister and give you a home! It seemed for the best.'

There was a tentative knock at the door and a bashful footman appeared with a tray of refreshments. He looked so startled to see Lady Seagrave and Lucille sitting next to each other that he would have dropped the tray had Peter not moved swiftly to intercept it.

'Of course, we lost touch with what happened to you and your sister,' Lady Seagrave resumed. 'I was

not even aware until quite recently that Gilbert
Markham had died. An old friend, unaware of my
connection with the Kellaway family, was recounting
the scandalous tale of how your sister came to become—' She caught Seagrave's eye again, and
cleared her throat. 'Anyway, she told me that it was
entirely because you had been left destitute on the
death of your adoptive father that Susanna had turned
to…her profession. I took this with a pinch of salt,
for I knew George Kellaway was still alive and
thought that he must have provided for you. It was
only when I received the letter that I realised!'

Seagrave stirred in his armchair. Lucille jumped.
She had almost forgotten he was there—almost, but
not quite, since it was impossible to ignore his physical presence.

'The letter, Mama?' he said patiently.

'From Churchward and Churchward, of course!'
The Countess turned back to Lucille. 'They wrote to
me, enclosing a letter from your father. They are our
family lawyers, you know, and quite by chance they
also looked after George Kellaway's estate. They also
held his will.'

Lucille frowned. 'I was not aware that he had any
estate, ma'am! And as for his will—did he not die
intestate?'

The Countess snorted. 'Certainly not! Kellaway
may have been a ramshackle fellow, but he knew better than that!'

'But Susanna said that there was no will! Her man
of business had checked! She was entitled to nothing
but the lease of Cookes!' Lucille blushed as she
caught Seagrave watching her. 'I beg your pardon,

sir, I understand that the lease of Cookes is within your gift! But the fact remains that there was nothing else for her to inherit except the contents of the house!'

'There was nothing for *her* to inherit because she was not in the will!' Lady Seagrave said, with asperity. 'George explained it all to me. At the last, he was remorseful that he had been abroad when Markham died, and that he had never done anything to help you both. He had heard that you had become a teacher, Lucille, and I think he admired you for that. He hoped that you had inherited some of his interest in scholarship. Perhaps he even regretted that he had never had the opportunity to discuss it with you.' She saw the cloud that touched Lucille's face and sighed. 'Anyway, he left it too late. And the only recompense he could think of was to leave you his fortune.'

'That is nothing in comparison, ma'am—' Lucille said, in a choked voice.

'True.' Lady Seagrave looked approving. 'I imagine that you must sometimes have wondered about him, longed to meet him… He asked me, as your godmother, to try to find you and acquaint you with the news of your inheritance. Unfortunately, he did not say where you were teaching, and I was not at first able to find your direction. I had lost touch with the Markhams long ago, so first I had to trace them to ask after you. I finally found Mrs Markham about four weeks ago, and was directed by her to Miss Pym's school. Of course, by the time I had discovered the school, you had left for Cookes… So here I am, my dear, mightily glad to have found you at last!'

Lucille spared a thought for Mr Kingston, who had

been left to hold the fort at Miss Pym's and must have
been quite taken aback by the sudden and inexplicable popularity of their junior mistress. First Hetty, and
then Lady Seagrave seeking her out!

'Dare we ask about George Kellaway's estate,
Mama?' Peter enquired with a grin. He turned to
Lucille. 'I apologise for my curiosity, Miss Kellaway,
but I now view you quite as one of the family, and I
hope that excuses me!'

Lucille met Seagrave's sardonic gaze again and
blushed. It was impossible to believe that he could
hold the same sentiments. How he could feel at discovering this unwanted link between them, she dared
not even imagine.

'George Kellaway asked me to be utterly discreet
about his fortune,' Lady Seagrave said, virtuously.
'He had no wish to publicise his daughter's prospects!
He knew it would give rise to an ill-bred curiosity!
However,' she added to Lucille, her dark eyes sparkling, 'your father was an unconventional man, my
dear, so it is no surprise that he made his fortune
working for a Chinese warlord! Make no enquiry into
the service he rendered him—suffice it to say that the
gentleman in question paid him in precious stones and
solid gold bars!'

As Lucille gasped in shock, Seagrave and his
brother exchanged a look.

'Now that,' Seagrave said with feeling, 'is a story
well worth putting about, Mama!'

'Extraordinary business,' Peter Seagrave said,
chalking the end of his billiard cue. 'And Miss
Kellaway an heiress! I don't mind admitting, Nick,

when you ushered her through the door this morning I thought Mama would cut up rough! When she fell on Miss Kellaway's neck like a long-lost relative, you could have knocked me down with a feather! Thought she was touched in the upper works, though I dare say I shouldn't say such a thing.'

Seagrave laughed. The brothers had been imperiously banished from the drawing-room by their mother, who had declared that she wanted to spend some time getting to know her goddaughter. They were now playing a desultory game of billiards whilst they waited for their idiosyncratic parent to summon them again, though both of their thoughts were preoccupied, if for different reasons.

'Mustn't forget about Miss Markham in all of this,' Peter said suddenly. 'It's all very well Miss Kellaway suddenly being rich and respectable, but where does that leave her adoptive sister?'

'Don't worry, Peter.' Seagrave measured his shot and sank the ball with expert precision. 'If I know Miss Kellaway, she'll be confessing all to Mama at this very moment! By the time we see them again,' he added sardonically, 'they will have hatched some plot to explain Miss Kellaway's masquerade and have saved Miss Markham's reputation into the bargain!'

There was a note in his voice which made Peter glance up at him curiously. 'Miss Kellaway told you, then? What did you make of it all?'

'An extraordinary business,' Seagrave echoed his brother's words dryly. 'Miss Kellaway must have more of her father's wildness than one might have previously imagined! And now she is so rich, you see, she will be tolerated as an Original! No doubt she will buy a cottage, keep cats and hold bluestocking soirées!' This time there was no mistaking the undertone of bitterness in his voice.

Peter hesitated a moment. 'Did she tell you why she did it?' he asked tentatively, uncertain how far he could trespass. Despite their seven-year age gap he had always been close to Seagrave, but there were times when Peter knew better than to pry.

'Yes.' Seagrave turned to look beyond the formal gardens to the meadows, shimmering in a heat haze. His expression was distant. 'I understand from what she said that she wanted to escape; the school stifled her and the society in which she found herself was not stimulating... She is fortunate that she now has the means to indulge herself without having to resort to subterfuge!'

Peter almost said that he would expect his brother to sympathise with Miss Kellaway, since one of the features of his own existence had been the overriding boredom that had beset him in civilian life. However, one glance at Seagrave's face suggested that this would not be wise. The Earl was looking angry, an observation which was borne out by his next shot, which was wildly off target and played with more force than accuracy.

Peter sank his shot and won the game.

'Damnation,' Seagrave said emotionlessly. 'Something else for which to blame Miss Kellaway!'

'Devil take it, Nick!' Peter was moved to protest, against his better judgement. 'She's a nice girl, not up to snuff in the ways of the world, perhaps, but scarcely the hardened deceiver you make her out to be! Why, I'll wager the trick was a schoolgirl game, one sister pretending to be the other! I'm sure Miss Kellaway never imagined it would get her into trouble—'

He broke off at the look of cynical amusement on Seagrave's face. 'Now there,' he said, 'I must agree with you, little brother! Miss Kellaway had no notion of the difficulties in which she would find herself!' His amusement died. 'An innocent abroad,' he said softly, as he had done the night he had discovered the masquerade, 'and with no more idea of how to go on!'

Peter stared. He had never heard that tone from his brother before. And as their eyes met there was an expression there he had never seen before either.

'I think you should know that I would have done a great deal to save Miss Kellaway from the consequences of her own folly.' For once Seagrave's voice was devoid of mockery. 'Now that circumstances have changed, though, I imagine it will not be necessary, and I find that…disappointing…'

Peter paused, resting on his cue, and viewed his brother with a mixture of amazement and disbelief. 'Nick! Are you saying—?'

Seagrave turned away. 'I find Miss Kellaway…interesting, Peter. She is not at all in the common style! And she is hardly an antidote, is she?'

'Hardly,' Peter agreed with feeling. He found himself standing with his mouth open. He had never, ever heard his brother admit to an *interest* in a woman, other than in the purely physical sense.

'Do you know whether she intends to stay in Dillingham for long?' he asked, obliquely trying to discover the precise nature of his brother's feelings. Seagrave was not deceived. He grinned.

'I believe that Miss Kellaway would flee Cookes immediately were I to let her! However, I have managed to persuade her that it is in Miss Markham's best interests for her to stay a little while, and by the time you and Miss Markham are formally betrothed—' he gave his brother a look of sardonic amusement '—I shall have persuaded Miss Kellaway to marry me!'

Peter swallowed hard, running a finger around the inside of his collar, unsure how many shocks his constitution could take in a single morning. 'You're very sure of my intentions towards Miss Markham,' he said, with a grin. 'And what of yourself, Nick? Are you suggesting another marriage of convenience?'

'Like my proposal to Miss Elliott?' Seagrave smiled slightly. 'At that time I thought that if I had to marry someone then she would be as good as any! An insufferably arrogant attitude, although I console myself by thinking it would have been as much of a business arrangement on her part as mine! But Miss Kellaway...' His voice softened with a betraying tenderness. 'She is a very different matter. Not least because I wonder if she would accept me!' His smile faded. 'I *do* care for her, but I find I can love her no more than I could anyone else. I would not wish to delude myself or deceive her. I wonder, is it truly fair to offer marriage to such a woman on those terms?'

Peter expelled his breath on a long sigh. He had been afraid of this, afraid that Seagrave's coldness, although showing all the signs of thawing, would not melt into love for his future bride. Perhaps a strong mutual regard was the best that could be hoped for, but it seemed very sad, and a pale reflection of what could be…

'No,' he said quietly, 'it is not fair to offer Miss Kellaway marriage on those terms. But—you will do it anyway, will you not, Nick?'

Their eyes met. 'Yes,' the Earl of Seagrave said slowly. 'I do not intend to let her go.'

With his own perceptions heightened by his feelings for Hetty Markham, Peter was ready to dispute his brother's claim that he could not love Lucille Kellaway. He suspected that Seagrave's feelings ran far deeper than he might know himself, and hoped that he would not discover this too late.

'You seem very certain that your heart will remain untouched, Nick,' he said with gentle satire. 'I think you mistake! You have so much reprehensible experience, and yet you still do not realise that your feelings are truly engaged this time!'

Upon which challenging statement he sauntered out of the room, whistling under his breath, and leaving his brother staring at the door panels with a suddenly arrested expression on his face.

Lucille had indeed confessed to Lady Seagrave, for she felt that she could do no other. The story of her impersonation of Susanna came out haltingly and shamefacedly, whilst her godmother sat quietly listening and asking the odd question here and there for clarity. Lucille said nothing of her feelings for Seagrave, or of his offer of *carte blanche*, for her feelings on the subject were too raw, but Lady Seagrave was no fool and could discern a great deal about the state of Lucille's emotions simply from her narrative.

'Well, my dear,' she said, at the end of this recital of woes, 'it is a sad tangle, is it not, but do not despair! Mrs Appleton had the right of it when she said it was a foolish idea from the start! But enough of that—you have castigated yourself far too much as it is! I think it best if we call Nicholas and Peter back in now, for it seems they both have a stake in the matter!' She did not miss the betraying blush which came into Lucille's cheeks and patted her hand encouragingly. 'I know Nicholas seems formidable at times,' she said comfortingly, 'but if he has said he has forgiven you, you must believe it, Lucille. He does not bear grudges.'

Lucille felt less confident of this, but had no time to dispute the Countess's words, as she was ringing the bell briskly and sending a footman to summon the brothers. Once again, the sight of Seagrave strolling carelessly into the room made Lucille's heart do a somersault. It was not fair, she thought resentfully, that her feelings should be in such a turmoil when he appeared utterly impassive, not a flicker of emotion visible on his face.

The Countess went straight to the point. 'Lucille has told me everything,' she said, with a very straight look at her elder son, 'and it seems our first concern must be for Miss Markham. May I count on help from both of you in this?'

Peter nodded immediately. Seagrave was slower, and Lucille's heart sank. She was not to know that he had been momentarily transported back to childhood and was suffering from the guilt both he and Peter had always felt when confronted with some misdemeanour. Surely Lucille could not have told his mother *everything*? Once again, he remembered with perfect clarity the warmth and sweetness of her mouth beneath his own, the softness—

'Nicholas?' His mother's voice was sharp. 'You will, I hope, support my efforts to restore Miss Markham's reputation?'

'Certainly, Mama,' Seagrave said, obligingly, dragging his thoughts away from certain aspects of Lucille which he had an urgent need to explore further. His gaze was very dark and unreadable as it rested on her. 'And what do we do about Miss Kellaway's situation?'

Lady Seagrave waved a dismissive hand. ''Tis a simple matter! The only two facts which people know for certain are that Susanna Kellaway claimed Cookes, and that Miss Markham went to stay there. The rest is complete speculation!' She sounded most pugnacious. 'So we put it about that I invited Lucille, my *goddaughter*,' she stressed the word, 'to visit me at the Court, but my journey was delayed and so she was obliged to stay at Cookes in the meantime. Being a girl from a sheltered background, Lucille was not aware that people would take her for Susanna and did not realise this for some considerable time. When she discovered the fact, she sought you out for advice, Nicholas!' She saw the look of sardonic enjoyment on Seagrave's face, and hurried on.

'To compound Miss Kellaway's problems, she had invited Miss Markham to join our party, and now discovered that her adoptive sister was also tarred with the brush of Susanna Kellaway's reputation.' She caught Peter's eye. 'It will not help the tale if it becomes known that Miss Markham ran away from home, Peter, but I know I may rely on your discretion there!'

Peter nodded. 'And then, I imagine, you arrive, Mama, and decide that the best course of action is for us to make the true facts known, explaining that it was Miss Lucille Kellaway in residence all the time and not her sister. Miss Markham is vindicated and no one will care to dispute us, I think!'

'With Miss Kellaway's fortune to sweeten the pill,' Seagrave said sarcastically, 'I do not doubt that you are right, Peter!'

Lucille flushed and Lady Seagrave turned on her son. 'You are become monstrous disagreeable all of a sudden, Nicholas! Perhaps it is the heat! So, do I have your agreement to the plan?'

Three heads nodded solemnly. 'Excuse me, ma'am,' Lucille said suddenly, 'but must the solution depend on my remaining at Cookes? I have told Miss Pym that I shall be returning to Oakham shortly and the school holiday will soon be at an end! Would it not be better for you to take Miss Markham up, out of your kindness, and for me to return to my teaching?'

Lady Seagrave looked up and caught the expression in Seagrave's eyes as they rested on Lucille's downbent head. So that was how the land lay! It seemed that, despite her feelings, Lucille wanted only to escape from both Dillingham and the Earl, and that for his part, Seagrave was not inclined to allow her to do so. Her heart lifted. She did not yet know her goddaughter well, but already liked what she knew. And, if Seagrave had formed a *tendre* for Lucille, she was fairly certain that he would manage the situation to his advantage. And she would do her best to help him.

She framed her words carefully. 'I think, my love, that you must resign yourself to staying at least a little while.' Lucille's unhappy blue eyes met hers and she smiled encouragingly. 'The story of Miss Markham's predicament will ring true only if you are present to give the lie to the fact that Susanna was at Cookes. Once Miss Markham is creditably established, you may, of course, do as you please. And indeed, you have your own future to think of now that you have your own fortune!'

She saw Lucille's shoulders slump. Never had a newly discovered heiress looked so unhappy! 'You look worn out, poor child! So much to consider in one morning!'

Lady Seagrave knew only half the story, Lucille reflected tiredly. She could not believe that it was not yet luncheon. Half a century seemed to have passed in the brief time since she had stepped out from Cookes that morning. In a daze, she heard Seagrave ordering his carriage to be brought round to take Lucille back to Cookes, and Lady Seagrave murmuring that she would write to both Miss Pym and Mrs Markham, to acquaint them of the latest situation. Lucille nodded wearily. Mrs Markham would be beside herself to hear that Hetty was being taken up by the Countess of Seagrave.

Lady Seagrave pressed her hand in concern. 'Why, you are done up, are you not, my love! Well, we shall leave our plans until tomorrow! I shall call on you in the morning! Oh, we shall all have such fun! And

Miss Markham will be just the companion for Polly—
it is all working out so perfectly!'

Lucille wished she could summon up just an ounce
of Lady Seagrave's delight. To be obliged to prolong
her time in Seagrave's company was well-nigh intolerable. Amidst the pleasure of Lady Seagrave and
Peter, his own silence stood out markedly. His tone
was cool as he handed her into the carriage and bid
her farewell, and as the coach rumbled over the rutted
tracks taking her back to the village, Lucille allowed
two solitary tears to run down her cheeks. The dis-
covery of an anonymous letter waiting for her at
Cookes felt like the last straw and she tore it up with
a viciousness that went a long way towards relieving
her feelings.

Chapter Eight

'I cannot match the colour of the sea,' Lady Polly Seagrave was saying, laying down her paintbrush and shading her eyes against the dazzling sunshine. 'It is so bright, today! Only look, Lucille, I have made it appear the same colour as Mrs Ditton's turban!' She sighed. 'I fear I shall never be an accomplished artist!'

Lucille put her book down on the rug and went to look over Polly's shoulder at the water-colour on the easel. 'You have made The House of Tides look very pretty,' she pointed out consolingly. 'Lady Bellingham will be so surprised that she will want to buy your painting!'

Polly giggled. 'It is an ugly house, isn't it! I cannot understand why such a character as Lady Bellingham should choose to live there!' She smiled shyly at Lucille. 'I was so very glad to meet her—and surprised that Mama permitted it!'

Lucille had been surprised too. When she had expressed her intention of calling on Lady Bellingham that afternoon, a silence had fallen in the Dillingham

Court drawing-room, broken only by Thalia Ditton
saying in her fluting voice that her mama would never
allow her to call on a former actress. Miss Ditton had
then fixed Lucille with her limpid blue eyes and said
that she supposed that Miss Kellaway must, through
her family connections, have met some utterly *fascinating* people, but not those of whom the respectable
members of the *ton* could possibly approve.

It was left to the Earl of Seagrave to break the
uncomfortable silence, saying that for his part he had
always found Lady Bellingham to be absolutely
charming, and that he would be glad to escort Lucille
to The House of Tides. Miss Ditton had pouted, but
brightened when Peter had hurried to the rescue by
suggesting a picnic outing to Shingle Street, given
that the weather was so fine.

The Earl had caught up with Lucille in the drawing-room doorway. 'I see that you are loyal to your
friends, Miss Kellaway,' he observed, with a lazy lift
of one eyebrow. 'A number of people come so newly
into fortune and fashion might be tempted to drop
their previous acquaintances…'

Lucille's clear blue gaze met his. 'I collect that you
mean Lady Bellingham? But she was very kind to me
when…' her gaze fell '…before…' she finished
lamely. 'I find it tiresome that society judges on out-
ward appearance and not character. You will not find
me snubbing Lady Bellingham, I assure you!'

'Bravo, Miss Kellaway!' Seagrave said warmly. 'It
is what I would have expected of you and I admire
you for it! Now, Polly has told me she would like to
come with us, but what a pity Miss Ditton cannot be
one of our party!'

Lucille gave him a sharp glance, but Seagrave's face was as bland as ever.

'I find I cannot regret Miss Ditton's absence,' Lucille said sweetly. 'She is not at all the sort of person that Lady Bellingham would wish to meet with!'

Seagrave's laughter followed her out of the room.

And now here they all were, seated on the springy turf, out of the cooling east breeze and having partaken of a delicious picnic. Peter and Hetty were sitting a little way off, the two dark heads close together, under the watchful eye of Lady Seagrave. Nearer at hand, Miss Ditton was chatting engagingly to Seagrave, her parasol at a flirtatious angle as she gazed up teasingly into his face. Mrs Ditton was looking on with the calculating expression of an ambitious mama who has her quarry within her sights. Lucille found that the scene put her out of humour. She put her book down and looked out to sea.

How dramatically life had changed at Cookes since Lady Seagrave had taken them up, Lucille reflected. As Lady Seagrave's goddaughter and an heiress to boot, Miss Kellaway was no longer to be scorned and ignored. Several prominent members of Dillingham society had soon been overheard to say that they had always known that so sweet and prettily mannered a girl could not have been the Cyprian, despite the fact that they had never actually met her. Thalia Ditton had actually had the temerity to claim a friendship, based on the unpleasant encounter in Woodbridge, and had brought her brother to call. It became apparent that Mr Tristan Ditton did not regard his previous relationship with Susanna as a bar to courting Lucille for her fortune.

Lucille's failure to disclose her true identity had been neatly glossed over and put down to a becoming modesty—or possibly the allowable eccentricity of a bluestocking of independent means. Many expected the schoolmistress-turned-heiress to be both original and quaint, and applauded her for it. Local society wished to take her to its bosom and so she became fashionable. Hetty considered it to be a great joke, and Lucille, who privately found it both shallow and hypocritical that she should be fêted wherever she went, tried to tell herself not to be so pompous.

Lucille had swiftly discovered that Lady Seagrave's plans for presenting Hetty into society meant that she would have to make some concessions. She had tried to resist, but the Dowager Countess was adamant.

'I understand your reluctance to appear in society, my love,' Lady Seagrave had said sympathetically, 'for I know that you are interested only in more bookish occupations. And clearly a lady of your independent means and…' she paused delicately '…and your age will not be concerned to be settled creditably. But it is essential that we establish Miss Markham's good reputation, and you did offer your help in that. I am afraid that it will involve a degree of self-sacrifice.'

Lucille had reluctantly acquiesced, knowing that to refuse would appear ungracious when Lady Seagrave had done so much for them. As for her own plans, she had seldom considered marriage in her scheme of things, for she had known from an early age that her prospects were not bright. She had had no family, fortune or opportunity to help her, and now that she had suddenly acquired all these things, she was obviously considered too old to be making a brilliant match. Lady Seagrave had hinted that there might now be many dubious fortune hunters dangling after her for her money, but had suggested that her best course of action might lie elsewhere.

'I realise that you do not have any ambitions towards the married state, Lucille,' she said carefully, 'being of scholarly inclination and possibly a follower of the ideas expressed by Mary Wollstonecraft in her *Vindication of the Rights of Women*.' She wrinkled up her nose. 'A very good sort of woman, I am sure, but some of her suggestions are most impractical. Now, where was I? Oh, yes, I think that under the circumstances you might consider buying yourself a cottage, hiring a companion and spending your time reading and so forth. I am persuaded that you would find such an existence most agreeable.'

Lucille, who six months previously would have said that such a life would be her idea of bliss, found that this suggestion made her want to cry. The Dowager Countess's next words made her feel even worse, and forced her to confront the truth rather painfully.

'Of course,' her godmother had said in a kindly tone, 'should you discover that you are not averse to the married state, you would do best to settle for a solid country squire, the type of man like Charles Farrant, who is so *reliable*.' She gave Lucille an affectionate smile and continued, 'Such men may not be very exciting, of course, but you are past the age of wanting romance! A sensible match to a worthy man—what could be better?'

Lucille had missed the look of wicked amusement on Lady Seagrave's face as she contemplated her god-daughter's pale, unhappy expression. The Dowager Countess had already observed that the mere mention of her elder son's name could put Miss Kellaway to the blush and she was determined to keep him at the forefront of Lucille's mind. Lucille was not naturally unsociable, but her attempts to avoid the Earl of Seagrave were making her appear so. If there was the slightest chance that he would be present at a break-fast or *fête champêtre*, Lucille would cry off, em-ploying a range of half-truths and creative excuses. It was therefore both disconcerting and annoying to find that somehow her avoidance tactics did not appear to be working.

On one occasion she had pleaded a sick headache, only for him to call on her in the afternoon to ask after her health. Worse, she had refused an invitation to the Dittons at Westwardene, an outing on which she was certain he would be present, only to stumble across him as she took a walk. He had fallen into step beside her and had invited himself back to Cookes for afternoon tea. His manner towards her was faultless but she seemed unable to escape his company, which, given that it gave her pain just to see him, was very difficult for her. Her feelings gave her no rest—Nich-olas Seagrave haunted her thoughts when she was awake and walked through her dreams at night.

Meanwhile, Peter Seagrave was paying serious court to Hetty, whose schoolgirl prettiness was blooming into luminous beauty in the warmth of his attentions. He would call at Cookes each day to take her driving through the country lanes, or to visit with friends, or simply to walk together in the gardens. The blossoming romance clearly had the blessing of Lady Seagrave, who would sigh extravagantly over young love, thereby making Lucille feel even more as though she were at her last prayers.

It was in Polly Seagrave's company that Lucille found some solace. For some reason she had expected Lady Polly to be a female version of Peter, extrovert and vivacious, and had been surprised to discover her to be both shy and studious. Polly had the Seagrave features, the rich chestnut hair and gold-flecked eyes, but there was a gravity in her manner that resembled the Earl more than his younger brother.

Early on, Polly had confided in Lucille that she was in disgrace with her mother for being too particular over her suitors; she had rejected eight potential husbands in her first season and had thereafter been labelled as 'the fastidious Lady Polly.' She was now three and twenty, and considered herself to be firmly on the shelf. Once again, Lucille felt the weight of her own twenty-seven years crush her. It could not be wondered that Seagrave would not look twice at such a faded spinster!

Charles Farrant was a regular caller at Cookes these days and was happy to escort Lucille into Woodbridge or on any expedition she chose. Together they were making a study of the history of the wind-mills in the area, and would spend hours poring over old maps and documents. Hetty was thrilled, convinced that her sister and the bashful Mr Farrant would make a match of it, and she had done all she could to encourage him. She was so in love that she wanted everyone else to be happy too. And it was not Mr Farrant's fault, Lucille thought fairly, that he had kind blue eyes rather than dark, gold-flecked ones, and that his gentle, slightly stammering tones had none of the mellow timbre of the Earl's voice.

'Do you come with us on a walk along the beach, Miss Kellaway?' Thalia Ditton's piping voice cut across Lucille's thoughts. 'Lord Seagrave—' she cast a coy, sideways glance at him under her eyelashes '—suggested it. He has offered to show us a stone sculpture wrought entirely by the sea over the centuries! Too thrilling!'

Lucille knew that the last thing Miss Ditton wanted was for her to be an unwanted third to her tête-à-tête with Seagrave, and since Lucille had no wish to feel like an unwelcome chaperon, she graciously declined the invitation. Peter was pulling a reluctant Hetty to her feet in order to join them on the trip to the beach and Polly was packing up her paints and going across the grass to join her mother and Mrs Ditton in the sun. Lucille tilted the brim of her straw hat against the sunlight and settled down again with her book. Gradually the piping voice and girlish giggles of Miss Ditton faded away, as did the low tones of Peter and Hetty, engrossed in their conversation. A bee buzzed near at hand amid the sea thrift. Lucille's eyelids grew heavy, the dazzling bright light and the heat all combining to make her feel very sleepy.

It was a blade of grass tickling her nose which brought her back to the present. She opened her eyes to find that she was looking directly into those of the Earl of Seagrave, in much the same way as she had done the time he had found her asleep in Cookes's drawing-room. The difference this time was that he was smiling at her and the effect on her was consequently greater than before, both mesmeric and compelling. She felt light-headed at his proximity. Lucille blinked and cleared her throat, determined not to lose her common sense in the face of this unexpected attack on her emotions. The blade of grass was not now in evidence, but she was certain that he had been teasing her with it all the same.

'Surely you cannot have abandoned Miss Ditton on the beach, my lord? She may be swept away by the tide!' Lucille struggled to sit up straighter, aware that Seagrave's lazy gaze was appraising her in a way far too reminiscent of the looks he used to give her before she had been transformed into a respectable young lady. Since she had resumed her own identity, his behaviour had been impeccably proper, underlining to Lucille just what the differences were in the way society treated a lady and a Cyprian.

Only occasionally did she catch him looking at her with a watchful, almost calculating look which puzzled her, and once she was surprised to see in his eyes the same heat she remembered from their encounter in the woods, before his customary, cool detachment had closed his expression down again.

'I am sure Peter is capable of taking care of Miss Ditton, even given his preference for Miss Markham's company!' Seagrave said indolently.

'But it is not Mr Seagrave's society Miss Ditton sought!' Lucille said tartly, then realised that her waspishness could be easily attributed to jealousy. She changed the subject hastily. 'Are the rock formations very fine, my lord? I have read of some in Derbyshire which are accounted well worth seeing!'

'Well, ours certainly cannot compare with the Derbyshire peaks,' Seagrave acknowledged wryly. 'I think it must have been some drunken fisherman who first espied an outcrop of rock here and likened it to Queen Elizabeth's face! I cannot see the likeness myself! And any caves around here are used for more serious purposes than pleasure visiting!' He sounded quite grim for a moment.

'Smuggling, my lord?'

'That and other things.' The gold-flecked eyes were very serious as they met hers. 'Will you walk with me a little, Miss Kellaway?'

Lucille looked round. Polly had gone to join the others on the beach and Mrs Ditton was asleep, overcome by the warmth of the sun, her mouth slightly open as she snored quietly. Lady Seagrave also looked as though she were dozing, although Lucille could have sworn that she had seen the Countess's eyes open and close again very quickly a moment previously. In the meantime, Seagrave had, with his usual authority, decided that she would agree to his proposal, and had pulled her to her feet. He took her arm and steered her towards a path that was cut through the springy turf.

'Have you heard of the Fen Tigers, Miss Kellaway?' Seagrave asked as they fell into step together.

'I understood them to be the men who had originally drained the fenland in the seventeenth century, sir,' Lucille said, wondering what he meant.

'That's true,' Seagrave smiled down at her. 'How

very knowledgeable you are, Miss Kellaway! However, there is a band of men calling themselves the Fen Tigers who are currently roaming the land around Ely and Cambridge. They are mainly disaffected farm workers and even tenant farmers who claim that rents are too high and wages too low.' Seagrave sighed, looking out across the dazzling waves. 'I have always tried to preserve good relations with my tenants here at Dillingham, but I have heard that such unrest is spreading eastward. They burn barns down and attack farms and their owners. They have many hiding places, both for men and their weapons.'

Lucille shivered as the sun went behind a solitary cloud. For some reason the talk of unrest and discontent had made her think of the anonymous letter-writer and his threats to drive her from Dillingham. She had thought to receive no more letters after her true identity was announced, assuming that the author would realise his mistake. But the letter that had been awaiting her on her return from Dillingham Court that day had been followed by two more, always delivered after dark, and each more lurid than the last.

'That was what you meant about the caves being used for other purposes,' she said, shivering again.

Seagrave nodded sombrely. 'I have frightened you,' he said, watching her. 'I do apologise, Miss Kellaway. I have not, I hope, inadvertently touched on matters which are distressing to you?'

Lucille's startled blue gaze met his dark, unreadable one. The sun had emerged from behind its cloud and she suddenly felt far too hot. The words of the most recent anonymous letter seemed to burn into her mind, with their implication that she and Seagrave were lovers. Looking up, she realised that he was still watching her with that stilled, concentrated look that was far too perceptive. She gave herself a little shake.

'Gracious. my lord, how could that be so?' She knew that she sounded both shaken and unconvincing. 'I know nothing of secret hiding places or rural unrest! It all sounds most disagreeable!'

'As you say, Miss Kellaway.' Seagrave was still watching her intently. 'But there might be something else, something closer to home—'

'No, indeed!' Lucille bit her lip, realising immediately that she had betrayed herself with that hasty denial.

They had stopped walking, and were standing facing each other across the grass, almost in the manner of antagonists.

'You always were a bad actress,' Seagrave said softly, almost consideringly. 'I do not believe you, Miss Kellaway! Can it be that Cookes has some secrets too? Perhaps as a hiding place… But no—' it was frightening how quickly he could read her '—it is something else, isn't it, something more personal—?'

'Lucille! Nicholas!' Polly was coming across the turf towards them, dangling her straw hat from its ribbons. 'The others are ready to go now. Are you—?' She broke off, looking from her brother's tense face to Lucille's studiously blank one. 'I beg your pardon! I did not realise that I was intruding.'

'You were not, Polly!' Lucille was quick to reassure her friend. 'I shall be ready directly!' She slipped her hand through Polly's arm and turned gratefully away from Seagrave. She did not look back, but she knew that he was watching them as they made their way to where the carriages were waiting.

Seagrave chose to travel back with Mrs and Miss Ditton, a fact which made Lucille glad for once. She felt sure that the constant scrutiny of those dark eyes would have broken down her resistance. But as she was once again surrounded by the lively chatter of Polly and Hetty on the way home, she reflected that there were some undercurrents beneath the bright and happy surface of life in Dillingham, and some had already touched her too closely.

Lucille was not by nature given to melancholy, however, and by the time the night of Lady Seagrave's impromptu ball had come round, two weeks later, she had managed to throw off her low spirits and was looking forward to the event with almost as much excitement as Hetty. Lady Seagrave had helped her to choose a dress, a simple confection of sapphire silk and silver gauze which perfectly matched the blue of her eyes. That was one benefit conferred by age, Lucille thought wryly—she was not obliged to wear the whites and pastels of the younger girls! With her silver hair drawn into an artistic chignon rather than a severe bun, she felt agreeably chic in an understated way, which was perfectly appropriate for a lady of her mature years who would be seen rather in the light of a chaperon to Hetty than her older sister.

Hetty, heartbreakingly pretty in a plain white figured gown, was waiting in the drawing-room for Lucille to give her the seal of approval. When she saw her adopted sister she rushed forward to give her an impulsive hug.

'Oh, Lucy, you do look fine! You will not want for partners tonight!' She gave her a sly, sideways look. 'I'll wager Mr Farrant will be quite tongue-tied when he sees you!'

Lucille sighed, thinking Hetty was probably right. It was unlikely that the Earl of Seagrave would be affected in the same way.

She held Hetty at arm's length and smiled. 'Well, my love, you are no dowd yourself! I take it that Mr Seagrave cannot have arrived yet, or no doubt I would have found him paying you the most extravagant compliments!'

Hetty blushed. 'Oh, Lucille! He isn't...he cannot be trifling with me, can he? I try not to hope too much, but—' She broke off, her pleading blue eyes fixed on her sister.

Lucille gave her hands a comforting squeeze. 'Mr Seagrave has been most particular in his attentions,' she said thoughtfully, 'and I am sure that he would not be so careless of your reputation as to draw such attention to you only to dash your hopes. But you have not known him long, Hetty...' she hesitated '...are you certain of your own feelings?'

Hetty's eyes lit with a shine that was almost incandescent. 'Oh, yes! I knew from the moment I first saw him! Even when I was refusing his help, I knew my protests were in vain for—' she gave a delicious little shiver '—what happened between us was inevitable!'

Lucille did not have the heart to utter any warnings in the face of such transparent happiness. She heard the sound of the Seagrave carriage draw up outside and found herself hoping fiercely that matters would work out for Hetty. That way the Seagrave brothers would only have broken one heart between them rather than two.

The ballroom at Dillingham Court was brilliantly lit and already full when Hetty and Lucille arrived. This was Lucille's first ball, and she suddenly found herself daunted by the prospect. Clearly Lady Seagrave's idea of 'a small party for close friends' involved a hundred people and a monstrous amount of organisation. The Earl, looking immaculate in the severe black and white of evening dress, was waiting with his mother to greet their guests. Lucille, suddenly overcome by shyness, had to be almost pushed into the ballroom by Hetty, and found herself confronting Seagrave with all thoughts flown completely from her head. He gave a charming but entirely impersonal smile.

'Good evening, Miss Kellaway. I hope that you enjoy the ball.'

His indifference piqued Lucille. 'You are all goodness, my lord. I shall endeavour to do so.'

At that, his gaze focused properly on her face in the most disconcerting manner and Lucille's heart gave a little jump of apprehension. Why could she not have held her tongue! Then Seagrave smiled with genuine amusement.

'I had forgotten that you would probably have preferred to be at home with your books this evening, Miss Kellaway,' he said. 'No doubt our frivolous pursuits will not interest you!'

Lucille gave him a dazzling smile, reminiscent of

Susanna at her best. 'On the contrary, my lord, I am growing a little tired of the assumption that I am only interested in scholarship! It should be possible to dance every dance, I imagine!'

'Entirely possible,' the Earl murmured, with a cynical look at the ranks of men barely holding back from besieging her. 'But only if you spare one for me, Miss Kellaway! Astringent conversation is the antidote I shall need this evening!' He gave her his rare, heart-shaking smile and continued, 'But here is a gentleman who, I am persuaded, will do his best to entertain you in the meantime!'

He stood back to allow Charles Farrant to approach Lucille, and watched in amusement as Lucille's pack of admirers closed in.

Mr Farrant was delighted to see her and he was more tenacious than he appeared. Before anyone else could cut him out, he grasped her hand firmly and pulled her onto the dance floor. 'Miss Kellaway! How charming you look, ma'am! May I beg the honour of the first dance?'

One of Lucille's responsibilities at Miss Pym's was to teach the young girls dancing, so she was not entirely unfamiliar with the dances that were taking place. However, there was a great deal of difference between a schoolroom and a fashionable ballroom, and she was glad that it was Charles Farrant guiding her through the set of country dances. Had she been dancing with Seagrave, she reflected ruefully, she would have been so distracted that she would no doubt have stepped all over his feet.

Charles Farrant escorted her off the floor and stuck by her side like a limpet, his face becoming gradually more flushed as one man after another attempted to prise Lucille loose. She secretly found it a charming novelty to be so much in demand, although a natural cynicism, confirmed by the sardonic amusement she saw on Seagrave's face as he contemplated her, made her realise that it was mostly her fortune that was the attraction. She emerged from the mêlée with her dance card full for most of the evening and her new circle of admirers vying with each other to entertain her. The experience was not an unpleasant one, particularly in view of Seagrave's obvious indifference.

Lucille's exertions on the dance floor gave her little time to worry about Hetty, whom Lady Seagrave had promised to chaperon anyway, and it was not until the first break in the dancing that she had the chance to look around and espy her sister in the middle of a group of debutantes and their beaux. Hetty was tilting her head to listen to the words of a lovelorn potential poet, but her eyes were drawn repeatedly to Peter Seagrave, who was lounging just beside her chair in a distinctly possessive manner.

'Peter is *épris,* is he not, Lucille,' a soft voice said in her ear, and Lucille turned to find Polly Seagrave beside her, her warm brown eyes smiling. She was looking slender and fragile in silver gauze, but it seemed only to accentuate the pallor of her complexion and her faintly sad expression as it lingered on Peter and Hetty.

'I am glad,' Polly added consideringly, 'for Hetty is a lovely girl and she cares for him too.' She drooped a little. 'I wish—' she began, and broke off as her gaze alighted on a gentleman across the other side of the ballroom. She caught her breath on a slight gasp and dropped her fan, bending hastily to retrieve it.

Lucille, much diverted by this, wondered who the gentleman could be who had so disturbed Lady Polly's composure. She had made no secret of the fact that she found most of her admirers tiresome boys or men without anything to commend them. Lucille had wondered whether this dissatisfaction related to some disappointment in the past, or perhaps to some ideal with whom she compared everyone.

'Lady Polly, who is that gentleman—' she began, only to be interrupted by a flustered Polly, whose manners were usually immaculate.

'Gracious, it is so hot in here!' She plied her fan rapidly and nervously, and spoke with more animation than usual. 'Oh, look Lucille! That spiteful cat Thalia Ditton is here, and she has brought Louise Elliott with her, of all people! I had heard that the Elliotts were staying with the Dittons, but how Louise dares to show her face after throwing Nicholas over, I cannot imagine!' Polly wrinkled up her pert little nose. 'Did you hear that she tried to pass off the broken engagement as a misunderstanding? Perhaps she thinks to engage his interest again, but she'll catch cold at that! Nicholas had a lucky escape there!'

Lucille, distracted as Polly had intended her to be, turned to consider Miss Elliott with curiosity and jealousy in equal measure. She had never suffered from jealousy before, and found it too painful to view as an educational experience. Miss Elliott, plump and fair, was smiling up at her recently betrothed with a winning charm and Seagrave did not look in any way averse to her company. As Lucille watched, he mur-

mured something in Miss Elliott's ear and swept her
into the dance. Polly gave a snort of disgust.

'Lord, this ball is hardly better than the London
crushes! Silly girls, tiresome men—'

Lucille laughed. 'Are your admirers not to your
taste then, Polly?'

Lady Polly grimaced. 'They are such boys! Oh, I
know some of them are older than I am, but they are
so immature!' She saw Lucille's sympathetic smile
and said hastily, 'No doubt you think me too particular, for I know that I am generally held to be so!
But—'

'But what you need is a real man, Lady Polly!'

Polly jumped and blushed vividly, spinning around.
'Oh, Lord Henry, I did not see you there!' She got a
grip on herself although her colour was still high.
'Have you met Miss Kellaway before? Lucille, may
I introduce Lord Henry Marchnight?'

Lucille found herself being appraised by the gentleman she had seen across the room. He certainly
was a man who knew how to invest a look with all
sorts of meaning. His warm grey gaze started at the
top of her head and travelled languorously down her
in open appreciation, before returning to her face as
he gave her a broad smile.

'Miss Kellaway...' his voice lingered caressingly
over her name '...it is a pleasure to meet the new
sensation!'

Lord Henry was, Lucille thought, possibly the most
handsome man she had ever met. He was tall, well
built and fair, with a lithe physique which must be
the envy of every aspiring sprig of fashion. And there
was absolutely nothing about him which made her

heart beat any faster. Polly, on the other hand, had a becoming blush in her pale cheeks and was plying her fan rather fast to cool it. Reflecting ruefully on the unpredictable nature of attraction, Lucille held out her hand to him. Her smile was serene but it was belied by the twinkle in her eye. She could not help but like Lord Henry.

'How do you do, sir!'

The grey eyes widened as Lord Henry took in the self-possessed nature of her greeting, and his smile grew. It was not the response to which he was accustomed.

'So do I find you ladies bereft of suitable masculine company?' he enquired, raising a lazy eyebrow at Polly. 'Or should I perhaps say unsuitable company?'

Despite the lightness of his tone, Lucille picked up a barely detectable hint of bitterness, an impression confirmed when the colour rushed back into Polly's face and she answered with constraint, 'We were reflecting on the sad lack of serious conversation at such a gathering as this, sir!'

'Ah, conversation!' Lord Henry smiled satirically. 'But surely such is not the purpose of these events, for the more opportunity a lady and gentleman have to converse, the less likelihood that they will discover any ground of mutual interest! Surely, Lady Polly—'

'Your servant, Marchnight.' The shadow of the Earl of Seagrave had fallen across the three of them and his dark eyes moved thoughtfully from Lord Henry's amused face to Polly's flushed one, then lingered for a moment on Lucille, who was looking studiously blank. He turned to his sister.

'I believe you promised me the boulanger, Polly!'

Lord Henry watched them walk away, a slight, cynical smile on his lips. 'Seagrave doesn't approve of me making up to his little sister,' he said ruefully.

He sounded unconcerned, but once again Lucille picked up the nuance of bitterness and frustration and thought she briefly caught an expression of real unhappiness in those grey eyes.

'Why is that, sir?' Lucille was wondering whether Seagrave's willingness to leave *her* in Lord Henry's company sprang from indifference or the belief that she was too old or unattractive to warrant his attentions. 'Are you, then, considered very dangerous?'

Lord Henry almost choked at this. 'I believe the relatives of youthful females consider me excessively so,' he said drily. 'I wonder that you dare be seen in my company, ma'am!'

Lucille felt her lips twitch. 'Ah, but then I am not precisely an impressionable girl, am I, Lord Henry? No doubt Lord Seagrave believes me to be quite safe!'

Now it was Lord Henry's turn to grin broadly. 'Do not depend upon it,' he said seriously, allowing his admiring glance to linger on her animated face. 'However, if you are feeling really brave, you might consent to walk a little with me, ma'am? The Seagraves have a charming conservatory which would be most suitable for…furthering our acquaintance!'

Lucille held his eyes for several seconds, but could read there nothing but a limpid innocence. She did not believe herself to be in any danger from him. She had already divined that his real interest lay with Polly and that anything else was merely distraction. And she was curious to find out what barriers were

preventing Lord Henry's courtship of Lady Polly
Seagrave. Polly, for all her studious ways and pro-
claimed lack of interest in her suitors was not, Lucille
thought, at all indifferent to his lordship.

All the same, strolling with him in the conservatory
might not be the wisest course of action. She was
about to suggest a convenient alcove as a more suitable place for their conversation, when the dancers
turned and she saw Seagrave glaring at them from
across the set. That decided her. She gave Lord Henry
a dazzling smile.

'Thank you, sir. I should be delighted!'

She saw the quick flash of surprise in Lord Henry's
eyes before he offered her his arm and escorted her
around the edge of the dance floor. One set of double
doors were open and led directly into the conservatory, which was humid and dimly lit with paper lanterns. It was an intimate atmosphere, but the number
of couples strolling amidst the ferny darkness made
it an unlikely place for dalliance.

Which was just as well, Lucille thought, for that
was the last thing she wanted. They admired the pond,
with its series of waterfalls tumbling over rocks into
the central pool and Lucille stopped to identify a
number of exotic lilies. When they reached the stone
seat at the end of the glasshouse, she sank down onto
it with an encouraging smile at Lord Henry to join
her. He took the seat, saying, 'Now we may get to
know each other a little better, ma'am!'

Lucille sat up straight. 'Yes, indeed. I am so glad,
for I wished to talk to you of Lady Polly. She is a
charming girl, is she not?' She added thoughtfully,

'In fact, I noticed that you find her more than charming, Lord Henry!'

There was a long, chagrined silence.

'Miss Kellaway,' Lord Henry said at length, in tones of rueful amusement, 'you are possibly the only lady I have ever been in such a situation with, who did not wish to talk about herself! Or at least—' he sounded very slightly piqued '—about herself in conjunction with me!'

Lucille smiled at him apologetically. 'I am sorry, sir! I have been told my ways are somewhat unconventional! I had formed the opinion that you might wish to talk about Lady Polly, but if I was mistaken—'

'You were not, ma'am.' Lord Henry sighed. 'In the absence of being able to talk *to* Lady Polly, I suppose that talking about her is the best alternative! You must be most perceptive, ma'am, to have guessed my feelings for Lady Polly on so short an acquaintance. But the simple fact is that I shall never be considered suitable to pay my addresses to her!'

There was such a wealth of bitterness in his voice that Lucille felt her heart go out to him. 'But surely there can be no objection—' she said, knowing that he was a younger son of the Duke of Marchnight. 'Your family—'

'Oh, my family credentials are impeccable, Miss Kellaway!' Lord Henry could not stop himself once he had started. 'There could be no objection to the Marchnight name, only to me personally!' He sighed heavily. 'I met Lady Polly five years ago when she was first Out. Amongst all those silly debutantes she was like a breath of fresh air. I was attracted to her at once.' He paused. 'She had a friend—a lady I shall not name for reasons which will become obvious. She was forever in Lady Polly's company. I did not...' he hesitated, looking endearingly self-conscious '...I was not aware that she cherished any hopes for the two of us, for Lady Polly was the only one who occupied my thoughts! But one day the young lady contrived that her coach broke down in the neighbourhood of my house in Hertfordshire.' He sighed. 'She knew that I was out of Town and claimed to be passing quite by chance. Whatever the case, she was obliged to stay at Ruthford overnight. We were not alone, of course, for Miss—the lady—had a cousin travelling with her as chaperon and my housekeeper was, of course, in residence. Nevertheless, the gossip, much of it on the part of the chaperon, was harmful and it was made very clear to me that the honourable course of action could entail nothing other than a proposal of marriage.'

His unhappy grey eyes sought Lucille's. 'If only you could know, ma'am, the sleepless nights I spent trying to work out what I should do. I had been on the point of making Lady Polly Seagrave a declaration, you see, and I could not bear to consider deliberately cutting myself off from a future with her. It seemed hopeless. And in the end I made it clear that I would *not* be offering for Miss—for the lady who had stayed at Ruthford.'

He shook his head, staring into the dark pools of shadow between the lanterns. 'I then went to old Lord Seagrave, the current Earl's father, and asked his permission to pay my addresses to Lady Polly. I was foolish—I should have waited for all the gossip to die down, but I could not! Anyway, he turned me down flat, calling me a man without honour who trifled with young women! Everyone was shunning me for my behaviour—I was in despair! I could not see why I should be called upon to pay such a heavy price for a situation that had not even been of my contriving.' He shrugged uncomfortably. 'Oh, I know that as a gentleman I was supposed to take the responsibility, and under other circumstances I might possibly—' He broke off. 'But I was furious at being manipulated and even more angry at being condemned in such a fashion. I managed to see Polly alone and tried to persuade her to elope with me. She refused to go against her father's wishes.'

There was a silence but for the faint splash of the waterfall into the pool below. Lord Henry stirred. 'Since then I am afraid that I have achieved a well-deserved reputation for wildness. My amorous exploits are always loudly decried by the *ton* and seen as confirmation of my bad character!' He met Lucille's intent gaze and broke off self-consciously. 'I beg your pardon, ma'am, I cannot believe that I am broaching such a subject with you—'

Lucille raised a hand in a slight gesture of appeasement. 'Have no concern on my account, sir, for I have always been told I have no sensibility! You do not shock me!'

'I shock myself,' Lord Henry said feelingly. 'It is unpardonable of me to burden you with this story—I cannot think why—' He broke off again and finished, puzzled, 'Upon my word, Miss Kellaway, there is something remarkably sympathetic about your character! I do not usually confide in complete strangers!'

Lucille smiled slightly. 'I can believe it, sir! But I count Lady Polly my friend and I know that she is not happy. Is there anything I can do?'

'You are all goodness, ma'am, but I am persuaded that it is too late for Lady Polly and myself to settle our differences. And I am sure the current Lord Seagrave sees me in no kinder light than his late father did!'

'Well,' Lucille said, and this time the note of bitterness was in her own voice, 'I cannot offer to help you there, that is true! It would do your cause no good for me to approach Lord Seagrave!' She stopped before she betrayed herself completely, but Lord Henry had clearly sensed her distress and put a hand comfortingly on one of hers.

'Then it seems you are in no better case than I—' he had begun, when Seagrave himself interrupted them. Neither of them had noticed his approach.

'Miss Kellaway! I am come to escort you to supper!' Lucille looked up to see him at his most inscrutable, but there was a wealth of meaning in his voice if not his face, and it made her bristle instinctively. She had no idea whether he had been close enough to hear her last comment, but she certainly resented the way his gaze lingered suggestively on Lord Henry, and in particular on their clasped hands. She began to withdraw her own, and Lord Henry let her go with what appeared to be deliberate and regretful slowness. She knew that he was only doing it to annoy Seagrave.

'Are you constituted as my Nemesis for this evening, Seagrave?' Lord Henry was saying, with lazy disdain. 'To be torn away from the company of not one charming lady but two seems more than mere coincidence!'

'If you wish to consider it deliberate, Marchnight,' Seagrave said pleasantly, 'then please do so!' There was an ugly expression in his eyes. He turned back to Lucille. 'If you please, Miss Kellaway—'

'I believe that Mr Farrant is my escort for supper,' Lucille said, feeling a secret pleasure at being able to thwart Seagrave's high-handed tactics, but rather ashamed of herself at the same time. 'Oh, look, here he is come to claim me! If you two gentlemen will excuse me…' She bestowed a particularly warm smile on Lord Henry, and got to her feet.

'Good God, I am falling over your admirers tonight!' Seagrave said, with a rare show of ill temper. He turned on his heel and strode out of the conservatory.

Chapter Nine

Lucille enjoyed her supper with Charles Farrant, Polly Seagrave and Polly's partner, George Templeton, who was evidently considered to be far more suitable than the luckless Henry Marchnight. As she watched Polly picking at her food and attempting to appear animated, Lucille reflected on the story which Lord Henry had told her. Polly could only have been eighteen at the time of the proposed elopement, and it was quite understandable that she would not have dared to flout her father's wishes. What seemed so sad now, however, was that Polly had clearly had a regard for Henry Marchnight—feelings which had not faded or been replaced with the passage of time. To be obliged to see him socially, to be drawn to him and yet to be forever separated from him must, Lucille thought, be a torment to her.

Across the room, Henry Marchnight was ostentatiously feeding grapes to a fast-looking lady in vivid red. There was much banter and flirtatious laughter, and Lucille saw the shadow that touched Polly's face. Nearer at hand, Hetty was laughing with shy coquetry at some comment of Peter Seagrave as he sat beside her. Peter's attentions were becoming so marked that it could not be long before he made Hetty a declaration. Lucille had no doubts that he was in earnest. His feelings were clear from the way his gaze lingered on Hetty's piquant little face, the proud possessiveness with which he watched her.

Lucille felt as though a hand had squeezed her heart, both sad and happy in one complicated rush of feeling. Hetty was very lucky, she thought fiercely, and perhaps did not know how fortunate she really was. She prayed hard that Hetty would never know the pain of being disillusioned in love.

As if in an echo of her thoughts, the Earl of Seagrave crossed her line of vision, leading Thalia Ditton into the first set after dinner. A romance in that quarter would certainly strain the friendship between Miss Ditton and Miss Elliott, Lucille thought, digging her spoon viciously into her ice. Miss Elliott was looking very sulky.

Lucille danced the next with Charles Farrant and was expecting to sit out the following dance, which was a waltz. She was rather diverted to find Henry Marchnight approaching her. He swept her onto the floor with aplomb.

'The next time you wish to make Seagrave jealous, you may rely on me, Miss Kellaway,' Lord Henry said, with one of his dizzying smiles. 'I have not had so much entertainment in an age!'

Lucille tried to looked severe and could not repress a smile. 'I do not know what you mean, sir!'

'Oh, come! Since we are already such good friends, Miss Kellaway, I should tell you that I have never seen Seagrave behave so! He is notorious for having no feelings, and yet he betrayed plenty tonight!' Lord Henry's smile deepened. 'Do not mistake me,' he added hastily. 'I actually like Seagrave, and in common with many of his acquaintances I was distressed to see the change wrought in him by his time in the Peninsula. He used to be far more…approachable. But I truly believe that if anyone can reach him, it must be you, Miss Kellaway.'

Lucille looked up into his face to see if he was teasing her, but Lord Henry looked completely sincere. For one glorious moment she allowed herself to believe him, to think that perhaps she might be able to make Seagrave return her regard. But only for a moment. Lord Henry did not know about the masquerade, after all. Had he done so, he could never for one minute have thought that Seagrave would hold her in anything other than contempt. At that moment the movement of the dance brought them round in a circle, and Lucille saw that Seagrave was waltzing with Louise Elliott. Miss Elliott was pressing herself against him with far more abandon than the dance required, and was smiling archly up into Seagrave's face as she did so.

The light went out of Lucille's eyes. Lord Henry, following her gaze, gave an exaggerated sigh.

'What a tiresome little piece Miss Elliott is! Do not regard it, Miss Kellaway. Unless I miss my guess, Seagrave is only doing his duty dances!' He cast a sly look down at Lucille. 'And if it has the added benefit of making you jealous, Seagrave will consider it well worthwhile!'

Lucille shook her head. 'I wish you would not persist in this mistaken belief that Lord Seagrave could in any way care about my reaction,' she said tiredly. 'You could not be further from the truth, sir!'

Lord Henry seemed unconvinced. 'There is a simple way to put it to the test, ma'am,' he drawled. 'You have only to show a modicum of interest in flirting with me to bring Lord Seagrave to heel! I would stake on it!'

For a moment, Lucille was tempted. But she knew that, whatever the effect on Seagrave, it would twist a knife in Polly's heart. She shook her head reluctantly, giving him a slight smile to temper her rejection.

'I am vastly flattered by your offer, sir, but it would not serve.'

Lord Henry was not despondent. As the music stopped he let her go, raising her hand to his lips. 'Should you change your mind, ma'am, just let me know! It would be no hardship!' He gave her one last, wicked smile and took himself off into the cardroom.

It was unfortunate that the movements of the dance had left Lucille standing just to the left of an alcove, and one which contained the Misses Ditton and Elliott. They had found a way to be united, Lucille discovered, and that was by denouncing her as the common enemy.

'…thirty years old, if she's a day,' Miss Ditton was saying, 'no style, no air, no address…she would have done better to stay in the schoolroom! Flirting in that ill-bred way with Harry Marchnight, whom everyone knows will take up with any woman if she throws herself at his head!'

'It will take more than a fortune in gold to improve

her chances of marriage,' Miss Elliott agreed, with a spiteful laugh. 'The Cyprian's sister! What man would wish for that connection in the family!'

Lucille turned aside a little blindly, and went out into the hall, taking the first door that she found. Her gaze was blurred with tears and she was suddenly afraid that she might disgrace herself by fainting. She found that she was in the library, a room which was fortunately deserted and lit only dimly with a lamp at either end. She sank gratefully into an armchair.

How strange that Miss Ditton's cruel jibes could hardly touch her, when Miss Elliott, who was only stating the truth after all, had made her feel so exposed, so vulnerable. It *is* true, Lucille thought hopelessly. No one, not even Lady Seagrave, had been blunt enough to point it out to her before, but how many men would want to marry a woman whose sister was a notorious courtesan? Certainly not the sons of noble families, with a proud name and title to uphold. Not even the country gentlemen such as Charles Farrant, whose upright moral ideas would be outraged at the thought. Lucille had never wanted to marry before and so her sister's situation had never affected her in that way—now she suddenly saw it as the biggest stumbling block of all.

She looked up, dry eyed. So she must put any secret dreams of marriage to Seagrave behind her, and just be grateful that she now had her fortune to sweeten the pill of her inevitable loneliness. And perhaps, given time, she might no longer be haunted by those dark, perceptive eyes, the mellow cadences of that voice…

'Are you unwell, Miss Kellaway?'

The Earl of Seagrave was coming down the library towards her. Lucille felt hot and then cold. How curious, a part of her observed, that the brilliant charm of Harry Marchnight had left her unmoved when the slightest word from Seagrave could throw her into complete confusion. She cleared her throat.

'No, my lord, I thank you. I am quite well.'

'Then why are you hiding away in here? Your hordes of admirers are quite desolate, I assure you!'

Seagrave took a chair opposite Lucille and scrutinised her carefully. His tone softened.

'What is the matter, Miss Kellaway? And do not try to fob me off with the answer that nothing is wrong, for I shall not believe you!'

Lucille hesitated. The temptation to tell him about Miss Elliott's carelessly spiteful words was very strong, but she knew she had to resist. Such a confidence could only lead on to dangerous ground.

'I am tired, I think, my lord,' she said, avoiding his too-observant gaze. She tried to smile. 'This is my first ball, after all, and I am accustomed to living quietly. I came in here for a little solitude.'

Seagrave's steadfast gaze had not faltered and she knew that he did not believe her, but after a moment he said lightly, 'This is a fine room, is it not, Miss Kellaway? Perhaps you include an appreciation of architecture amongst your interests?'

Lucille looked at her surroundings properly for the first time. The library was indeed beautifully proportioned, with arches at either end and long windows opening onto the terrace outside. As well as the shelves of books behind their glass cases, there was a fine collection of sculpture and some paintings which she could not see clearly in the dim light.

'A part of the sculpture collection was accumulated by my father on his Grand Tour,' Seagrave was saying, 'but your father also brought back pieces for him over the years. You may have realised from what my mother has said that your father and mine were great friends. He was both a prodigious scholar and also a traveller who had remarkable stories to tell of his time abroad. I used to come to Cookes when I was down from Cambridge, to hear tell of his adventures.'

'I have read some of his manuscripts,' Lucille admitted. 'He must have been a fascinating man to talk with.'

'Indeed he was.' Seagrave was looking at her with that same watchful consideration that Lucille found so disconcerting. Then he smiled at her suddenly, which was even more disturbing. 'He would have liked you, I think, Miss Kellaway! In some ways you have much of the same unconventionality. Tell me, what were you discussing with Henry Marchnight?'

How clever of him, Lucille thought, with reluctant admiration, to lull her into a false sense of security before springing on her the question that really mattered. No doubt his concern for Polly was prompting the enquiry—he must be concerned that Henry could not make an approach to his sister through Lucille. Suddenly she felt reckless. She might have to let go of her own hopes, but she would do her utmost to help Henry.

'Lord Henry was telling me of his regard for your sister,' she stated boldly. 'He has not, I believe, recovered from the disappointment he suffered in that direction several years ago.'

There was a short, sharp silence.

'He hides his disappointment remarkably well,' Seagrave said drily. 'And how does Polly feel?'

'I have not asked her, sir,' Lucille said calmly. 'I had intended to speak to Lady Polly, for I saw that Lord Henry's presence discommoded her. However, if you prefer, I shall not broach the topic. I imagine that you would not wish to encourage a friendship between your sister and myself!'

Seagrave's eyes narrowed slightly. 'A curious assumption, Miss Kellaway! I assure you that I have been pleased to see the growing friendship between the two of you! Polly has lacked friends within her own circle—whilst she enjoys all the usual society diversions, there is a seriousness about her that relishes sensible conversation. I understand that, for in some ways she and I are very alike. So please do not imagine that I would wish to discourage you from spending time together. But Lord Henry is another matter, perhaps.' His voice took on a reflective quality. 'I have always liked him, but there has been an undeniable rake's progress in his behaviour in recent years.'

'Perhaps it is the aimless seeking after distraction of one who has lost the only woman he truly cared about,' Lucille said boldly. She could not believe that she was speaking thus. Perhaps the lemonade had contained a secretly alcoholic component which had loosened her tongue.

'Lord Henry seems to have gained a champion in you very swiftly,' Seagrave said, and there was an element in his tone which Lucille could not interpret. Nor could she read his face, which was in shadow. 'I should perhaps warn you that Lord Henry is accounted very dangerous!'

'So I understand!' Lucille said tartly. 'That is, however, rather like Satan rebuking sin, is it not, my lord!'

Again there was a sharp silence, then Seagrave laughed. 'Once again you have surprised me, Miss Kellaway. I would have you know that Harry Marchnight has far worse a reputation than I have!'

'In general terms that may be so, sir,' Lucille allowed fairly, 'but I can only speak as I have found and Lord Henry has always treated me with perfect chivalry. However,' she added kindly, 'I daresay that you have had more provocation than he did, sir!'

Seagrave was shaking his head in amused disbelief. 'I cannot dispute your words, Miss Kellaway! I have indeed behaved towards you like the veriest rake, but yes, the provocation has been excessive!'

He stood up, and a sudden ripple of anticipation went through Lucille.

'There is something about you, Miss Kellaway,' Seagrave continued reflectively, 'that makes me wish to live up to my reputation!'

He put a hand down and pulled her to her feet, and Lucille wondered whether he was about to kiss her. The orchestra had stuck up for a waltz in the ballroom next door, and the faint strains of the music floated into the library.

'You promised me a dance,' Seagrave said, softly. 'Dance with me now.' He pulled her into his arms before she had time to reply. Lucille's eyes widened as she felt the response of her body to his proximity.

Waltzing with Henry Marchnight had not been like this. Just the brush of his thigh against her was sufficient to send a shiver of sensation right through her. His arm was hard around her and she seemed acutely aware of every line of bone and muscle in his body.

The dimly lit room, with the sculptures watching them with unseeing eyes, the soft lilt of the music, the darkness outside, all seemed to combine to create that secret, magical atmosphere which spun its web around them. Once again, as in the churchyard in Dillingham, Lucille scarcely dared to breathe for fear of breaking the spell.

Her dress brushed against a sheaf of lilies arranged in a large basalt pot, and their scent suddenly filled the room, heady and sweet. Seagrave's face was in shadow, defeating her attempts to read his expression once more, although she thought that he was smiling slightly. The music swept on, the distant notes all part of the dream. Lucille could feel the warmth of his body and had to fight against the surprisingly strong urge to slide her hands beneath his coat and press closer to him.

This time it was the sound of voices from immediately outside the door that interrupted them. Their dancing feet faltered and Seagrave's arms fell away from her as he stepped back.

'I believe that I hear Miss Markham's voice.' He glanced at the clock. 'No doubt she is ready to leave for home, as I understand that you did not wish to stay the night at the Court.' His voice had regained its habitual coolness. 'Good evening, Miss Kellaway!'

That had dropped her down to earth with a bump, Lucille thought resentfully. When would she learn?

As she slipped out of the door, she saw Seagrave
reach for a book and settle himself in an armchair.
He seemed to have forgotten about her already.

In the hallway she was pounced on by Hetty who,
together with Lady Seagrave and Polly, had been
hunting for her.

'Lucille! Are you all right? We looked for you everywhere but could not find you!'

Lady Seagrave's observant brown eyes were scan-
ning her face and Lucille could feel a betraying
warmth rising in her cheeks. She tried not to look
towards the library door, and found it almost impossible not to do so.

'I am sorry to keep you waiting, Hetty,' she said
hastily. 'I had a headache and went to sit down quietly for a while.'

Hetty chattered about the ball all the way back to
Cookes, and only fell silent when she saw the lines
of genuine strain and tiredness in Lucille's face. She
parted from Lucille in the hall at Cookes and wafted
up the staircase on a wave of euphoria after a barely
coherent good-night. Lucille, in comparison, felt bone
tired. Mrs Appleton had left a tray of food out for her
in case she had wanted anything, but all she felt ready
for was her bed. She picked up the candle and as she
turned to go upstairs, her gaze was caught by something white lying on the tiles of the hall floor.

Lucille bent closer, then recoiled as she recognised
the bold black writing on the white envelope. Another
anonymous letter! But surely, now that her identity
was so well known in the neighbourhood there could
be no reason— Very gingerly, she bent down and
picked the letter up. It must have been left there after

Mrs Appleton had retired to bed, which could only mean that her mysterious accuser was out wandering the village that very night. The thought made her uneasy and she glanced towards the door to make sure that it was securely locked. Taking the letter in one hand and the candle in the other, Lucille made her way slowly upstairs. Suddenly she had never felt less like sleeping. In her room, she put the candle down on the washstand, and ripped open the envelope.

'You are still pretending to be a respectable lady, you slut, but we all know the truth. You are Seagrave's whore and if you are not out of this house within a sen'night it will go badly for you.'

Lucille held out the letter to the candle flame with a hand that shook. Not just insults, but threats as well now! Either the writer did not believe the story of her identity, or he thought her of easy virtue anyway. Lucille remembered the kiss in the garden, this time with a shudder of horror rather than pleasure. Had someone been spying on her then? Perhaps, even now, an unseen watcher was outside, his gaze trained on her window where the faint light still burned, knowing that she must have read his letter... The flimsy ashes of that letter stirred in a slight breeze from the casement. Lucille shivered. Now she was getting fanciful, and at all costs she could not let her imagination run away with her. Perhaps, if she told Seagrave... She paused for a moment, all too aware of the difficulties of explaining to the Earl that an anonymous member of the village thought that she was his mistress. And yet, the matter was becoming too dangerous to be simply ignored.

There was a scream, sudden and shocking in the

quiet house. Lucille grabbed the candle, leapt to her feet and rushed to the door. On the landing she collided with Mrs Appleton, resplendent in a voluminous nightdress and lacy bedcap, and grasping her bedroom poker very firmly in her right hand.

'Miss Kellaway, what on earth is going on? Was it you who screamed just now?'

'Hetty!' Lucille grasped Mrs Appleton's sleeve with an urgent hand. 'Go and waken John the coachman, Mrs Appleton! I will—'

She got no further as the door of Hetty's room burst open and her sister ran along the landing and flung herself into Lucille's arms, sobbing wildly. Lucille nearly dropped the candle.

'Lucille, there was someone in my room just now!' Hetty cast a terrified look over her shoulder towards the half-open door. 'I opened my eyes and saw a face looking at me through the bedcurtains! I thought I would die of fright!'

As Lucille wrapped an arm around the terrified girl, Mrs Appleton took the candle and advanced purposefully towards the door.

'Oh, no!' Hetty gasped fearfully. 'Mrs Appleton, do not! He may be dangerous!'

Lucille, who would have wagered any day on Mrs Appleton against any unknown intruder, drew her sister into her own bedroom and encouraged her to curl up under the eiderdown. Hetty was still pale and shaking, her hair a mass of tumbled curls, her thin nightgown providing no warmth against the shivers that assailed her. She clung to Lucille's hands.

Lucille tried gently to free herself, but Hetty clung harder. 'Do not leave me, Lucille!'

At that moment, Mrs Appleton appeared in the doorway, shaking her head. 'There is nobody there, ma'am. I have checked thoroughly, behind the furniture and under the bed, but there is no one.'

Hetty gave another sob. 'I know he was there! I saw him!' She looked at Lucille defiantly. 'I know you think I was dreaming, but I swear I was not! I had not even gone to sleep, and I turned over and opened my eyes and there was a pale face staring at me through the curtains!' She gave another shudder and looked as though she was about to burst into tears again.

Lucille hugged her. 'Of course we do not think you imagined it! It is just difficult to see where the man can have gone!'

Hetty looked mutinous. 'I don't know, but I know he was there!'

'What manner of man was he?' Lucille asked. 'Tall or short, dark or fair, young or old?'

'I don't know!' Hetty burrowed under the covers, drawing her knees up to her chin. 'He was dark, I think, and not old...I only saw his face for a moment!' Her voice wavered and she shuddered.

'I shall make us a nice pot of tea,' Mrs Appleton interposed comfortably, 'and no doubt we shall all feel better for it. Miss Kellaway, if you have a moment...'

Lucille tucked Hetty up and went out on to the landing. Mrs Appleton was holding something in the palm of her hand. It looked like grey dust.

'I did not say anything in front of the young lady, ma'am,' she began, 'but I thought that you should see this. I found it in the room, by the side of the fire-place.'

Lucille touched the powder and held it up to her nose. She almost sneezed as the pungent smell filled her nostrils. 'Snuff! But—'

Her puzzled gaze met Mrs Appleton's. 'I cleaned that room only this morning, ma'am,' the house-keeper said quietly, 'and there was no trace of this then. But someone has been in the room tonight—there can be no doubt!'

They looked at one another in silence for a moment, then Mrs Appleton patted her arm reassuringly. 'Let us leave it until the morning, Miss Kellaway! I'll go and make us that tea!'

None of them slept very well that night, and the morning saw Hetty keep to her bed pleading tired-ness. Lucille took breakfast alone, knowing she looked pale and drawn, her mind full of anonymous letters and unknown intruders in equal measure. She scoured the room, with Mrs Appleton in attendance, but they could find no further trace of the mysterious trespasser. Yet there was no denying the small pile of snuff which Mrs Appleton had carefully collected and put in a little glass bottle.

Lady Seagrave and Polly called in the afternoon, and were distressed to find Hetty indisposed and Lucille looking so wan. Lucille told them of Hetty's experience, but did not mention the snuff. For the time being she thought it better that the episode be explained away as a bad dream. She had still not de-cided whether or not to tell Seagrave. Polly too, was looking a little jaded, and Lady Seagrave seemed rather annoyed that such a splendid social occasion had left all her protégées looking rather the worse for wear.

'Here's a to-do!' she said, crossly. 'I thought you young people would have had more stamina! Peter is nursing a sore head, and Seagrave is in some kind of bad mood! I despair of the lot of you!'

Lucille laughed, but as they were leaving she took the chance to draw Polly aside for a quick word and promised to visit her the next day. Polly smiled at her, but still looked sad.

That night, both Lucille and Hetty had retired to bed early, Hetty having been moved to the second guest bedroom and the door of her original room locked. The house was very quiet. Lucille was attempting to read and was experiencing the most enormous difficulties in keeping her mind on the written page. Why was somebody apparently waging this campaign against them? Surely it could not be Seagrave, still intent on ridding the village of them? It would take the greatest hypocrisy to fall in with his mother's plans whilst simultaneously working secretly against them. She could not believe it of him. And were the letter-writer and the intruder one and the same? Lucille sighed, blew out her candle and lay down with no real hope of going to sleep.

Surprisingly, she fell asleep almost immediately, and did not dream. It was an unquantifiable time later that she woke suddenly, unsure what had disturbed her. The wind had got up during the night and was sighing in the trees outside. The house creaked a little.

Lucille's nerves prickled. She opened her eyes and stared into the dark. Then she heard it again, the noise which must have woken her. It was a soft, scraping sound, and it came from immediately outside her window.

Lucille slipped silently out of bed and crossed the bare boards to the window, hesitating only slightly before she slipped behind the heavy curtains. The night was dark, for the wind had brought up some cloud which was harrying the full moon. Its silver light was fitful, one moment lighting the whole garden, the next plunging everything into darkness as it disappeared. A branch tapped against the glass and made Lucille jump. Nothing moved in the silent garden.

Then, as she was about to return to her bed, Lucille saw a shadow detach itself from the side of the house just below her. There was the quietest of clicks as the window was closed behind him. The moon disappeared behind a cloud. When it came out again, there was nothing to be seen.

Lucille returned to bed and sat shivering beneath the covers in much the same way as Hetty had the previous night. There was no doubt that there had been someone there—someone who had broken into the house for some secret purpose, and had left like the thief in the night that he was. Lucille had absolutely no inclination to go downstairs and investigate. She lay awake until the first hint of dawn light crept into the sky outside.

'This is a very serious business, Miss Kellaway.' The Earl of Seagrave had been with his agent in the estate office when Lucille had hesitantly asked to see him, but he had sent Josselyn away immediately and gestured to her to take a chair. He leant on the desk, viewing her unsmilingly.

'Since the end of the wars there have been many masterless men roaming the countryside trying to find a living. I suppose it is hardly surprising if some of them have turned to crime, though it is puzzling that you could find nothing missing this morning.'

'No, sir.' Lucille had also seen the men in tattered uniforms who had been dismissed immediately after Waterloo. Some swept the streets or cleared the gutters, but it was humiliating for them to have sunk so low when they might justifiably have expected their country to treat them as heroes. 'I checked the house thoroughly, but none of the contents appeared to have been stolen.'

'There has been unrest on the land, as well.' Seagrave straightened up and drove his hands into the pockets of his casual shooting jacket. 'We talked about it that day at the beach, did we not? I have heard that the rick burning and rioting have moved closer. I wonder…?'

He seemed lost in thought for a moment.

'Wool prices were higher during the war, were they not?' Lucille observed thoughtfully. 'That cannot have helped. And I have read that the enclosure of common land has deprived those who used to use the land for grazing. It must be very difficult for them to earn enough to feed their families.'

'Yes, indeed. Unless one can farm enough land, there is little money in it,' Seagrave agreed, 'and with many clergymen and landowners putting up rents, it is no wonder that there has been arson and damage to farm buildings. But your problem, Miss Kellaway, appears to be more specific than this.' He held the small bottle of snuff up to the light and took a careful sniff. 'Is there anything else which might throw some light on the activities of your mysterious intruder?'

This was what Lucille had dreaded. It had almost been sufficient to prevent her from seeking his help at all. Since the day at the beach she had been afraid that he would try once again to prise from her the secret of whatever was troubling her. She had hoped that he had forgotten, but now he was watching her once more with that unsettling perspicacity. Nothing would have induced her to mention the letters and their malicious accusations. Even so, she felt a blush rising to her cheeks and met his eyes defiantly.

'No, my lord, that is all.'

'I see.' His gaze, searching and too penetrating, lingered thoughtfully on her face, noting her high colour. 'Well, if you remember anything else, be sure to tell me. I cannot imagine that you will have any more trouble, but perhaps it would be a good idea for the three of you to remove to the Court? The whole village must be aware that three women are living alone at Cookes, even though your coachman is close at hand in the coach-house. I would feel better were I to know that you were all under my roof.'

He spoke with only the most impersonal concern, and once again Lucille was reminded of the burden that they already constituted to him. She shook her head slowly. To be in such close proximity to Seagrave and be obliged to treat him with the same indifferent courtesy that he was showing her could not be borne.

'You are very good, sir, but I am sure we will do very well where we are. As you say, we are unlikely to encounter any further trouble.' She got to her feet.

'As you wish.' To her faint disappointment, Seagrave made no attempt to press her to change her mind. Once again, Lucille castigated herself for wishing that he would do so. How contrary of her to wish to avoid him and yet be annoyed when he showed her nothing but impersonal concern! It put her out of all patience with herself.

Seagrave held the door open for her with scrupulous politeness. Lucille found that even this was beginning to irritate her. 'We shall see you tonight at Mama's card party, I hope,' he was saying, still with that irritatingly casual lack of interest. 'The Dittons and Miss Elliott shall be here, amongst others! Good day, Miss Kellaway!' And Lucille was left standing in the passageway reflecting that even for Hetty's sake she was unprepared to make such a sacrifice as that evening would entail.

When she got back to Cookes, to complete her ill-humour, the latest anonymous letter was waiting for her.

Chapter Ten

In the event, neither Hetty nor Lucille were able to go to Dillingham Court that night for the card party. When John went to put the horses to, he discovered that someone had sawed very neatly through the front axle of the coach, making it completely unusable. There was no doubt that the damage was deliberate and malicious. Lucille sent him over to Dillingham Court with a message for Lady Seagrave, and settled down to play a hand of whist with a disappointed Hetty. Before long, however, there was the sound of wheels on the gravel outside and then Peter Seagrave's accents were heard in the hall, greeting Mrs Appleton. Hetty threw down her cards with a glad cry and rushed out to greet him.

'Oh, Peter, how glad I am to see you! The most extraordinary things are going on here—it makes me quite frightened!'

Over her tangled curls, Peter's eyes met Lucille's. She had tried to make light of the incident to Hetty, but could not deny that the atmosphere of tension in the house was strong and she felt as uncomfortable as anyone. Peter put Hetty gently away from him, but retained a grip on her hand.

'Miss Kellaway, my mother has sent me to convey you all at once to Dillingham Court. When she heard of this latest accident that had befallen you, she felt that the best thing would be for you to come to stay with us until the matter is resolved. If you could all pack a few necessities, I can take you straight back to the Court and we may return for the rest of your belongings in the morning.'

Lucille looked at his guileless face suspiciously. For some reason she was certain that Seagrave's high-handedness was behind this, presented in its most acceptable form by Peter and Lady Seagrave. Hetty, however, was looking so relieved that Lucille did not have the heart to refuse and it was with very little real reluctance that she went to pack a case for their remove to Dillingham Court.

Life at the Court gave Lucille a real insight into how a family like the Seagraves would live when they chose to take up their appointed place in the neighbourhood. There was no doubt that they were considered to be the first family in the locality. Invitations to the Court, or to join the Seagrave party on some outing or assembly, were highly prized. The family breakfasted late, usually at ten or eleven, for the previous evening's entertainment would only end in the small hours.

After breakfast Seagrave would often go off to the estate room to attend to business, or go out riding or shooting with Peter and a number of their male acquaintances. Lady Seagrave, Polly, Hetty and Lucille

would embark on a round of visiting in the neighbourhood, often staying out for luncheon with friends,
or returning to the Court to read, wander in the gardens or play croquet on the lawns.

Dinner was a vastly formal occasion. The family
rarely dined alone and seemed to have guests almost
every night, sometimes staying, sometimes not. The
meal was served in splendour, with footmen behind
every chair and much plate on display. Later, the
ladies withdrew to the drawing-room and the men
smoked, drank and chatted before joining them for
cards or impromptu dancing. It was a relentlessly so-
ciable if superficial existence, and Lucille, who had
been daunted by it to start with, soon found it bored
her.

She was considered odd because she often wished
to stay in her room to read, or wandered off alone in
the gardens. The indulgence with which her eccentricity had been treated at first was now declining and
a vociferous minority, led by Thalia Ditton, were both
open in criticising her obliquely for her unconventional ways and decrying her connection with so
disreputable a person as Susanna. Lucille knew Miss
Ditton's sniping sprang mostly from resentment, but
it hurt nevertheless. She rarely thought of Susanna
these days, except to wonder how long it would be
before her sister reappeared to throw Dillingham into
turmoil. She longed to return to Oakham, but Lady
Seagrave was still adamant that Hetty needed her.

Under the circumstances, Charles Farrant's uncom-
plicated admiration was balm to her soul, particularly
as Seagrave was an attentive but wholly indifferent
host. It shook Lucille to realise that this aloofness on

his part made no difference to her feelings for him. She had learned more about love in the space of three months than she would ever have wanted to know, she told herself sadly. That led her thoughts on to Polly Seagrave, for Henry Marchnight had apparently left Suffolk for London. Lucille saw that Polly was pining, and her heart ached for her, but it seemed that in Polly's case as in her own, nothing could be done.

At the end of the second week of their stay at the Court, Lucille let herself out of the house just as the sun was starting to set. She made her way cautiously through the gardens, heavy with the scent of honeysuckle and night-scented stock, and set off up the path that led up to Dragon Hill. She paused to look at Dillingham Court, illuminated by the rosy rays of the setting sun. How tranquil it looked! But this world was not for her. Lucille made a secret promise to herself that as soon as Hetty was officially betrothed to Peter, she would make her excuses and return to Miss Pym's school. That would give her a little time to decide what she wanted to do with the fortune she had so unexpectedly inherited—and start to recover from the effect that the Earl of Seagrave had had on her life.

She had reached the place where the path left the Dillingham park and climbed up beside the wood, had even placed her foot upon the stile, when her name was called from close at hand.

'Miss Kellaway! A moment, if you please!' The Earl of Seagrave himself was striding down the bridleway towards her in the dusk, a deep frown on his brow. Lucille bit her lip. Damnation! Was the man omniscient? She had laid her plans so carefully, crying off from an evening party at Westwardene, the home of the Dittons. As far as she knew, the entire Seagrave family had been intending to go—but it seemed she had been mistaken. And now Seagrave was bound to cut up rough and spoil her outing. She took her foot from the step and placed her basket upon it. It was starting to feel heavy.

Seagrave reached her side in five strides. 'What the devil can you be doing out alone at this time of night, Miss Kellaway?' he said, without preamble. 'Have you taken leave of your senses?'

Lucille looked mutinous. 'I felt in need of an evening constitutional, my lord,' she said, knowing she sounded sulky. 'It is such a delightful night, is it not? I see that you too are enjoying the evening air!'

Seagrave's lips twitched. 'Cut line, Miss Kellaway! You do not go for an evening walk with a heavy basket! Now, what's afoot?'

Lucille gave up. He would insist on escorting her back to the Court, so it mattered little if he knew the truth.

'I was going up the hill to look for the comet, my lord,' she said baldly.

There was perfect silence. A pheasant scuttered away from beneath their feet, uttering its harsh cry. Far away in the wood, a tawny owl called. Then Seagrave stirred.

'You never cease to surprise me, Miss Kellaway,' he said affably. 'I did not realise that your scientific leanings had recently taken an astronomical turn. I take it that you refer to the comet discovered recently by Sir Edmund Grantly, who put a paper on it to the

Royal Society? I recollect reading about it in the *Morning Post.*'

'Yes, sir.' Lucille looked up at the sky, which was already darkening to a deep blue. 'I discovered an old treatise in my father's library which predicted that a certain comet would return seventy-one years hence, a date which brought it close to the present. I then remembered reading a report of the same scientific paper you mentioned, sir. So I concluded that it could be the same comet and decided to look for it myself.'

'You fascinate me, Miss Kellaway,' Seagrave said, with perfect truth. 'A most enterprising adventure! And in the basket?'

Lucille pulled the rug aside and produced a telescope in a battered leather case. Seagrave took it and considered it thoughtfully. 'I remember this, for your father used to allow me to look at the stars through it when I was a boy! Good lord, I had quite forgot...' He handed it back to her and looked curiously into the depths of the basket. 'And a picnic as well! How well prepared you are, Miss Kellaway! Do I detect some of Mrs Appleton's famous pastries? And a Cornish pasty? You will be telling me next that you have a bottle of wine tucked away in there as well!'

'I have port wine, sir,' Lucille said primly, and could not resist smiling at his laughter. 'I thought it would be useful against the cold!'

'Capital! Then we have all we need, though I suppose—' he slanted a look down at her '—we shall have to share the glass—unless you intended to drink it from the bottle!'

'We?' Lucille was all at sea. Bemused, she watched

him pick up the basket and climb over the stile in one lithe movement.

'Yes, indeed!' He was holding out an imperative hand to help her over. 'I cannot permit you to go star—or comet—gazing alone, so I shall accompany you. That way, you shall be quite safe!'

Lucille doubted that severely. Whilst his recent behaviour towards her had been irreproachable, he was a threat to her peace of mind at the very least, and could be far more dangerous than that, as experience had taught her. Her recent forays into society had confirmed that Seagrave was much sought after as a matrimonial prize, but the same calculating mamas who threw their daughters in his path considered him to be both cold and unfeeling. Privately, Louise Elliott was thought to be the veriest fool for throwing Seagrave over, but there were those who thought she had had a lucky escape.

Cold, unemotional, heartless, were all words which Lucille had heard used to describe the Earl of Seagrave and they were impossible to equate with her experience of the complex, charismatic man who was now proposing that she take a midnight picnic alone with him. As she stepped over the top bar of the stile, his strong hands caught her about the waist and swung her to the ground. Breathless and dizzy, she felt her spirits soaring. No matter that he was a dangerous threat to her hard-won composure—for one moonlit evening he was hers alone, and though it would be cold comfort when she was back in the narrow world of Miss Pym's school, memories would be all she had.

He kept a hold on her hand as they climbed Dragon

Hill together. The sun was setting in the west in a flurry of blues and gold, and a sliver of moon was rising above the hill. There were only wisps of cloud and a breath of wind. It was indeed a perfect night. Seagrave spread the rug for them in the shelter of the wall and watched with amusement as Lucille unpacked the picnic. 'Not just pastries, but tomatoes, strawberries... You are a remarkable woman, Miss Kellaway!'

The light was draining from the sky, leaving Seagrave's face in shadow. Deep within her woollen coat, Lucille shivered. It was only a slight movement, but he saw it.

'I hope you are well wrapped up, Miss Kellaway. Sitting still at night is a cold business! I used to go out looking for badgers with the gamekeeper's son when I was a lad, and a long cold night we had of it sometimes!'

'Did you see any?' Lucille enquired, pouring some port into the glass and passing it to him. Their fingers touched. She repressed another shiver.

'Yes, and charming creatures they were too! We found one ancient sett in the woods behind us— doubtless it is still there, for I imagine it has been inhabited for centuries! Have you ever seen a badger, Miss Kellaway, or do you not rate natural history as highly as astronomy?'

Lucille laughed. 'Being a girl, I led a more circumscribed existence than you, my lord! I fear I was not allowed out at night to look for badgers, owls, or any other creatures—much to my regret!'

'I am surprised that you did not escape from under

your adoptive parents' vigilant eye and go anyway,' Seagrave observed.

'I expect Susanna would have told tales,' Lucille said thoughtlessly, then stopped. Seagrave appeared not to have noticed.

'Were you close to your sister?' he enquired, draining the glass and passing it back to her.

'As a child, I suppose…' Lucille paused '…we were quite close, but always very different. I always had my nose in a book, whilst Susanna hated bookish things. She could not wait to escape from the constraints of school!'

'And of everything else,' Seagrave said dryly. He was stretched out beside Lucille, propped on one elbow, and his nearness was having its usual disturbing effect on her senses. But tonight was so extraordinary, so unexpected, that she had at last given in to the impulse which was telling her to forget the future and simply relish the pleasure of his company whilst she could. 'Despite her wildness, though, it must have been a severe shock to you all when she decided to go on the Town!'

Lucille giggled. She could feel the port wine warming her inside—and prompting her to further confidences. 'Oh, it was terrible! Mrs Markham went into a spasm and had a fit of the vapours that lasted a week. We had to call the doctor! I tried to persuade Susanna against it, but she was adamant! She said it was the only career for which she had a talent!' Lucille sobered. 'We practically lost touch with each other after that, which was a pity. I would have given a lot…' Her voice trailed away.

'It was a shame for you to lose what family you

had,' Seagrave agreed, sinking his strong white teeth into one of Mrs Appleton's excellent pasties. 'But mine have taken you to their bosom! I am glad that Polly has found such a friend in you, Miss Kellaway, and with the connection between Peter and Miss Markham about to be formalised... I am breaking no confidences when I tell you that he plans to travel to Kingsmarton tomorrow to ask Mrs Markham's permission to address her daughter.'

Lucille was silent, thinking of the bleak future she had mapped out for herself by comparison. It seemed that her release would come sooner than she had realised. 'I am so very glad for Hetty,' she said sincerely, deploring the self-pity she could not help feeling.

'And what about you, Miss Kellaway?' Seagrave asked softly. 'What plans do you have?'

He was too quick, Lucille thought resentfully. Perhaps having the Earl of Seagrave's undivided attention was not such a good thing after all.

'Now that I know Hetty is settled suitably I shall go back to Oakham,' Lucille said, expressionlessly. 'Once I am back at the school I shall have time to decide what to do in the future.'

'The school, yes...' Seagrave sounded thoughtful. 'How different can two sisters be, I wonder? You are evidently both well-read and enthusiastic about learning, and whilst I can claim only the barest acquaintance with Susanna, I do remember hearing her say she would rather die than read a book, an over-exaggeration which no doubt accounts for why I remember it!' He turned sideways to look at Lucille, whose clear profile was etched against the darker sky.

'Miss Kellaway, when you were pretending to be your sister, how much of what you said was true?'

Lucille hesitated. Though he had spoken casually, she sensed somehow that this was a very important question. Her impersonation of Susanna had never been mentioned between them since the day the Dowager Countess had come to Dillingham. On Lucille's part this was because she had no wish to expose herself to Seagrave's scorn and denunciation once again, and she had assumed that he had not spoken to her of it because he deplored the whole episode. It was an uncomfortable issue which lay between them, only partially resolved, and added to the barriers which kept him remote and her unhappy. But now he was actually asking her...

She fidgeted with the edge of the rug, unable to meet his eyes. 'Oh, most of it was nonsense, my lord! I do not know Susanna well enough to know what her opinions would be on most things, so I made them up! I imagine that I was in danger of creating a most ridiculous caricature! And...' her voice took on a desperate edge '...the deeper I got, the more guilty I felt. I was on the point of abandoning the whole sorry charade and going back to Oakham on the very day that Hetty arrived and put a spoke in my wheel!'

'Your assumptions about Susanna's opinions were quite accurate, I believe,' Seagrave said. It was too dark to see his expression, or tell what he had made of her words. 'But it must have been difficult, when your own thoughts and tastes are so well established.' His voice took on a reflective quality. 'I cannot believe that it took me so long to realise! I knew Susanna hated reading, yet you left your novels lying about the place, and a fine variety of them there were too! I knew she hated walking and travelled everywhere in her carriage, yet I found you out walking on more than one occasion! And when we talked you would step out of your part every so often when you forgot yourself! You do not even really look like Susanna, since you evidently refused to lard yourself with cosmetics, or drench yourself in chypre!'

'No,' Lucille said slowly. 'I would have expected that anyone who knew Susanna really well would quickly see through the masquerade for the sham it was! That was why I was so grateful that you got rid of the Comte De Vigny so quickly, my lord! That, and—' She stopped, colouring up.

'That and his distressing inclination to refer to your sister's undoubted talents between the sheets!' Seagrave finished drily. 'Yes, you were most shaken by that, were you not, Miss Kellaway! The penalty for deception?'

'If that were the only penalty, then I would consider myself to have been let off lightly, sir,' Lucille said, subdued. 'To lose—or never gain—the good opinion of those one respects—that is of more serious consequence!'

'If you value such things, that must be true,' Seagrave agreed, pensively. 'Not everyone would believe that it mattered. But how important is that to you, Miss Kellaway?'

Lucille felt as though she were suffocating. There seemed to be a great lump wedged in her throat. She had said nothing of any stronger feelings—she knew she could never have his love. But just to know that he liked her a little, respected her even...would that not be enough?

'It means a very great deal to me, my lord.' In her desperation she dared more than she would have thought possible. 'Through my own folly I have forfeited the right to your respect, and when this whole sorry episode is just a memory that knowledge will stay with me forever!'

There was a silence.

'It must have been difficult for you to remain at Dillingham for Miss Markham's sake, when all you must have wanted to do was escape,' Seagrave observed. Lucille cursed the darkness and his own inscrutability, which made it impossible for her to judge his response to her words.

'It was.' Lucille knew there was still a raw edge to her voice and suddenly wished she had never started this painful soul-baring. It was too humiliating. If he were to say something cutting after all she had revealed, she would probably run away down the hill in tears.

'You explained to me at the time what had prompted your actions,' Seagrave said, still in that same contemplative tone. 'Let me tell you something, Miss Kellaway. I was never proud of some of the things I had to do whilst on campaign with Wellington. I saw some hideous atrocities, and was obliged to take some actions which would haunt any man. Such experiences change people, and when I was invalided out I was profoundly glad.

'Imagine, then, my horror on discovering that I could not simply adapt back to civilian life! I missed the uncertainty, the challenge, the excitement of the army. I was deeply bored.'

He shifted slightly. 'I ran through every pleasure that life in Town had to offer! Women, gambling, any dangerous sport, and the more hazardous the better! I was a fool, and I was able to indulge that folly because I had the means to do it.'

His voice took on the same bitterness that Lucille had heard that evening in the churchyard. 'Poor Harry Marchnight is pilloried for one youthful indiscretion, and yet I revelled in every kind of reckless behaviour and it was all forgiven me because I was a supposed hero! The more I tried to tarnish the image, the more people indulged me. And after a year of foolishness, during which I lost more money and trifled with more women than I care to remember, I was challenged to a duel by one outraged husband, and let him shoot me because I could not be bothered to defend myself and knew in my heart that I deserved it! Such madness eclipses anything that your boredom could ever have driven you to, Miss Kellaway, so let us hear no more of that!

'And the worst of it is,' Seagrave finished savagely, 'that when this temporary madness had gone, I found I still cared little, felt nothing! Oh, I care for my family, perhaps, for I owe them a great deal, but my estates, my responsibilities, the lady to whom I was betrothed…they meant nothing to me! I am still uncertain whether anything ever will!'

Lucille was silent. All words seemed inadequate, platitudes he must have heard from well-meaning friends a hundred times. She remembered Polly confiding in her how much the War had changed

Seagrave, and how Henry Marchnight had said how sorry his friends were to see this remoteness in him.

Instinctively, impulsively, prompted only by the love and concern she felt, she reached out a hand and touched the back of his in a gesture of comfort. She was about to draw back, appalled at her own effrontery, when his fingers closed over hers, warm and reassuringly alive after all that he had said.

'The stars are coming out, Miss Kellaway,' Seagrave said a little huskily, pulling her closer.

It was true. Engrossed in their conversation, Lucille had not realised that the sky had turned a deep velvet blue and that the first stars were shining far above them. The sky was clear but for a few scattered clouds, and the new sickle moon swooped low over the wood. The owls were calling again. It was a beautiful night.

She got to her feet a little stiffly, helped by Seagrave's hand under her elbow. He was standing very close to her.

'Where is this comet to be found, Miss Kellaway?'

'In the constellation of Cassiopeia, sir,' Lucille said, as briskly as she could. 'There…above the point of the central star. Why, I can see it even without the aid of the telescope! How beautiful!' She raised the telescope to study that smudgy pinpoint of light. 'Why, it has a tail rather like one of your tropical fish, my lord! Only look—'

Excitedly she passed him the telescope and waited whilst Seagrave focused on the heavens. After a while he sighed. 'It is…quite awesome, is it not, Miss Kellaway? And all those stars—how very humbling!'

The breeze rustled in the woods behind them. Some

small creature of the night scattered away through the undergrowth. Lucille shivered. There was a strange timeless quality about the night as though it were not really happening.

'Are you cold, Miss Kellaway?' Seagrave turned to her. 'Would you like to go back?'

'No!' Lucille saw him smile in the moonlight and added hastily, 'That is, it is such a beautiful night, my lord, that I did not wish to go back inside immediately, but—'

'But you must not get cold,' Seagrave observed. 'Here, take my coat!'

He draped it around her shoulders. It smelled of the fresh air and a faint cologne, and whatever that indefinable smell was that was the essence of Nicholas Seagrave himself. Lucille breathed it in and felt herself go weak at the knees.

'Oh, no!' She realised how husky her voice sounded. 'You will be cold yourself, my lord! Please—I have my coat—'

'And I have my jacket, Miss Kellaway, and will do very well with that.' Seagrave stooped to pick up the rug and the basket. 'Come, I will show you the lake in the moonlight. It should look very pretty.'

They went slowly down the hill to the stile. As Lucille stepped over the top bar, Seagrave picked her up as he had before, but this time he did not swing her down to the ground, but let her slide slowly down against him. When her feet touched the ground he did not let her go. Lucille's heart started to hammer. A most delicious, terrifying anticipation was causing butterflies in her stomach.

'I have tried,' Seagrave said, with a note of exasperation in his voice, 'God knows, I really have tried to behave with circumspection, Miss Kellaway! But it is impossible—' He put a hand under her chin and turned her face up to his. 'Lucille,' he said softly, consideringly. His fingers traced the line of her jaw with the gentlest of touches before he bent his head to kiss her.

The flash flood of desire swept through Lucille immediately, as though it had only been waiting for this moment and all her attempts to deny it had been in vain. She could feel the heat of Seagrave's body, feel the racing of his heart against her hand, where her palm rested against his shirt. She slid her arms around him, and heard him groan against her mouth.

'Lucille…' he said again, gently, caressingly, his breath stirring her hair. 'Who would have thought…?'

Lucille's senses were full of the scent of his skin. She ran her fingers into the thick dark hair at the nape of his neck, and drew his mouth back down to hers. His arms tightened about her. Then she remembered their encounter in the wood, her heated response to him, the danger she was in from her own wayward senses, and she drew back slightly.

'Don't be afraid…' Seagrave murmured, his lips touching the hollow at the base of her throat.

'Last time…' Lucille said, uncertainly.

'I know.' He sounded as though he really did understand. 'But this is different, Lucille. It will never be like that again, I promise.'

'Oh…' It was more a sigh than a word, and Lucille heard the betraying note of disappointment in her own voice. So did Seagrave. He laughed softly.

'Unless, perhaps, that is what you want. But that wasn't what you meant, was it, Lucille?'

It was so difficult to concentrate, Lucille found, when the brush of his lips against the tender skin of her neck was making her shiver from head to toe. Shiver, but with a consuming heat that burned into her soul.

'I know you meant only to punish me.'

'To start with there was something of that in it,' Seagrave agreed softly, thoughtfully, 'but I wanted you, Lucille. From the very first moment I saw you, I wanted you…' His lips returned to hers again with a searching insistence that robbed her of all thought.

Neither of them heard the approaching footsteps until the stranger was almost upon them in the darkness, and then the effect on Seagrave was electric. He pulled Lucille further back into the shadows, held hard against him, but this time it was his hand across her mouth that silenced her.

'My lord! Are you there?' The quiet whisper barely reached them. Swearing under his breath, Seagrave let Lucille go.

'The devil! Jem, you scared me half to death!'

'Sorry, sir.' The man came out into the moonlight, and Lucille recognised him as one of the grooms at the Court. 'But it's past the time we said we'd meet, and there's trouble over at Cookes, sir. Evening, ma'am,' he added to Lucille, showing not the least surprise that she was there.

The change in Seagrave was remarkable. Lucille was still in a dazed and dreamlike trance, but he had snapped back to reality without appearing to draw breath in between. 'Right, Jem.' His voice was hard

and incisive. 'You get back to Cookes and stay with
Will—I'll join you as soon as I've escorted Miss
Kellaway back to the Court—'

'Too late, sir!' Jem turned to point to the hill behind them. 'They're coming this way. About twenty
men, my lord, armed with pitchforks and scythes in
the main, but in an ugly mood! Walter Mutch kept
the weapons at Cookes—'

Lucille woke up. 'Cookes! But how—?'

'There's no time!' Seagrave took her arm tightly.
'Jem, get over to Martock Farm and warn them. I'd
heard word that they would be heading that way
sometime soon. Take the fastest horse—and don't let
them see you. I'll send someone to call out the yeomanry and follow you over there. Now, Miss
Kellaway—'

'Sir!' Jem's urgent whisper cut across his words.
'Look, there!'

There were torches flaring at the top of the hill.
The mob were making no secret of their approach.
The tramp of feet echoed through the still night, a
ragged rhythm with an undertone of violence. Voices
were raised in angry clamour. Lucille saw with a
shock that their faces were blackened, emphasising
the bright, atavistic excitement in their eyes. She
shrank back into the enveloping thickness of the
bushes, pulled close against Seagrave's body. The
warmth and strength of his arms was reassuring, but
she was still trembling with fear.

The mob passed over the hill and the torchlight
flickered and died behind them, the roar of voices
fading away. The bushes rustled beside them and Jem
was gone. Lucille and Seagrave stepped out onto the

path. The moonlight was as bright but the night had lost all its magic. Lucille shivered convulsively in the cold breeze and folded her arms tight against her.

'The Fen Tigers!' she said in a choked whisper. 'And you knew that they were connected with Cookes—'

'I will tell you everything later, Lucille,' Seagrave said in a tone which brooked no opposition. He had set off for the house at a fast pace, obliging her to run to keep up. 'For now, you will oblige me by going back to the Court and not stirring a foot outside until I return!'

Lucille clutched his arm. 'You will not go to Martock Farm alone? The danger—'

She saw Seagrave grin in the darkness. 'Never fear for me! I have faced far worse than this!' He gave her a brief, hard kiss and was gone.

Chapter Eleven

Lucille did not even try to read, but sat by the window in her room, looking out over the darkened gardens. Her mind was split; half of it was marvelling over the magical evening that she had spent with Seagrave and the precious, fragile rapport that seemed to be building between them, and the other was wrenched with fear for him. Every moment she spent with him only served to make her fall deeper in love, but Lucille had long given up trying to explain her feelings to herself or to dismiss them. She knew now that the life she led at Miss Pym's school, which had already begin to pall when she had come to Dillingham, could never be fulfilling again. She did not know if there was an alternative.

A diversion to her thoughts was caused by the return of the rest of the family from Westwardene. Hetty knocked on the door on her way to bed, and regaled Lucille with a highly amusing account of the card party. Both Miss Ditton and Miss Elliott had been as mad as wet hens, she said, to discover that Seagrave was not of the party, and the odious Mr

Ditton had declared himself desolated at Lucille's absence. Yawning, Hetty had kissed her sister and gone off to bed, having extracted a promise from Lucille that she would join them on their visit to the ruins at Allingham Castle the following day.

The minutes ticked past and Lucille dozed in her chair. She was just wondering whether Seagrave would wait until the morning to acquaint her with the events at Martock Farm, when there was a knock at the door. She opened it to find an impassive footman on the landing.

'His lordship's compliments, ma'am, and would you join him in the drawing-room.'

There were no concessions to politeness: if she would be so good, if she were not too tired... A prickle of apprehension ran down Lucille's spine. She looked at the man's face, but he appeared quite blank. It seemed that none of Seagrave's staff were going to question their master's right to peremptorily summon one of his guests in the middle of the night.

Her first view of Seagrave did nothing to allay her fears. He was standing before the fireplace, his arm stretched along the mantelpiece and one booted foot resting on the fender. There was a moody scowl on his face which even the dim, shadowed room could not disguise. It was almost impossible to equate this man with the one who had held her so tenderly in his arms only a few hours earlier. Lucille's heart sank.

'Sit down, Miss Kellaway.' His tone was curt. 'There are a couple of matters I wish to discuss with you. I regret that they cannot wait until the morning!'

Lucille was starting to feel very nervous. She sat

on the edge of her chair, looking up at him. He turned away.

'You should know that I have had Cookes under surveillance ever since you told me of the curious occurrences there,' he began, without preamble. 'That was why I wanted you all out of the house and installed here at the Court, but as usual, your damnable independence—' He broke off, glaring at her, and ran a hand through his ruffled dark hair. 'I had already received intelligence that the Fen Tigers intended a strike in this neighbourhood, the fenland becoming too hot for them. Walter Mutch's name was mentioned. Your cousin, I am sorry to say, is a young man who has been involved in various dubious enterprises over the years.'

Seagrave's dark eyes searched Lucille's pale face thoughtfully. 'The Kellaway wildness runs deep in him, they say. Walter had anticipated that Cookes would be his before Susanna's unexpected claim overset his plans. He had already begun to use the house as a base for his activities.' Seagrave shrugged. 'A little smuggling, perhaps; storage of stolen goods, certainly... In addition, he had been accustomed to helping himself to the contents of the house during your father's prolonged absences abroad. He is always fathoms deep in debt, for he is an extravagant gambler, and he found it useful to take the odd item here and there to settle his bills. I believe the house to be so cluttered with artefacts that no one would have noticed.'

Lucille nodded tiredly. 'No, I am sure no one would have realised... Oh, dear! And then Susanna upset his plans by moving in! I suppose that it was Walter that Hetty saw that night?'

Seagrave nodded. 'Yes. I imagine he was hoping to scare you all away, since he seems to have deliberately set out to frighten Miss Markham. I had heard that Walter is partial to snuff—it is one of his extravagances—which was one of the reasons I suspected him when Mrs Appleton found the snuff dropped by the fireplace. I imagine he must have slipped out in the confusion after Miss Markham screamed and before you all came running. As he knew the house, it would not be difficult for him to slip away unnoticed. Certainly your presence at Cookes was very unwelcome, especially with Walter's connection with the Fen Tigers. He had a quantity of arms hidden in one of the outhouses—I have been over there tonight after the insurrection at the farm was put down—and I imagine that he was on tenterhooks lest you discovered his secret.'

Lucille was momentarily distracted. 'The farm! I almost forgot! Whatever happened?'

Seagrave smiled for the first time. 'Very little, Miss Kellaway! These mob outings are usually characterised by a lot of shouting and swearing but very little real violence! When I reached Martock, Jem had already warned the farmer and the place was barricaded. The rabble were milling about threatening to burn the place down. Then the farmer doused them all with buckets of water which he had thoughtfully filled in advance in case of fire, the yeomanry arrived, and the whole thing degenerated into an ignominious retreat!'

His smile faded. 'Walter Mutch was taken by the

yeomanry. I understand that he has…acknowledged the error of his ways, and decided that a future in America might possibly be for the best!'

Lucille considered him with misgiving. 'You mean that you have persuaded him! Oh, poor Mrs Mutch! How dreadful for her!'

'Better to have a son emigrate than have a son denounced as a rabble-rouser and a thief!' Seagrave said strongly. 'I imagine that you would not have wished to press charges and cause trouble in the family, Miss Kellaway, but the contents of Cookes actually belong to your sister, who may not be so forgiving!'

Lucille hesitated, certain that he was right. Were Susanna to return and consider herself defrauded, no consideration of family feeling would be likely to sway her. An idea occurred to her. 'Perhaps I could settle his debts,' she said eagerly. 'After all, now that I have a fortune at my disposal—'

She stopped as Seagrave held up a hand, a look of amused resignation on his face. 'You are most generous, ma'am, but I have to tell you that I have already instructed Mutch to seek settlement of his debts through Mr Josselyn, and have included, in addition, a sum to speed him on his way abroad!'

Lucille's heart sank. Was there no end to the responsibilities that her family would lay at his door? She got to her feet. 'Then you must let me repay—'

'Certainly not.' Seagrave was standing over her, awesomely authoritative. 'You will not argue with me, Miss Kellaway.' The gold-flecked eyes scrutinised Lucille's pale face with a hard look. 'The matter is closed. But I infinitely regret that there is a more important issue which I need to discuss with you.'

Lucille sensed something in his manner—tension? Anger? She was not sure, but her nerves tightened in response.

'That day at the beach, I asked you if you were hiding something from me,' Seagrave was saying. 'I wondered if you had, in fact, discovered Walter's cache of arms, and were too afraid to say anything, but I thought it unlikely.' He was taking from his jacket pocket what looked like an envelope, a white envelope with black writing. 'And now,' Seagrave said grimly, holding the letter out to her, 'I realise just what it was you were omitting to tell me, Miss Kellaway.'

'Oh!' Lucille recoiled in horrified remembrance. She had left the last anonymous letter carelessly discarded on a table in Cookes drawing-room and had forgotten about it completely. And Seagrave had said that he had been to Cookes that evening, and must have gone inside, into the drawing-room, where he would have seen the letter... She remembered what was written there, and the colour flooded into her face.

'Well might you look so!' Seagrave said, with soft vehemence. He was very close, his physical presence, trapping her, intimidating her completely. 'Why did you not tell me, Miss Kellaway?'

Lucille tried to speak calmly though her heart was hammering. Those furious gold-flecked eyes were only inches from her own.

'Oh, because such letters are best ignored, my lord! They were spiteful and malicious, and I did not care to take them seriously! And I was embarrassed—I admit it!' She met his eyes defiantly. 'I did not wish you to see what was written there!'

Seagrave moved slightly away from her, although his angry gaze never left her for a moment. 'How many letters have there been, Miss Kellaway?'

'I don't know…five…six, maybe. I threw them away!' Lucille was horrified to find that she was nearly in tears, more upset by his anger than she had ever been by the hurtful accusations of the anonymous writer. The lamplight blurred into puddles of gold as she felt her tears spill over and she dashed them away.

'Forgive me for pressing you on this, but I must know—' There was constraint in Seagrave's voice now. 'Were they all like this? Did they all suggest that there was an…illicit relationship between the two of us?'

Lucille looked miserably down at the carpet. 'No. The first two were purely personal attacks on me— on Susanna. It was only after I…resumed my real identity that the letters suggested that I—that we…' Her voice trailed away.

'I see.' Seagrave sounded quite expressionless. He came across to her once again. She sensed that he was standing close to her, but she could not look up into his face. 'Miss Kellaway—' his voice was very gentle '—I understand that aversion to such poisonous malice as this might make you wish to destroy the letters; pretend, perhaps, that they never existed. Unfortunately, in a small place such as Dillingham it is not so easy to escape such spite. Although country society appears to have taken you to its heart, below the surface, not everyone is so generous! A word here or there, and a reputation dies. Your reputation, Miss Kellaway.' He tapped the letter. 'There are plenty of people who would be willing to believe this libel.'

Lucille looked up at him then, her eyes very bright. 'But I am going away soon—it does not matter!'

Seagrave was shaking his head. 'Such malevolence travels, Miss Kellaway. By devious means it will work its way back to the school, back to the parents of the children in your care... They will hear that Miss Lucille Kellaway is not a fit person to take charge of their offspring, that she is a woman of shady morality, perhaps.' He sighed regretfully. 'Or suppose that you decide to use some of your fortune to settle in some comfortable town, a seaside resort, perhaps. How long would it be before someone hears a rumour, a tantalising tale of a lady and a nobleman...scandalous details...Miss Lucille Kellaway is, after all, the sister of a notorious Cyprian. How piquant, that the respectable sister should, after all, be proved as licentious as the courtesan... You will never be free of it, Miss Kellaway!'

He looked down into her face and gave a short laugh. 'You look horrified, Miss Kellaway! Had it never occurred to you that *this* might be the natural outcome of your masquerade? I see it had not!'

'No, sir.' Lucille's voice came out as a shaken thread of sound. 'I had never thought that my good name would be compromised...not my own name... I know I pretended to be Susanna, but I always intended to resume my life as before, and no one had ever questioned my own integrity...'

Seagrave took her hand and pulled her round to face him. 'Nor mine, Miss Kellaway. This touches my honour. But fortunately the solution is easy to hand. You will marry me.'

Lucille withdrew her hand hastily. 'Oh, no, sir! I could not possibly allow—'

'I was not asking you, Miss Kellaway,' Seagrave said, with a hint of humour, 'I was telling you. The only way I can protect your reputation—and restore my own—is for us to wed. So perhaps we can dispose of your objections relatively quickly?'

He took the chair opposite hers and raised a quizzical eyebrow. Lucille sat down a little abruptly. Her mind was spinning. To be Countess of Seagrave—it was all that she had wanted; all that she had dreamed of. But not like this! This quixotic proposal, borne out of necessity...

'I am very sensible of the honour that you do me, my lord...'

'But? Do, please, be frank, Miss Kellaway. If you have any objections to me personally—'

'Oh, no!' Lucille was struggling already. 'But I am a schoolteacher, sir—'

'Yes?'

'And as such must be a most unsuitable person to become a Countess.'

Seagrave waved a hand. 'A trifling objection, Miss Kellaway! I cannot regard it! Your family is an old and respected one in this County. What could be more suitable?'

'But I do not fit into County society—it bores me.'

'It bores me too,' Seagrave agreed affably. 'We shall not mix with our neighbours if we do not wish!'

Lucille was thinking of Louise Elliott's cruel

words. 'And my sister is a Cyprian, sir! A barque of frailty, a—'

'Say no more, Miss Kellaway!' Seagrave was actually grinning. 'I understand you perfectly! But I think you misjudge your sister!' He lips twitched again. 'The next time you see her, I confidently predict that she will be Lady Bolt, and as such above reproach!'

'And I deceived you, sir!' Lucille finished tragically. 'I pretended to be the Cyprian!'

To her amazement, Seagrave still had that wicked grin on his face. 'Yes, I own that I shall be very interested to see how you intend to further your impersonation in the marriage bed!'

The hot colour flooded Lucille's face. 'But—'

'Lucille,' the Earl said, suddenly losing patience, 'if you have no more substantive points to make, I suggest that you accept!'

'Yes, my lord,' Lucille said, slowly. 'It does seem to be for the best...'

'A little more enthusiasm might not go amiss,' Seagrave said humorously. He got up and pulled her to her feet. 'Before I let you go, perhaps we should seal our bargain...'

It was impossible, Lucille thought, to resist that dizzying, demanding spiral of desire that overcame her at his lightest touch. But she was remembering the words he had spoken only that night when he had told her that he could never care deeply for anyone ever again... He had told her he wanted her and the urgent claim of his hands and his mouth was now making that very clear. But love? When she loved him so much, was it not the ultimate folly to accept this compromise and marry him? For she would always be striving to make him love her, making herself unhappy when it was obvious that he did not feel as she did. The subtle, sensuous touch of his tongue parting her lips distracted her thoughts for a moment and she struggled to free herself.

'My lord—'

'Yes, Lucille? I really think that you should call me Nicholas now.' Seagrave's lips were just grazing the soft skin beneath her ear, sending ripples of feeling along all her nerve endings. His mouth moved, brushing her neck, to pause at the base of her throat and slip even further to the hollow between her breasts. Lucille gasped.

'My lord…Nicholas…an intense physical awareness is not a good basis for a marriage…'

'True, my clever little Lucille—' Seagrave's words were barely above a whisper '—but it is intensely pleasurable, is it not?' He raised his head and looked down at her, his eyes brilliant with desire. 'I like to tease my cool, practical Miss Kellaway…' His mouth was doing precisely that, following the marauding hands that were sliding the lace edging of her bodice aside.

'Nicholas…' Lucille tried again, although she was finding it almost impossible to remember what she was trying to say. His thumb was skimming the tip of one breast whilst his tongue savoured the delicate curves he had uncovered.

'If I am not to take you here and now, I must let you go,' Seagrave was saying huskily, regretfully, his glance lingering on her flushed face and feverishly sparkling eyes. He gave her one last, deliciously leisurely kiss. 'But we shall be married very soon! On that you may depend!'

'Oh, Lady B., what am I to do!' Lucille put down her cup of chocolate and fixed her visitor with anxious blue eyes.

Lady Bellingham, awesome in puce velvet with matching turban, raised her eyebrows. 'Do? I do not immediately perceive your problem, my dear!' A humorous light entered her dark eyes. 'You are an heiress who is to be married to one of the County's most eligible bachelors in less than a sen'night! What could be more suitable? Why do you have to do anything?'

'I am wondering,' Lucille said slowly, 'whether I should cry off from the marriage!'

When Lady Bellingham's huge coach had lumbered through the gates of Dillingham Court that morning, Lucille had been both surprised and very glad. She had been intending to call at The House of Tides, but had never seemed to have a moment to herself from the time the engagement had been announced.

Good news had travelled fast. The morning after her passage of arms with Seagrave had taken place, the maid who brought Lucille's hot chocolate dropped a respectful curtsy and told her how pleased all the staff were that she was to be Lady Seagrave. Five minutes later, the Dowager Countess, in a dashing negligee of lace and gauze, had swept into the room and enfolded Lucille in her warm embrace.

'My love! I am so happy!' She had paused to look indulgently at her future daughter-in-law. 'I knew you were just right for Nicholas the moment I met you!

Oh, this has all worked out so much better than I dared to hope!'

Hetty had been no less ecstatic. 'Now we shall be sisters twice over!' she had declared, hugging Lucille tightly.

Peter and Hetty were to be married the following spring in St George's Church, Hanover Square. Seagrave, however, had decreed that he had no intention of making a fashionable spectacle out of his wedding, and had declared that the service would take place in two weeks' time in the Dillingham village church. This announcement had thrown his mother into a frenzy of preparation. She had sent to London for her own dressmaker, and Lucille had then undergone what seemed to be endless fittings for her wedding dress and talk of nothing but trousseaux. And in less than a week...

Recalled to where she was, Lucille looked up to see Lady Bellingham watching her with the same humour still lurking in her gaze.

'A change of heart?' she mused. 'But what are the alternatives? A country cottage and a country companion? Or perhaps a home by the sea, with your books? And yet I could swear that you were in love with him!'

The words, delivered in the best tradition of melodrama, caused Lucille to start and look round nervously, but they were alone in the library.

'That is the problem,' she acknowledged baldly. 'I am in love with him—but he does not love me, Lady Bellingham!'

Lady Bellingham helped herself to another cup of chocolate from the silver pot, and took two of the bonbons which Lady Seagrave's housekeeper had thoughtfully provided.

'You are in the habit of thinking too much, Lucille,' she observed equably after she had munched her way through the sweets. 'You should, in common parlance, let nature take its course. Seagrave is much attracted to you—furthermore, he finds you interesting.' She wrinkled up her nose thoughtfully. 'On the day he escorted you to The House of Tides, I noticed that he scarcely took his eyes from you the whole time! Men can be notoriously foolish when it comes to discovering their feelings—I fear you will just have to give him time.'

'Will you come to the wedding?' Lucille asked eagerly.

Lady Bellingham's eyes twinkled. 'My child, I would not miss it for the world! To be Received and Recognised—' she rolled her 'Rs' impressively '—in the County! It is beyond my wildest dreams!'

Lucille viewed her with misgiving. 'Now, Lady B., you are not going to be naughty, are you? I doubt Mrs Ditton would be able to cope with it!'

Lady Bellingham opened her eyes to their widest extent. 'You may rely on me, my dear! But what a pity your sister cannot be present! Lord, I would give a monkey to see Mrs Ditton's face were the Cyprian to make an entrance!' She stood up and pulled on her gloves. 'I have it in mind to go travelling again,' she added. 'I leave next week. Mayhap I shall see your sister whilst I am abroad!' She presented her cheek to Lucille to kiss. 'I shall give her the new Countess of Seagrave's greetings!'

Lucille felt bereft as she watched the carriage roll

away down the drive. Suddenly she could not bear the thought of dress fittings and interminable talk of weddings. She let herself out of the French windows and set off down the Green Walk towards the lake.

The thick tree canopy shaded her from the heat of the sun and the dappled grassy glades were filled with the scent of summer flowers.

A slight figure was sitting on the stone bench beside the lake. With surprise, Lucille recognised Polly Seagrave, her shoulders slumped beneath the gay parasol, one hand shading her eyes against the bright reflected light from the water. She turned at the sound of Lucille's approach and her melancholy expression lightened slightly into a smile.

'Have you escaped Mama's clutches, Lucille? It is too fine a day to be indoors, bridal fittings or no!'

She turned away slightly, but Lucille's observant gaze had already noticed the betraying tears drying on Polly's cheeks, the hastily concealed handkerchief that seemed suspiciously damp. Polly had seemed genuinely happy when told the news of Seagrave's betrothal to Lucille, but Lucille had wondered on more than one occasion whether all the talk of weddings was not putting a strain on her friend. Polly was even quieter and more withdrawn these days.

Lucille sat down beside her on the bench. 'If you would rather I went away, just tell me,' she offered. 'I know that sometimes, when one is miserable, it is far better to be left alone!'

Her words had the desired effect. Polly looked as though she was about to deny that she was in any way unhappy, then she took a deep breath.

'No, Lucille, please stay! The truth is...the truth

is…' she hesitated, then went on in a rush, 'You will have heard that Lord Henry had returned to London? I keep telling myself that it must be for the best, but in my heart…' She burst into tears.

Lucille passed her a dry handkerchief and waited until Polly's sobs had subsided a little before giving her a hug.

'I thought that all this talk of weddings would be upsetting to you,' she said regretfully. 'Oh, Polly, I am so very sorry! Is there no chance—?'

But Polly was shaking her head. 'I think not. Yet now, after five years, I can no longer deny that I love him! If he asked me to run away with him now, I would not hesitate a moment! Yet of course, I know he will not!' She sighed despondently. 'Enough of this! I do not wish to dwell on it!'

She stood up and took Lucille's arm, saying with studied brightness, 'You must come and see the new greenhouses! Mama swears we shall soon be able to feed an army on our own produce! It was Nicholas's idea, you know—he has become a model landowner! I believe Mr Josselyn is quite overcome!' The brittle cheerfulness of her tone softened a little. 'Oh, Lucille, this is all your influence, you know!'

Then, as Lucille tried to demur, she insisted, 'No, indeed! It is on your account that Nicholas has stayed in Dillingham and found an interest in the estate. He has become much more the brother I remember!' She frowned. 'Oh, no! There is Mrs Hazeldine come to fetch us.' She gave an involuntary giggle. 'She looks very hot and bothered, rushing around in the full sun!'

In the light of Polly's genuine praise, Lucille thought a little wryly, her half-formed plan to run away from the wedding seemed rather ungracious. She allowed the housekeeper to catch them up and submitted obediently to dress fittings for the rest of the afternoon.

Chapter Twelve

The wedding was a great success and Dillingham Church was packed to the rafters. A proud Mrs Markham sat in the front row with Hetty on one side and her sister Mrs Pledgeley on the other, that matron puffed up out of all proportion at her tenuous connection with the nobility. Miss Pym was there, celebrating the occasion by forsaking her customary dress of black bombazine for one of grey instead, adorned with a string of pearls. Best of all was Lady Bellingham, magnificent in jet black taffeta and the most outrageous diamonds that the County had ever seen.

Mrs Ditton, already furious at the failure of her daughter to catch the Earl, seethed with envy and outraged respectability across the aisle. She had been silenced totally by the cordial way in which Lady Seagrave had greeted Lady Bellingham, and had only managed to murmur *sotto voce* to Mrs Elliott that she could not imagine what the County was coming to when an *actress* was thought fit to grace such an event.

The only absentee was Mrs Mutch, who had been
so distraught at Walter's downfall that she had taken
to her bed and not re-emerged. However, her second
son, Ben, was there with his young family, and
Lucille had made a point of speaking to him, to Mrs
Ditton's further disapproval. Ben Mutch was a pleasant young man, with none of Walter's unsteadiness,
and Lucille was sure that, given time, she might heal
the breach with her father's family.

Lucille had been horribly nervous at the start of the
day, but felt nothing but happiness all through the
service and the long wedding breakfast which followed at the Court. Just the presence of Seagrave beside her, his attentiveness, the warm approval in his
eyes, made her feel wonderfully cherished. At the
back of her mind was the thought of the night that
was to come, and a shiver of anticipation and awareness went through her as Seagrave's hand brushed
against hers.

It was very late when all the guests left. Lady
Seagrave escorted Lucille upstairs and helped her out
of the beautiful embroidered dress of white satin and
into one of the delicious filmy concoctions from her
trousseau which passed as a nightdress. Lucille sat
dreamily before the dressing-table whilst the maid
brushed her hair, the nervous expectation just starting
to stir within her. Lady Seagrave fussed about, picking items off the table and putting them down again,
and finally dismissing the maid a little abruptly. She
sat down on the end of the bed and fixed Lucille with
her bright gaze.

'With no mother of your own to speak of such

matters, Lucille, I feel that I should be the one to broach the subject of the intimate side of marriage—' Lady Seagrave broke off in annoyance as the maid slipped back into the room and whispered something in her ear. She frowned.

'Well, tell him that I shall be but a moment! Really—!'

The maid whispered something even more urgently, and Lady Seagrave sighed and stood up. She swooped on a bewildered Lucille and wrapped her in her scented embrace, kissing her soundly. 'You look beautiful, my love! I wish you very happy!'

It was only as her new mother-in-law's exit was followed immediately by her husband's entrance into the bedroom that Lucille realised why Lady Seagrave had left so rapidly. Clearly the Earl had been in a hurry to claim his new bride. Lucille was suddenly gripped by shyness as Seagrave's intent gaze swept over her, lingering on the diaphanous lines of the nightdress as they softly skimmed her body.

In the candlelight he looked more magnificent than ever. He had discarded his coat and his white linen shirt was open, revealing the strong, brown column of his neck. He strolled across the room with his customary easy grace, and leant one hand against the bedpost, still studying her. Lucille's tension grew, particularly as Seagrave had neither smiled nor spoken since he had entered the room, had done nothing but contemplate her with that inscrutable, lingering regard.

And then, at last, he spoke.

'You look...' The Earl hesitated and Lucille held

her breath. Perhaps radiant, or lovely, was the word
that he was looking for? But no...

'You look tired, my dear,' the Earl of Seagrave said
to his new wife, with a chill courtesy that struck
Lucille in the heart. 'I shall bid you goodnight.'

He kissed her forehead gently, passionlessly, and
went out of the room.

At the end of the third week, Lucille acknowledged
to herself that her new husband appeared to have no
interest in consummating their marriage. She had no
idea why his feelings for her appeared to have undergone so sudden a change. He had said that he
needed her, wanted her, and yet it seemed that that
was no longer so. At first Lucille had been perplexed;
now she was beginning to feel hurt and angry.

During the day, they appeared to live their lives in
charming harmony. They took breakfast together, then
Seagrave would attend to estate business and Lucille
would continue her instruction with Lady Seagrave on
the art of running a great house. There were endless
visits to be made about the estate and equally endless
calls from their neighbours; they dined out or enter-
tained at home; they were seldom alone.

Gradually the warm respect of the servants had
given way to commiserating looks; conversations
were broken off hastily as she entered the room. The
visitors, with an ear for scandal, probed gently but
implacably. And through it all, Seagrave was attentive
but distant, as impossible to read as he had ever been.

At the start of the fourth week, when it became
apparent to Lucille that she was to spend another

night alone, she put her book to one side, and slipped out of the huge bed, pulling her lacy negligee on over the entrancing confection of lace and gauze that was her nightdress. Its transparent, silky lines mocked her. Evidently it took more than this to tempt the Earl of Seagrave. To tempt an Earl... For a moment she hesitated, her nerves almost persuading her back to bed—alone. Then she steeled herself and turned to the door.

The landing was deserted. At the bottom of the stairs, the grandfather clock struck eleven-thirty with its melodious chime. It felt like a very long way across to the door of the Earl's bedroom. Lucille raised her hand and knocked softly on the panels. There was no sound. She knocked again, a little louder. A sound from downstairs made her start, and without conscious thought she turned the handle. The door was unlocked. And the bedroom was empty.

'I beg your pardon, madam.' It was Medlyn who was standing behind her, his face its usual impassive mask.

Lucille jumped and spun round. Under other circumstances she might have been embarrassed to be found thus, particularly considering the filmy nature of the nightgown, which Medlyn was studiously avoiding looking at too closely. Now, however, her anxiety over Seagrave's disappearance overrode all other concerns.

'The Earl, Medlyn—do you know where he is?'

She waited in an agony of doubt for the shadow to fall across his face, the shadow which would suggest that her husband had left her and gone up to London,

or was gambling away his substance to avoid having
to face his responsibilities, or, worse still, was in the
arms of another woman...

Medlyn looked thoughtful, grave. 'His lordship
went out about an hour ago, my lady,' he said, carefully expressionless. 'He did not say where he was
going. However...' he hesitated '...I believe he may
have gone to Cookes, ma'am. He has been there twice
before in the last couple of weeks.'

'To Cookes?' Lucille was dumbstruck. 'But why?
The house is closed.'

Medlyn was shaking his head. 'I do not know,
ma'am. However...' again he hesitated, before putting considerable weight on his words '...if you were
seeking him, ma'am, I believe that you would find
him there.'

Their eyes met. 'Thank you, Medlyn,' Lucille said,
slowly. 'I am persuaded that you are right.'

The butler nodded. The faintest suspicion of a
smile seemed to touch his lips for so brief a moment
that Lucille was sure she had imagined it. 'Good luck,
my lady,' he said.

Lucille dressed swiftly and donned a warm cloak,
before slipping down the stairs and out of the house.
A light was still burning in the hall, but she saw no
one, not even the man whom Medlyn had instructed
to follow her and keep her safe. It was a clear night
and she had no difficulty in following the track to
Cookes, a journey which took her a mere twenty
minutes. She was not afraid. The necessity of confronting Seagrave was the sole thought in her mind.

She reached the village green with its slumbering cottages and paused, a little out of breath.

The front of Cookes was all in darkness. Holding her breath, Lucille tip-toed up the drive and around the side of the house. The drawing-room curtains were drawn, but a thread of light showed beneath them. She knew that the French door must be unlocked, for Walter Mutch had tampered with the latch when he had broken in and unless Seagrave had had it mended it would still be damaged.

Her heart was suddenly beating in her throat. She pushed the door open, and stepped into the room.

The Earl of Seagrave was sprawled in one of the faded velvet and brocade chairs before the fireplace. He had discarded his coat and loosened his cravat, and was staring into the fire, an empty brandy glass held carelessly in one hand. As Lucille closed the door behind her with a soft click, his gaze came up and fixed on her with unnerving intensity. With a slight shock she realised that he was not as drunk as she had at first imagined, although the half-empty brandy bottle at his elbow was testament to the fact that he was also nowhere near sober.

'What the devil are you doing here?' he demanded unceremoniously, the mellow voice much harsher than usual.

Lucille took off her cloak and folded it over the back of a chair, trying to ignore the shaking of her hands as she did so. This was going to be even more difficult than she had imagined. Sheer determination had brought her this far. She raised her chin. She was not going to let her courage desert her now.

'I came to find you, my lord,' she said, with far

more calmness than she was feeling. 'I was somewhat…concerned to discover you from home.'

'Very wifely,' the Earl said coldly. 'Well, since you
are here, my dear, you may as well join me in a drink
to toast this hollow marriage of ours!'

Lucille began to feel angry. It was the only way to
keep out the hurt that she knew would destroy her if
she let her defences slip for one moment. She moved
over to the table and poured Seagrave another glass
of brandy—and a generous one for herself.

'A pity that you did not discover this aversion to
my company before we were married rather than after, my lord,' she observed sweetly, as she sat down
opposite him. 'Your timing is rather unfortunate.'

Her anger was growing now, warming her. She saw
his eyes narrow on her and continued recklessly, 'Do
you wish to be released from this marriage which you
contracted so hurriedly? If so, you need only say the
word!'

'Are you suggesting a divorce?' Seagrave asked,
his tone so soft that Lucille could barely detect the
thread of anger than ran through it. Her own rage was
like a fire in her blood now, its effect as strong as a
rush of adrenalin.

'I thought more in the way of an annulment,'
Lucille waved her hand airily. 'It would be easy to
prove, after all! And think of the speculation, my lord!
Why, no one would know which were the greater
piece of gossip—to suggest that the Countess of
Seagrave was so unattractive that her husband found
her repellent, or that the Earl was incapable of consummating his marriage!'

She swallowed half her brandy in one go. It was

making her feel quite marvellously uninhibited. Seagrave's gaze was now a dark glitter focused on her unwaveringly. There was a tension in him that Lucille recognised, the tautness of a man who is barely holding himself under control. He said slowly, 'I understand that you are trying to provoke me, Lucille. Appearances may be to the contrary, but I am not a patient man. Take care that you do not push me too far!'

Lucille shrugged carelessly, although her frustration and the need to hurt him were consuming her. 'My words can have no power to move you, my lord, since you do not care for me. At least in *that* you have been honest! You never pretended to love me! But I would have settled for much less, for what you offered on the night you proposed to me! Now it seems you intend to deny me even that!' She downed the rest of her brandy with a gulp.

Seagrave's very stillness was terrifying. His face was inscrutable. 'It is not as you imagine, Lucille. You do not understand—'

'Oh, I understand very well!' Lucille's bitterness spilled over. 'It is simply that you regret what you have done!' She leant across for the brandy bottle. Seagrave moved it out of her grasp. Suddenly infuriated, she got up and reached across him, determined that in this small matter at least, she would have her way.

Seagrave's hand closed around her wrist. 'The only thing I regret,' he said very softly, 'is not doing this sooner.' He gave her arm a sharp tug. Lucille was caught off balance and the brandy, which had gone straight to her head, did the rest. She tumbled on to his knee.

'And now, my Lady Seagrave,' the Earl said, through his teeth, 'you will be able to judge for yourself whether your husband is incapable of consummating his marriage!'

Despite his anger, it soon became apparent that the Earl of Seagrave was in no hurry. The kiss was long, insistent and utterly inescapable. Lucille was immediately assailed by the same treacherous weakness that always invaded her senses when he touched her. She gave a little sigh deep in her throat, the telltale sign of her pleasure. Instantly, the fierce sweetness of the kiss intensified. Seagrave entwined one hand in the cloud of silver hair, holding her face upturned to his so that he could plunder her mouth at will. Still kissing her, he stood up, holding her in his arms. Lucille tore her mouth away from his with an effort.

'What—'

'Hush.' He silenced her again. The searing passion washed through Lucille in a tide that left her trembling. This time when he raised his head she did not speak, simply resting her cheek against his broad shoulder as he carried her out of the drawing-room and up the stairs into her own bedroom. Her eyes were closed, waiting for the onslaught on her senses to begin again, wanting nothing but to touch him, taste him, explore the sensations which she still only half-understood. Seagrave kicked the bedroom door shut behind them.

The curtains were not drawn, but neither of them paid any attention. Seagrave tossed her down into the middle of the big bed and was beside her before

Lucille had time to draw breath. His mouth reclaimed hers immediately, but Lucille was aware that his fingers were busy with the buttons at the back of her dress, skilfully unfastening it to slide it off her shoulders and down to her waist. When he realised that she was wearing no chemise beneath, wearing nothing beneath, Seagrave paused, a slow smile curving his lips.

'Well, Lucille, whatever were you about to forget to dress properly?'

'I was in a hurry,' Lucille whispered, and saw his smile deepen as he lowered his head to her exposed breasts.

Lucille arched upwards against the demand of his lips and fingers. She tugged hard at his shirt and felt it come loose, sliding her hands beneath the linen and gasping as she touched his naked skin for the first time. Her quick, indrawn breath was smothered against his lips.

Seagrave drew away a little to pull off his boots and toss them with an impatient hand into a corner of the room. He discarded the rest of his clothes in a couple of quick movements before rejoining her on the bed. Lucille watched the silver moonlight slide over his muscular physique and reached out to pull him down beside her. She ran her hands over his chest, spellbound by the texture of his skin, wanting to feel it against her own. Her fingers drifted lower, over his stomach and across his ribs, and he groaned, pulling her against him.

Lucille had never seen a naked man before and the classical statues she had seen in pictures, whilst beautiful, were in no way as compelling as the real thing. Her exploring hands stilled as coherent thought returned for the first time in a long while. Her reading and observation of real life had given her an understanding of how animals mated, but as to how that would apply to her—

'Nicholas…' There was a thread of anxiety now in her whispered words.

Seagrave heard it and was quick to reassure her. 'Trust me.' His voice was soft. 'It will be all right. You will see…'

He was still stroking her skin and the gentle touch was both relaxing and at the same time oddly exciting. Lucille felt her worries slip to the edge of her mind as pleasure began to cloud her thoughts again. Her skirt was tiresomely in the way, she thought crossly, and she was grateful as she felt Seagrave easing it over her hips to fall, an empty shell, on the floor. She felt his hand run the whole length of her near-naked body and opened her eyes. Seagrave was looking at her, her silver hair spread across the pillows, her slender body illuminated in the sharp moonlight. His narrowed, concentrated gaze only served to excite Lucille further.

'Silk stockings?' he said musingly, a hint of amusement detectable in his voice. 'That was the only piece of underwear you stopped long enough to put on?' His hand was stroking her silken thigh, slowly, tantalisingly, and its touch was deliciously stimulating. Lucille remembered vaguely that the stockings, part of her trousseau, had been nearest to hand as she had dressed and before her haste to find him had overcome her. She tried to form the words to explain to Seagrave, but he was already kissing her again. Anyway, he did not seem to mind, Lucille thought hazily, for he had not taken them off. As his hands lingered on her thighs a feeling of unbearable anticipation was growing in her, warming the pit of her stomach, demanding satisfaction. She felt his fingers part her legs, still stroking persuasively, urgently. Lucille dug her fingernails into his shoulders.

'Nicholas, please…'

She did not know exactly what she was asking, but he did. He slid into her, hard and deep, and Lucille's instinctive gasp of pain was lost as he moved inside her, replacing pain with pleasure, such unimaginable pleasure that she cried out as the inexorable tide of sensation tumbled over and through her. She was dimly aware of Seagrave gasping her name as the same hot, sweet tide took hold of him almost immediately.

It was a long time before the ripples of that pleasure died away, and Seagrave rolled over, pulled Lucille into the crook of his arm and wrapped the blankets firmly around them. She felt wonderfully warm and secure there, her head resting against his shoulder, watching the taut lines of his face relax into sleep. Her own eyelids grew heavy. Soon she too was asleep.

When Lucille awoke again the moon had moved round and the room was in near darkness. It was still night outside and she could hear the wind in the trees. She propped herself on one elbow to look down at her husband. He looked boyish in sleep, the thick dark lashes resting against the hard line of his cheek and the tousled dark hair falling across his brow. Lucille was swept by an intensely strong, protective love. She also felt rather pleased with herself and was half-ashamed to be so brazen.

Seagrave might not love her, but she had made him consummate the marriage in an entirely satisfactory manner. Her body ached pleasantly with the aftermath of an unfamiliar pleasure and a little smile curved her lips. It was then that she realised that Seagrave was awake and watching her. In one swift movement he had pulled her beneath him.

'That was a very self-satisfied smile I saw just now,' he said huskily. 'No doubt you are pleased with yourself, madam?'

Lucille's eyes widened. She was unable to gauge his mood and her heart began to race with a mixture of genuine nerves and anticipation. What if he was angry with her for provoking him and pushing him too far? He might have genuinely intended an annulment. She stared up at him. If he repudiated her now, she did not think she could bear it...

Seagrave's gaze shifted from her face to her bare shoulders, and Lucille suddenly became acutely aware of her nakedness. Worse, she became aware of his nakedness, of his body poised above hers. That strange but delightful ache was invading her body again, making her want to offer herself shamelessly to him again. She frowned. How very odd to discover such wayward impulses that she had never before suspected... She was just debating with herself whether a study of genetics would be instructive, when Seagrave's mouth took hers roughly at the same time as his hand came up to her breast. Lucille gasped with shock.

'This is no time to be thinking scientifically, my

demanding little wife.' Seagrave had read her thoughts. His voice was soft, but with a mocking undertone. 'I understood you to have found me lacking in my husbandly duty. Allow me to make up for lost time!'

Lucille's eyes widened still further. 'Nicholas, again? But…' Once again she lost her train of thought as his mouth plundered the softness of hers.

'Yes, again,' Seagrave confirmed with a grin. 'You will find that I can also be a demanding husband!'

It was quite different from the first time, less gentle but no less exciting. The relentless rhythm of their bodies was building now, pushing them both over the edge once more and leaving them exhausted with pure pleasure, to doze, wake in the dawn, love again and finally fall into a fulfilled and dreamless sleep.

It was very late when Lucille finally awoke. The room was filled with daylight and she was alone. She lay still for a moment, wondering whether she had dreamed the whole of the previous night, but the tumbled bedclothes and the indentation in the pillow where Seagrave's head had lain suggested that it had been real. So did the faint marks on her body, the unaccustomed but wholly pleasing differences she felt in herself. The colour rose to her cheeks as she remembered all that had happened.

How innocent she had been, and how he had delighted in instructing her, promising that this was only the start… Lucille frowned. But where was Seagrave now? Surely he could not just have left her… Even as the first doubts began to infiltrate her mind, she heard a sound downstairs and, wrapping the sheet tightly around her, hurried down to see if he was there.

The scene which met Lucille's startled gaze was a chaotic one. The entrance hall was full of empty packing cases, and from the dining-room came the rustle of paper and the chink of china and glass. Lucille pushed the door wider and walked in.

Susanna was standing at the table, a frown marring her brow as she tried to wrap a pair of outlandish china figures, whose outstretched arms were defying the tissue paper. She looked up crossly as Lucille came in.

'So there you are!' she said, peevishly. 'Where is Mrs Appleton? I need her to help me wrap these pieces. How am I to take it all away with me if I have to do it all myself?'

Her petulant blue gaze took in the hastily wrapped sheet and Lucille's sleep-filled eyes and tumbled fair hair. 'Well, upon my word! Country living must have wrought some strange changes in you! It is high noon! Whatever can you have been doing?'

As if in answer to that precise question, there was the sound of the front door closing and the Earl of Seagrave strolled into the room. He was dressed casually in breeches and a linen shirt. In one hand was a can of milk and in the other a loaf of bread and a pat of butter. His dark brows rose as he saw the two sisters, Lucille in her sheet and Susanna in plunging emerald silk.

Susanna's face was a picture. 'Lucille! Seagrave! What—! Surely—!'

Seagrave, a wicked grin on his face, put the food down carefully and crossed to Lucille's side, sliding his arm around her waist and pulling her intimately close.

'You look entirely delightful, my darling,' he said softly, his breath stirring her hair. 'I hoped to be back before you awoke.' He dropped a kiss on her bare shoulder. 'How I look forward to exploring again what is hidden beneath that sheet…' He straightened up.

'Your servant, Lady Bolt,' he said easily. 'Congratulations on your recent marriage. Is Sir Edwin with you, or in London?' His gaze took in the packing boxes and the serried ranks of glass and china. 'I take it you are removing from Cookes? Do not trouble to pack for yourself—my agent will arrange to have all the items you wish transported to your new home, or pay you for those you wish to leave behind. I have a new tenant for Cookes, but no doubt Josselyn and your man of business can sort matters to your satisfaction.'

Susanna's avid gaze was travelling from one to the other. There was only one matter that interested her at the moment, and for once it was not money. 'Seagrave, surely you have not seduced my sister!'

'On the contrary,' Seagrave said smoothly, 'she seduced me! You must have more in common than might immediately be apparent!'

Lucille was scarlet. 'Nicholas…' she said, beseechingly.

Seagrave relented. He took her hand. 'You may wish us happy, Lady Bolt,' he said softly. 'Your sister became my wife a month ago.'

'Your wife! A Countess!' Susanna's face was working like milk coming to the boil. 'Lucille, you

sly minx! To think that I leave you here to impersonate me and return to find you married to Seagrave!
Of all the conniving starts! Why, it could have been
me—' She broke off at Seagrave's look of amused
disbelief. 'Well,' she said grudgingly, getting a grip
on herself, 'I suppose I must wish you happy! And—'
she was recovering herself fast and gave Seagrave a
flirtatious look '—I must beg your lordship's indulgence for the masquerade! I hope you will forgive
me!'

There was a silence. Seagrave looked thoughtful.
'I believe I owe you my thanks, Lady Bolt,' he said
coolly, at length. 'Had it not been for your idea to
change places with Lucille, I should never have met
her. And now...' his warm gaze dwelled on his wife
and he smiled gently '...I discover that I love her with
all my heart.'

Lucille caught her breath as their eyes met. There
was such a deep tenderness in those brown eyes that
she felt quite dizzy. 'I am so very fortunate,' he said,
softly, 'to have found out how much I love you,
Lucille, and I think you love me too, do you not?'

'Lud, how affecting,' Susanna drawled. They had
both temporarily forgotten that she was there. She
picked up her gloves. 'There is nothing so tiresomely
unfashionable as a husband and wife in love with
each other,' she continued. 'I will leave the two of
you to bill and coo! You may find me at the Hope
and Anchor in Woodbridge when your agent wishes
to talk terms!'

She swept out and slammed the door behind her.
There was a silence, then Seagrave sat down, pulling
Lucille onto his lap. 'When we first married, I had

truly not realised the depth of my feelings for you, Lucille,' he said quietly. 'On our wedding night, the truth hit me with such a blinding flash that I think I was in shock with it. I did not know what to do or what to think. Suddenly all the feelings and emotions that had deserted me years ago returned with such intensity that I could not believe it. You had the most terrifying power over me, for I knew that to lose you would be my undoing. And whilst I tried to come to terms with that fact, I almost did lose you in the process!'

Lucille snuggled closer, turning her face into his neck. 'I am so very glad,' she said, muffled, 'for I love you so much I do not think I could bear it if you did not care for me!'

There was a contented silence whilst they just held each other, then Lucille said, 'What did you mean when you told Susanna that you had a new tenant for Cookes?'

Seagrave smiled. 'Ben Mutch, Walter's younger brother, has petitioned to take over the house. I think he will make an admirable tenant and I hope it will go some way to healing the breach with Mrs Mutch caused by Walter's misdeeds.'

Lucille kissed him. 'And now Susanna will exact a high price for removing herself from Cookes—she will fleece you!'

Seagrave pulled her closer. 'This time,' he said, with a smile, 'it is a price I am willing to pay!' He had found the end of the sheet now and was starting to unwrap it with single-minded concentration, raining little kisses over her bare shoulders. Lucille pushed him away.

'Really, Nicholas! When you had gone to all that trouble to fetch some food! Can we not have something to eat first?'

Seagrave paused, appearing to give the matter his consideration. 'In a little while, perhaps. First...'

Susanna Kellaway, returning a minute later to collect the reticule she had accidentally left behind, and to surreptitiously pick up a rather attractive silver watch chain she had earmarked to pay the landlord of the Hope and Anchor, found them equally entwined in the sheet and in each other's arms, oblivious to interruption.

'Disgusting!' she said, to her waiting coachman, as she closed the door of Cookes and hurried out to her carriage. 'There is nothing so odious to a Cyprian as a husband who prefers his own wife!'

*   *   *   *   *

PRESENTS

SIRENS OF THE SEA

The brand-new historical series
from bestselling author

Ruth Langan

Join the spirited Lambert sisters in their
search for adventure—and love!

THE SEA WITCH
When dashing Captain Riordan Spencer arrives in
Land's End, Ambrosia Lambert may have
met her perfect match!

On sale January 2001
THE SEA NYMPH
Middle sister Bethany must choose between a
scandalous highwayman and the very proper
Earl of Alsmeeth.

In June 2001
THE SEA SPRITE
Youngest sister Darcy loses the love of her life
in a shipwreck, only to fall for a man who
strongly resembles her lost lover.

MONTANA MAVERICKS

Bestselling author

SUSAN MALLERY

WILD WEST WIFE

THE ORIGINAL MONTANA MAVERICKS HISTORICAL NOVEL

Jesse Kincaid had sworn off love forever.
But when the handsome rancher kidnaps
his enemy's mail-order bride to get revenge,
he ends up falling for his innocent captive!

RETURN TO WHITEHORN, MONTANA, WITH

WILD WEST WIFE

Available July 2001

And be sure to pick up
MONTANA MAVERICKS: BIG SKY GROOMS,
three brand-new historical stories about Montana's
most popular family, coming in August 2001.

HARLEQUIN®
Makes any time special®

Visit us at www.eHarlequin.com   PHWWW

Harlequin truly does make any time special. . . . This year we are celebrating weddings in style!

To help us celebrate, we want you to tell us how wearing the Harlequin wedding gown will make your wedding day special. As the grand prize, Harlequin will offer one lucky bride the chance to **"Walk Down the Aisle" in the Harlequin wedding gown!**

There's more...

For her honeymoon, she and her groom will spend five nights at the **Hyatt Regency Maui.** As part of this five-night honeymoon at the hotel renowned for its romantic attractions, the couple will enjoy a candlelit dinner for two in Swan Court, a sunset sail on the hotel's catamaran, and duet spa treatments.

A HYATT RESORT AND SPA®   Maui • Molokai • Lanai

To enter, please write, in, 250 words or less, how wearing the Harlequin wedding gown will make your wedding day special. The entry will be judged based on its emotionally compelling nature, its originality and creativity, and its sincerity. This contest is open to Canadian and U.S. residents only and to those who are 18 years of age and older. There is no purchase necessary to enter. Void where prohibited. See further contest rules attached. Please send your entry to:

Walk Down the Aisle Contest

In Canada	In U.S.A.
P.O. Box 637	P.O. Box 9076
Fort Erie, Ontario	3010 Walden Ave.
L2A 5X3	Buffalo, NY 14269-9076

You can also enter by visiting www.eHarlequin.com
Win the Harlequin wedding gown and the vacation of a lifetime!
The deadline for entries is October 1, 2001.

Makes any time special ®

HARLEQUIN WALK DOWN THE AISLE TO MAUI CONTEST 1197
OFFICIAL RULES
NO PURCHASE NECESSARY TO ENTER

1. To enter, follow directions published in the offer to which you are responding. Contest begins April 2, 2001, and ends on October 1, 2001. Method of entry may vary. Mailed entries must be postmarked by October 1, 2001, and received by October 8, 2001.

2. Contest entry may be, at times, presented via the Internet, but will be restricted solely to residents of certain geographic areas that are disclosed on the Web site. To enter via the Internet, if permissible, access the Harlequin Web site (www.eHarlequin.com) and follow the directions displayed online. Online entries must be received by 11:59 p.m. E.S.T. on October 1, 2001.

    In lieu of submitting an entry online, enter by mail by hand-printing (or typing) on an 8½" x 11" plain piece of paper, your name, address (including zip code), Contest number/name and in 250 words or fewer, why winning a Harlequin wedding dress would make your wedding day special. Mail via first-class mail to: Harlequin Walk Down the Aisle Contest 1197, (in the U.S.) P.O. Box 9076, 3010 Walden Avenue, Buffalo, NY 14269-9076, (in Canada) P.O. Box 637, Fort Erie, Ontario L2A 5X3, Canada.

    Limit one entry per person, household address and e-mail address. Online and/or mailed entries received from persons residing in geographic areas in which Internet entry is not permissible will be disqualified.

3. Contests will be judged by a panel of members of the Harlequin editorial, marketing and public relations staff based on the following criteria:

    - Originality and Creativity—50%
    - Emotionally Compelling—25%
    - Sincerity—25%

    In the event of a tie, duplicate prizes will be awarded. Decisions of the judges are final.

4. All entries become the property of Torstar Corp. and will not be returned. No responsibility is assumed for lost, late, illegible, incomplete, inaccurate, nondelivered or misdirected mail or misdirected e-mail, for technical, hardware or software failures of any kind, lost or unavailable network connections, or failed, incomplete, garbled or delayed computer transmission or any human error which may occur in the receipt or processing of the entries in this Contest.

5. Contest open only to residents of the U.S. (except Puerto Rico) and Canada, who are 18 years of age or older, and is void wherever prohibited by law; all applicable laws and regulations apply. Any litigation within the Province of Quebec respecting the conduct or organization of a publicity contest may be submitted to the Régie des alcools, des courses et des jeux for a ruling. Any litigation respecting the awarding of a prize may be submitted to the Régie des alcools, des courses et des jeux only for the purpose of helping the parties reach a settlement. Employees and immediate family members of Torstar Corp. and D. L. Blair, Inc., their affiliates, subsidiaries and all other agencies, entities and persons connected with the use, marketing or conduct of this Contest are not eligible to enter. Taxes on prizes are the sole responsibility of winners. Acceptance of any prize offered constitutes permission to use winner's name, photograph or other likeness for the purposes of advertising, trade and promotion on behalf of Torstar Corp., its affiliates and subsidiaries without further compensation to the winner, unless prohibited by law.

6. Winners will be determined no later than November 15, 2001, and will be notified by mail. Winners will be required to sign and return an Affidavit of Eligibility form within 15 days after winner notification. Noncompliance within that time period may result in disqualification and an alternative winner may be selected. Winners of trip must execute a Release of Liability prior to ticketing and must possess required travel documents (e.g. passport, photo ID) where applicable. Trip must be completed by November 2002. No substitution of prize permitted by winner. Torstar Corp. and D. L. Blair, Inc., their parents, affiliates, and subsidiaries are not responsible for errors in printing or electronic presentation of Contest, entries and/or game pieces. In the event of printing or other errors which may result in unintended prize values or duplication of prizes, all affected game pieces or entries shall be null and void. If for any reason the Internet portion of the Contest is not capable of running as planned, including infection by computer virus, bugs, tampering, unauthorized intervention, fraud, technical failures, or any other causes beyond the control of Torstar Corp. which corrupt or affect the administration, secrecy, fairness, integrity or proper conduct of the Contest, Torstar Corp. reserves the right, at its sole discretion, to disqualify any individual who tampers with the entry process and to cancel, terminate, modify or suspend the Contest or the Internet portion thereof. In the event of a dispute regarding an online entry, the entry will be deemed submitted by the authorized holder of the e-mail account submitted at the time of entry. Authorized account holder is defined as the natural person who is assigned to an e-mail address by an Internet access provider, online service provider or other organization that is responsible for arranging e-mail address for the domain associated with the submitted e-mail address. **Purchase or acceptance of a product offer does not improve your chances of winning.**

7. Prizes: (1) Grand Prize—A Harlequin wedding dress (approximate retail value: $3,500) and a 5-night/6-day honeymoon trip to Maui, HI, including round-trip air transportation provided by Maui Visitors Bureau from Los Angeles International Airport (winner is responsible for transportation to and from Los Angeles International Airport) and a Harlequin Romance Package, including hotel accomodations (double occupancy) at the Hyatt Regency Maui Resort and Spa, dinner for (2) two at Swan Court, a sunset sail on Kiele V and a spa treatment for the winner (approximate retail value: $4,000); (5) Five runner-up prizes of a $1000 gift certificate to selected retail outlets to be determined by Sponsor (retail value $1000 ea.). Prizes consist of only those items listed as part of the prize. Limit one prize per person. All prizes are valued in U.S. currency.

8. For a list of winners (available after December 17, 2001) send a self-addressed, stamped envelope to: Harlequin Walk Down the Aisle Contest 1197 Winners, P.O. Box 4200 Blair, NE 68009-4200 or you may access the www.eHarlequin.com Web site through January 15, 2002.

Contest sponsored by Torstar Corp., P.O. Box 9042, Buffalo, NY 14269-9042, U.S.A.

PHWDACONT2

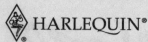